BOTH SIDES OF Love

BY
KIMBERLY WENZLER

BOTH SIDES OF LOVE

by Kimberly Wenzler

First Print Edition July 2014
First eBook Edition May 2014

ISBN 978-0-9905900-0-2

Cover design by *Suzanne Fyhrie Parrott*
Formatted for Publication by *First Steps Publishing Services*

Seaplace Publishing
Northport, New York

Please Provide Feedback

For Steve

꙰

Prologue

June, 1978

I pull into Nancy's driveway, four houses down from my own, and shift into Park. Her bedroom window is on the right corner, like mine. Every house on Maple Road was built by the same contractor in 1960; all were three-bedroom, one-car garage, brown, cedar shake ranches. The interiors were, by contrast, as diverse as the people inhabiting them. Nan's dark, cozy living room, brown and mossy green, is filled with velvet, oversized furniture on pumpkin orange, shag carpet while ours is sparse and light. Our low back sofa sits against neutral walls that are draped in large, floral prints over checkerboard floors.

We have our routine down to a science. A cursory glance shows me Nancy's *Be out in a minute* finger held up before she quickly ducks back inside. Paul Davis sings "I Go Crazy" as I tilt my head back to stare out of the open window and wait. The warm air is fragrant with cut grass, and the sunset left the sky an incredible shade of indigo. I squint, but can barely pick out the stars before the deep navy sets in. Bethlehem, Pennsylvania, nestled in the gently rolling hills of Lehigh Valley, may not possess the rich culture, fine dining or active nightlife boasted by large cities, like Philly and New York; but it has the most incredible view of the stars.

It's three am in England. Daniel's probably sleeping, but I like to imagine he's sitting on his grandparents' porch, gazing at the same stars, keeping us connected.

The screen door slams shut and I turn in time to catch her blow a quick kiss to her mom. Nan's saunter down the walkway makes me smile. She's wearing her Bicentennial Concert shirt we bought two years ago, at John F. Kennedy Stadium. At nineteen, it was our first time going into Philly on our own. God, we were batty for Peter Frampton. Her long skirt dances around her legs, tickling the daffodils that line the path. She climbs into my dad's Buick Skylark and immediately leans in for a quick, tight hug before settling back into the seat. A swell of optimism about the summer fills me, and just by being near her, the pain of missing Daniel is assuaged a fraction.

"Hey, girl. Missed you." she says, adjusting the radio while I back out of her driveway.

"Me, too."

Nan settles on soft rock, and pulls down the visor, to inspect her face. With a satisfied purse of her lips, she releases the mirror and it pops back into place.

"So, tell me. Did you get it?"

I offer a quick wave to Mrs. Shapiro, who is getting into her station wagon at the corner house, and make a right on Bradley. I glance at Nan with a shy smile. "Yup."

She gives me a wide grin and nods. "I had no doubt."

Nan is referring to the internship I applied for at the beginning of my senior year at college: an exclusive program at Rayston Field, supported by Juniata College, where I'll be immersed in forest ecology courses and projects. The internship pushes back my graduation by half a year, but I don't care. My dream of being an environmental scientist is within my grasp. Daniel happens to be graduating in December, too–a win-win for me.

"Teresa must be beside herself with this."

"What do you mean?"

"Well, you've been at Juniata for... what? Four years? And all you're coming out with is a degree and a career."

I laugh at Nan's perceptive assessment. What mother wouldn't be proud to have a child with such achievements and aspirations? Well, mine. Teresa's goal was to see her college-educated daughter sport around town in a tennis skirt, driving a Mercedes with a license plate ending with MD. Of course, the MD would be attributed to her son-in-law–not to me.

Honey, with your looks, you'll attract anyone you want. It's just as easy to fall in love with a rich man as with a poor one. Think of it: Dr. & Mrs....

Way to aim high, Mom.

I press on the accelerator, an unconscious reaction occurring whenever Teresa is mentioned, and peer over at Nan. "Well, I found more than my career at school."

She lowers the radio, lifts her skirt to her thighs and shifts in her seat to face me. "Do you mean what I think you mean?"

I nod, and cannot suppress a smile. I've been waiting to tell Nan about Daniel, wanting to do it in person and not over the phone. I'm glad I did. The look on her face was worth every painful minute of keeping my secret.

"Well, hell! Don't just sit there with that shit-eating grin. Gimme the skinny. Wait! Is he a doctor?"

"No. He wants to go into construction, like his dad. He's amazing and I love him and we're getting married after graduation."

Nan's big browns widen. "Married? Are you kidding me? He hasn't met my approval yet!"

"He will, Nan. He's my other half."

She retrieves a cigarette and matches from her crocheted bag.

"Out the window. My dad will freak." I warn, and am rewarded with an eye-roll.

"When can I meet him?" she says from the side of her mouth. I get a brief whiff of sulfur as the cigarette is lit.

"In the fall, I guess. He's in Bedworth, in England, for the summer. His grandfather had a stroke, and they called for him."

"England? Is he British? Does he have an accent?"

I shake my head. Daniel's warm, caramel voice is purely his, and not indicative of any specific region. I think of our last moments together before he boarded the plane, his declaration of love, and my cheeks flush.

At the airport terminal, we keep pace with a man and woman in front of us, also holding hands. I stare at the heels of her platform shoes, zoning out to the rhythm of the clopping as I get a glimpse of each sole in equal time. I am exhausted from hours of talking, making love, crying, and my eyes burn. Occasionally, a frustrated traveler jostles me awake. Without warning, the couple in front of us stops. She dropped something and is bending over, leaving us with the split-second decision to separate or maneuver around them. I loosen my grip, but Daniel tightens his and pulls me toward him, right before I would have rammed into the woman's rainbow pockets, surely knocking her off of those shoes. My sneakers squeak in protest as I trip over myself, grabbing Daniel before I fall in a heap to the tile. He mouths, You okay? I nod quickly, as my face grows hot.

"So, this guy…"

"Daniel," I say.

"Ah, Daniel. So, Daniel is in construction. Has Teresa met him?"

I shake my head as the traffic light on Main changes. I put the blinker on, pull into the right lane, and merge onto Route 9 toward Allentown.

Nan chuckles. "Oh, this is gonna be heavy. What I wouldn't do to be a fly on that wall. *What do you mean he's not a doctor?*" she says in a high-pitched wail that I suppose should be my mother's voice. "I can't wait."

Daniel is traveling tonight on a plane… Nan sings. I swat at her, but she ignores me and continues. *I can see the red taillights heading for Spaieein.*

There's a comfortable lull in our conversation as we both stare out of the windshield, lost in our thoughts. The Eagles' "Hotel California" drifts from the speaker, and Nan takes a long drag as she turns up the volume. As we sing along, I'm filled with a mixture of contentment and frustration, wanting to bring Daniel into my world—for him to meet Nan and my parents, and us to spend our first summer together. We have our whole lives to share; but I want it to start now. I can't wait three months. *79 days*, I hear Daniel correct me in my mind. I smile.

Nan lowers the radio. "What?"

I shake my head. "Nothing."

"Right," she says with a knowing wink. "Okay, one more question and then I'll leave you to your goopy thoughts. Did you do the nasty, or are you still the last standing American virgin?"

"Thank you." Daniel says.

"For what?"

We lie facing each other, our heads on pillows, naked under a thin blanket. Daniel leans over and kisses my shoulder.

"For waiting for me."

We just made love for the first time. My first time.

A tear trickles down the side of my face and falls silently to the pillow.

"I would have waited for you forever." I whisper.

His green eyes soften and he tucks a strand of my hair behind my ear. "You're mine." His mouth says, though I can barely hear him.

Slowly I pull my body onto his and look down at him. My hair drapes around his head, giving us a private curtain. I feel him respond to me and I smile.

"I will always be yours."

Nan leans over and looks into my full eyes while I try to contain myself and stay on the road.

"Good for you, Lizzie," she whispers, cranking the radio up again.

On my right, the moon plays on the fields surrounding the highway, and I'm reminded just how much I love it here. Nan leans back, her feet propped, the warm wind blowing her hair, and I know the moment is perfect. I'm with my best friend, waiting for my love to come home, and the freedom that summer brings is upon me.

The floor-to-ceiling window offers an uninterrupted view of the runway, lit along the edges, as planes creep up behind each other, idling. It is a gorgeous spring evening, though I can't feel the soothing air or appreciate the fragrance of the new earth from my air-conditioned post. The rumbling 747 is a blur through my tears, as it lifts up into the purple sky. The aroma of roasted coffee beans from a nearby kiosk reaches me and I gag, either because my stomach is empty, or the thought of being separated from the only man I've ever loved makes me physically ill.

When his plane is no longer visible, I turn to leave, passing the offensive kiosk, and wonder if I'll always associate coffee with this desolation, the way the smell of Pez candy reminds me of my youth, of happiness and security, or how garlic simmering in a pan makes me nostalgic for my grandmother. I head back down the concourse and see the couple again, the woman with the platform shoes who dropped something on the floor. I think of how Daniel wouldn't separate from me—how I am the one who would have let go.

Nan flips her butt out the window and belts out the chorus of Hotel California. I join her, an octave below. *Welcome to the Hotel California! Such a lovely place, such a lovely face….* We sing loud and out of tune, until finally, the song ends, leaving us in a fit of giggles.

"Thanks for convincing me to go tonight. I can't wait to catch up with everyone. It's been too long."

"Aw, I could convince you to climb Everest if I wanted to. You've always been good to me that way. I spoke to Jamie earlier. She can't wait to see you, too. It'll be bitchin. And Peter, Mike, Abby…"

Those are the last words I hear before I notice–too late–the truck veer from the left oncoming lane, barreling straight for us.

∾

Chapter 1

September, 1990
Beth

Indian summer. Nature's cruel joke. The green leaves have a hint of yellow in them: a sign that cooler weather is on its way. Where the hell is it? I shut the engine off and listen to the clicking of the cooling fan as the air inside the car quickly warms. My breath keeps time with sound of the dying motor. Inhale, click, exhale, click, inhale...

I pull the tag out of the glove box and hang it on the rear view mirror. Through my windshield, I watch three women walk into the building together, dressed in shorts and tanks. I look down at myself, in my chinos and cardigan, and pray silently that the AC is on inside.

Okay, Beth, get out.

At the curb, a woman glides effortlessly past me with an absent nod. She opens the door and turns to hold it for me, but I'm still several feet behind her. She is not sure what to do. I've seen this before. I'm not far enough to ignore, yet not close enough for it to make much sense to wait. She pastes on a smile, already committed. I struggle to speed up, biting my inner cheek, and try to ignore the bead of sweat meandering down my spine. Why did I come here?

"Take your time," she says, and I want to scream at her to go on—just leave me to myself! I smile back, apologize for holding her up, and grab the door, relieving her at last.

I follow the echoing voices around the corner and down the hall until I reach the cafeteria of Mayfair Elementary School. Long, white tables with attached benches are lined up along the length of the room. I assume they will be our seats for the meeting, though no one is sitting yet. Small groups of women congregate, catching up, commiserating. They laugh, comfortably, completely at ease.

I stare into the sea of faces. Okay, a river of faces; this is a Parent Teacher Association meeting, not a Who concert. At the entrance, I feel like my five-year-old daughter, who just days ago, had to be pried from my leg and escorted grudgingly to her kindergarten class. I'm not surprised at the absence of familiar faces. I've been out of touch, according to Alan, who had convinced me to come, practically pushing me out of the house. *It'll be good for you and Stacy. You'll meet other moms, make some friends.* We moved here three years ago, and though Hummelstown's entire population can squeeze into a large New York City apartment building, I've heard, I still know very few people.

Okay, you're doing this for Stacy, doing this for Stacy, I chant as I carefully navigate toward the back of the room, ignoring the curious stares and stuffy atmosphere. I hear an occasional shout from a child in a nearby classroom as I appraise the multi-colored underwater scenes painted on the light blue cinder blocks along the perimeter and envision Stacy doing the same in a few hours when her class has lunch. From my back-corner perch, flanked by the mixed aroma of Lysol and French fries, I take in the scene. The major players are easy to discern. These are the women who make the circuit, finding something to chat about with nearly everyone. As expected, the attendees are all women. The number is larger than I thought, though I am clueless as to what is involved in these meetings.

A small table against the center of the eastern wall is adorned with various muffins, bagels, pastries and coffee. I don't see tea, and decide the effort to get up to check is not worth the reward.

Trying not to stare enviously at the athletically-built woman by the table, laughing as she butters a bagel, I decide to preoccupy myself with the agenda and handouts I'd picked up at the door, thankful for the distraction. After a few minutes, I sneak a quick glance up from my papers and immediately regret the move. Across the room, near the stage, stands a small cluster of women, all of whom avert their gazes as my eyes reach them. I should laugh off their immaturity, but I don't. Maybe my imagination is at work. Perhaps they all happened to decide to look elsewhere at the same split second I peeked their way. I turn my focus in the opposite direction, through the window to the cloudless blue sky, searching for flying pigs.

During my senior year of high school, I was voted "Prettiest Girl", and "Most Likely to Succeed", the first time a student was awarded such contrasting titles simultaneously. My position as apex of the cheerleading pyramids at varsity basketball games off-set the Science Olympiad competitions I participated in throughout Central Pennsylvania. I had Nan, who shared everything with me–who would be by my side for the rest of my life.

Here I sit, seventeen years later, alone, hiding in a corner; the recipient of pitiful, curious stares; a stay-at-home whose husband had to push her out of the house for fear of becoming one with the interior walls and furniture. Oh, how the mighty have fallen. At thirty-four, I am faced with the sad reality that my best years are behind me.

I am wallowing inside of myself when a deep, throaty voice brings me back to the surface.

"Are you saving these for anyone?"

I lift my head to find a woman standing at the table. She is so beautiful that I can't help but gawk. Her eyes are an iridescent blue, swimming in a smooth, mocha plain of blemish-free skin. She has movie-star hair: thick, glossy tresses fall around her shoulders, almost reaching breasts that seem larger because of her tiny waist. She should wear a shirt saying,*Caution: objects appear closer than they really are.*

I notice her eyes shifting right and left while she bites her bottom lip, and finally realize she's still waiting for an answer.

"No. It's just me."

The relief on her face makes me smile. "Oh, thank God! I feel like an idiot. I have no idea what I'm doing. Noreen White, PTA virgin." She reaches out her hand, and we shake.

"Beth Butler."

She climbs next to me, so close, I get a whiff of Tresor. I barely move my purse off the bench before she plops down noisily, tossing her own bag on the table.

"I never thought I'd be one to come to these until I realized the highlight of my week was rearranging my husband's armoire." She raises her perfectly-shaped, dark eyebrows. "He has no fashion sense, so I was elbow-deep in plaid. Can you feel my pain?"

A laugh bubbles to the surface, and I tell her I can. Even though she makes me feel like a circus side-show, I am immediately taken with this woman. I'm drawn to her beauty, her candor.

The most exciting thing about Alan's wardrobe is his collection of ties. Everything else he wears is a replica of what he wore the day before. I shouldn't complain. I pretty much live in sweats when I'm home, which is, well, always.

"I'm a virgin, too," I say, and then blush. What?

She laughs and nods. "My daughter just started kindergarten."

"Same here. Stacy."

"I have Nicole. And a two-year-old at home, Devin. A boy, in case you think I'm cruel enough to name a girl Devin. He's with an underpaid sitter, so I can breathe for a few hours. What time do these things usually end?"

I shrug.

"Wonderful. Well, if it's over before eleven, then I'm going shopping. I'll let the babysitter earn her money."

The PTA president, Meredith Sullivan, (in bold, on all of our handouts), grabs hold of the microphone attached to the podium and spends some time adjusting the angle. Her short, blond bob doesn't quite reach her collared shirt, sleeveless to show off her tan, taut arms. She presses her lips together in intense concentration, until finally, she is satisfied the microphone is directly in front of her mouth. When she begins to speak, Noreen and I look at each other and simultaneously raise our eyebrows. A warm, happy feeling rises inside of me. Meredith starts the meeting with introductions to the board before addressing the new agenda for the year. The board consists of six members, who sit importantly along a dais facing the group. These are the women who had been in that clump, looking at me. Meredith points to her vice president, Sarah Lewing; treasurer, Linda Michaels; and works her way down the table.

I miss the rest of the names because Noreen is asking, in a whisper, who Stacy's teacher is. While Meredith explains how class parents are chosen and what's involved in supporting the teachers, Noreen is going on in my ear about fate and how we were destined to sit together since our girls are in the same class. I don't have the heart to tell her that as there are only four kindergarten classes in the school, we had a twenty-five percent chance of this happening. Her enthusiasm is contagious.

While clubs and activities are explained in meticulous detail, I steal glances at Noreen. She's got four inches on me, easy, and her shorts stop upper thigh, exposing brown, endless legs. Not a hint of stubble is evident. I want to touch her hair, and become nostalgic for my own long, blond locks. As part of my metamorphosis, after my surgeries, I cut off fourteen inches and colored it; now, short auburn wisps float about my head, barely covering my neck. A delicate gold chain hangs loosely on the thin wrist that holds up her head, as if she's trying to appear bored—the cool girl in Social Studies class who doesn't want to appear too interested in what the geeky teacher has to say. I knew those girls. I was one of them.

Class parents are to be picked at the next meeting in two weeks. After final announcements about what is planned for the children during the year (cultural events, the spring dance in March, fashion show), the meeting is adjourned and everyone stands at once, conversing and passing around sign-up sheets for various volunteer activities.

"Will you be putting in for class parent?" Noreen asks.

I look at her in horror. "What? I…I have no idea how that works. I only came here to see the school and meet people." And because my husband made me.

"Come on. It can't be that hard. Why don't we put our names in and see if we get picked? We can work together."

I wait for the others to leave before venturing back out to my car, embarrassed by my special parking privilege. Settling in behind the wheel, I think of how quickly I allowed Noreen, a stranger, to convince me to do something that scares the hell out of me. Maybe Alan is right. Maybe I'm ready.

Chapter 2

Noreen

"Hi, babe," he says when I pick up the phone.

"Perfect timing. I just got home."

"From?"

I plop my bag on the counter and sit at the kitchen table, relishing my last few moments alone before I go next door to pick up Devin.

"Don't laugh. I went to my first PTA meeting. It's official: I've become my mother. Feel free to leave me, if you must. I am a boring suburban housewife who goes to school meetings," I joke, but the dismal truth is no laughing matter. What has become of me?

"My hot Stepford wife," my husband says.

"Well, don't expect me to start cleaning. Not in my contract."

Dutch chuckles softly into the phone. "I wouldn't dare dream of such a thing. So, how was the meeting? Learn anything new?"

"Not much. A gaggle of stay-at-homes sat in a room, all cackling at once."

"Noreen, be nice."

"Fine. But most of them seem ridiculous and self-important." I sigh, trying to defuse my defensive thoughts before I start ripping people apart–namely that Meredith, who so far as I'm concerned, takes her title *way* too seriously. There was so much material in that room to work with; but Dutch doesn't always appreciate my acerbic witticisms.

"I did meet one woman, though–a newbie like me, and so I sat with her. She's got a daughter in Nikki's class."

"You made a friend. I'm so happy. Should I pay her?"

Please, Dutch, I want to tell him. *She wears a Raymond Weil watch and carries a Prada bag.* This one has money; I'm not sure if it's an adopted status, or something she's been privy to her entire life, since she holds no air of self-importance. Her face seems sort of deformed, which may explain her shyness. She practically folded inward. Maybe she won a lawsuit. Why is her cheek so sunken in? I had devoted a good portion of the announcements, trying to decide if she suffered from a birth defect or if something had happened to her. I'd been dying to ask, but managed to refrain. Not a good first impression: *Um, were you born that way or did you piss off a dog?*

I hold my thoughts back from Dutch, knowing he would reprimand me for being shallow. Which I am; but doesn't he swim along the surface himself? He never complains about my gym membership, bikini waxing, hair coloring, or manicures. I do it all for him. I also don't mention the real reason I sat with Beth. She looked as lost as I felt, and I knew I wouldn't be rejected.

"If you were here, I'd hit you." I say instead.

"Oooh. I've been bad." He smiles through the phone, and my heart thumps. I am missing him. "Listen, I've extended a few more days. I'm making some contacts. Jared at All Island hooked me up with a potential client. This could be our year, babe."

I roll my eyes, thankful he can't see me through the phone. "Great. Good for you."

"No. Good for us. I have to keep my wife in the lifestyle she's used to." I gaze around the small kitchen and sigh again. Right.

"Okay. In the meantime, your wife would like her husband home. She's used to sex."

"A few more days. I promise. Kiss the kids. Oh, and can you please water my plants? Love ya."

I put the phone down while Dutch's last words to me (*Love ya* –as if we're buddies), reverberate in my head. I shrug off the unsettling notion that his precious plants receive warmer expressions of affection as I head out to fetch our son.

Chapter 3

Beth

I walk into the restaurant, smile at Deloris, the hostess, and make my way past her to our usual booth. I shrug off my jacket while Candy fills my water glass. Paper placemats and rolled napkins stuffed with utensils line each table. The hockey game on the television over the bar is muted. The sounds of the bartender putting glasses away and waitresses chatting by the kitchen door echo around the large, empty dining room. Everyone's waiting for the lunch crowd to trickle in, which won't start until around noon, giving us an hour of solitude.

My father and I take turns being tardy, and it's now a running joke as to who's got the better excuse when we're late. It started with the harmless, *Had to rescue a cat stuck up in a tree,* and gradually our stories morphed into mini-sagas. I believe I hold the title with my last excuse, having been abducted by a group of aliens who all happened to resemble Paul Newman, taken to their planet, Hud, (all I could come up with at the moment), only to be rejected due to the "blue eyes only" rule, and so I was deposited right back where they picked me up, which explained my fifteen minute delay. Sometimes, I wonder if we actually *try* to be the slower arrival, so as to have the opportunity to impress one another with our active imaginations.

My dad walks in minutes later, sees me, and gives me a raised eyebrow with his warm smile.

"So," he says, settling into his seat, and I wait. He nods hello to Candy and waits for her to fill his glass with water and leave before he begins. "I'm at the traffic light on Main and Elm, minding my own business, enjoying The Moody Blues..."

"'Nights in White Satin'?"

"'Go Now.' May I continue?"

"Sorry."

"So, I was minding my own business when there was a ruckus in the car in the next lane. The driver next to me was banging on the window to get my attention. He was using crazy hand gestures, panic-like, right? Without thinking, I threw my car into park, jumped out and ran over to his car."

"What kind of car?"

"Um, a Chrysler. Anyway, in the back seat, there's a woman lying there…in labor."

I sit with my head resting on my hands as he continues with his tale.

"I was shocked at first, but my instincts quickly took over. I ordered the man to go find someone and call for help. While he was gone, I told the woman to relax and breathe. But she wasn't going to wait, and she started pushing! In the car!" He pauses to take a sip of water. "It was tough going for awhile. I mean, it's been several years since you arrived, so I was out of practice."

"Weren't you in the waiting room of a hospital while Mom had me?"

"Stop interrupting. Where was I? Right. I soon found my rhythm, and the coaching came back to me and *voila!* Out popped a baby boy. Unfortunately, we had no hot water available; but the guy returned and found some old towels in the trunk. Within minutes, an ambulance pulled up and the medics took over." He sits back, resting his hands on the table. "Mother and baby are doing fine. I jumped back into the car, and here I am."

I smile in pleasure as he goes on, enjoying himself.

"Only missed the light once. She was fast."

"Voila?"

He clears his throat and glances around. "Well, I'm shooting from the hip here. Cut your old man some slack. Did I get on you about Hud?"

I chuckle. "I'm sure the couple is very thankful."

"Oh, they are. Named the baby Patrick."

"Do they know their baby was delivered by a Sociology professor?"

Dad frowns and shakes his head. "Never came up." He shrugs and reaches across the table, taking my hands. "Enough about me. How are you, honey?" he asks.

My father and I enjoy a standing lunch date every Wednesday. We started meeting when his class schedule changed at Elizabethtown College, where he has been teaching for the past twenty-five years. He called me out of the blue, right after I moved from Reading, for lunch. I was so happy to have Dad to myself, we decided to make a weekly date of it. I used to bring Stacy, but now she's in school. I treasure these moments with my dad-when we can talk about anything and everything, without fear of judgment by my mother or questions from my husband.

After giving him a thorough update on Stacy–how she's doing in school (starting to read), her latest Stacyism ("Chiwi again?" Her complaint at my making chili for dinner one time too many)–I tell Dad about working with Noreen as class parents, and how good I feel about being a part of something outside of the home.

Dad listens intently, nodding. I spot a curious expression on his face.

"What?"

"Just glad you're making friends. It's been a while. I'm just… happy for you."

I nod and look down at the table.

Dad was instrumental in getting me back on my feet after the accident. The pain of my operations and therapies paled in comparison to the overwhelming grief of losing Nan. She was like a sister to me for eighteen years. We had been inseparable since Kindergarten. When I woke up in the hospital after a days-long morphine-induced coma and found out Nancy had died, I knew I'd never be the same. I just hadn't realized right then how much I'd lost.

I quit school, gave up everything, and crawled back to the sanctity of my childhood home to hide and try to heal. I existed in a foggy state of despair, never leaving the house, outside of the surgeries, and intense physical therapies. When I cried about the pain, Dad reminded me of the miracle the doctors performed in saving my leg. While I obsessed over my loss, he spent hours, trying in his gentle way, to make me understand all that still lie ahead. It took three years for me to want to live again. Dad is the one who saved me.

"I'm happy, too. She reminds me of her. She's funny and beautiful and..."

"Hey." He put his hand on mine. "You're beautiful. Don't forget it."

I shake my head as tears well up. He means well, but I hate to hear it. *Don't lie to me, Dad. I can see what I am.* Every glance in the mirror is a constant reminder of what I lost, what I gave up; how different my life would be if I had never been in that car. The worst part is that I was the one driving. Meeting Dad here, eleven miles from Hummelstown, is a huge step for me. Five years ago, I wouldn't drive more than three or four miles from my house.

Over hamburgers and fries, Dad fills me in on his classes and changes to his curriculum. I congratulate him on his recent nomination for Teacher of the Year (fourth time), and we joke about where in the house Teresa will let him display his award. (The bathroom vanity is a favorite. She will try to convince him this is the best place for it, as he will be reminded of this honor with his first constitution every morning). The two hours pass too quickly, and I have to get back home to meet Stacy at the bus.

Dad hugs me tightly in the parking lot. "I love you, kiddo."

"See you Sunday, Daddy."

In my rearview mirror, I watch him walk to his car. Stacy and I (and Alan, if he's not called into the office) will be at my parents' on Sunday for our bi-monthly visit; but it's these lunches I treasure most— this time with just Dad and me.

Chapter 4

Noreen

Beth and I are seated alone in the back of the cafeteria, near the windows. This is our third PTA meeting, and it's already a given that we'll sit together. I strategically chose this seat today to be able to assess the other women without looking obvious. I like to people-watch: take in hair, clothes and accessories. What someone needs to do is to get up on that pulpit and offer some fashion tips. Start with cardinal rule no. 1: Never wear sweats outside the home. No one should need to be told that after college. The drone of the lawn mower through the open window forces Meredith to squawk more loudly into the microphone.

"Should we move?" Beth asks me.

I lift my head from where it was resting on my hand, and turn to her. "Nah–make her work."

She covers her mouth to stifle a giggle, and I wait until I resume my position toward the president before I reward myself with a satisfied smile. I've started to look forward to these meetings, and to seeing Beth. It was exhausting trying to keep up with Dana and Bridget back at home: their clothes and hair worth more than my house in Westchester, their judging eyes always keeping me on edge. She thinks I'm unaware, but I notice Beth watches me a lot, sometimes stares—in a good way; a way that doesn't make me paranoid.

Today, we found each other in the parking lot, and confirmed the details of the upcoming class Halloween party while walking to the school. I didn't mention her limp; I'm waiting for her to volunteer what happened. As slow as I tried to walk— my legs are several inches longer–she was almost panting when we reached the door.

While Meredith drones on up front, I mentally review our plans for the class party, wanting everything to go well so I don't have to suffer the discrimination of twenty-five kindergarteners. This is my first time as class mom, and I have to set a precedent of pure fun. They'll be talking about me for years. *You remember Mrs. White, back in Mayfair Elementary? Do I! She threw the Best. Parties. Ever!* I lean in to Beth, who doesn't appear as concerned as I do. "Are you going to dress up for the parade and party?"

Her eyes widen in surprise and she immediately shakes her head, flushed.

I'd hit a nerve.

"Why not? Come on. Don't make me dress by myself. It'll be fun!"

Her head droops and I can see her struggling with something. I'm sorry to have embarrassed her, but I won't let her off the hook. I want to dress up, and I *won't* do it alone. This is the perfect excuse to throw a mask on and pretend to be someone else.

I watch her as she decides what to do. When she looks up, I am armed with my most charismatic smile.

Her face breaks open and I know I've got her.

"You must get everything you ask for," she says. "Fine, but I don't do parades."

"Fair enough," I say, relieved. "We'll go as something together. Like a couple."

Beth stares at me. Okay. I'm on my own now. I toss out ideas, having a dialogue with myself.

"How about Raggedy Ann and Andy… Nah, too much work. Lucy and Ethel? No one will know who we are. Witches..unh-uh. Not enough of a stretch for me. Think, Noreen!"

Beth chuckles as I entertain her with my banter, getting nowhere until finally, she lets me off the hook.

"My parents were a nun and a priest a few years back. I'll see if they still have the costumes."

I consider her suggestion. What would our PTA royalty have to say about that?! "Sounds great. Let's meet outside of the classroom half an hour before the party."

Chapter 5

Beth

The water runs through the pipes and I already feel the heat coming from the radiator, dissolving the chill inside me. In my flannel pants and shirt, I'm dressed for the winter weather outside, but in fact happily find myself tucked into bed with a book. I listen to Alan roving about downstairs, shutting the television and lights off, followed by the familiar moan of the steps as he ascends them.

"Did you lock up?" I say when he comes into the room.

"Of course. You ask me every night, and every night I tell you yes." He pulls off his sweats and drops them on the floor, leaving him in loose boxers, which make his thin legs appear birdlike.

I put my book down. "All I know is, one morning I woke up and the back door was open. Not unlocked– *open*. We're lucky we weren't robbed."

Alan sighs. "That was two years ago. We live in a safe neighborhood. Will you please let it go?"

"I'm just saying."

"Fine."

I return to my story as he climbs into bed, taking time to settle himself under the goose down comforter.

"So, what's the latest with the Supermoms?"

Alan is amused by my stories of the meetings, poking fun at the PTA group when appropriate, which is more often than not. I admit he's got a lot to work with.

"The same." I place my book on the night stand and shimmy lower onto the pillow, until my head is next to his. "Meredith and Linda are still not talking, and the Spring Dance is only a few months away. Whenever those two are in the same room, the tension is so thick you could cut it with a knife, I swear. Mer won't let up with her accusation that Linda misused the budget money, and now we have no way of paying for the DJ. I mean, where did the money go?"

Alan listens and smiles. "You get all worked up when you talk about this group."

"Well, I'm part of a live, celibate soap opera…although I can't be too sure Cybil and Jeannine don't have something going on between them. They're always together. Joined at the hip."

"You're just jealous. They have a best friend, and you don't."

This elicits a poke, and Alan smirks. He's pleased that I belong to something. My usual preference is a quiet night with him and Stacy, or with my parents. His partners' wives all keep busy social calendars, and I don't think he realized how unsocial I was until he became privy to the social lives of others.

Fortunately, this doesn't bother me.

"I suggested that we hold a quick fundraiser to bring in some money until we can determine where the nine hundred dollars went. Noreen is going to help me distribute the flyers tomorrow at school, so parents can place their orders by next week. We're collaborating with Mrs. Jensen, the art teacher, and we'll sell the kids' drawings on mugs, t-shirts, tiles, etc. Hopefully, it will work."

"You've been talking a lot about Noreen the past months."

"I like her. And Nicole and Stacy are growing close. I'm so happy because I don't think Stacy has a lot of friends."

"You should invite her here."

"I should."

I roll over and stare out of the window at the moon, considering the best plan to entertain Noreen and Nicole. Nancy flashes through my mind like an old newsreel, always taking me by surprise. Fragments of memories play on my psyche. We played a major role in each other's childhood. Often I wonder what she would be doing now, if she were here. I no longer cry when I think of her—twelve years is a long time to keep crying; but my heart does still ache. The aching is timeless.

In the dark, Alan's hand lightly skims my back, and I squeeze my eyes shut in frustration. As he moves from my shoulder to my hip, I recoil, and fight the urge to push him away. I don't want sex; but if we wait until I do, we'll live in celibacy. He doesn't ask why I never initiate our lovemaking–one of many topics we don't discuss. I swallow a cry and silently face him to endure the foreplay, willing myself to enjoy it; but I already know that I won't. I never have before.

I started seeing Alan mostly just as an excuse to get away from Teresa's incessant criticisms. For two years after the accident, I left the safety of my house only to go to my therapies. As I grew stronger, so did my mother's complaints about my reclusive existence, until I finally allowed her to set me up with her friend's son, who recently suffered a breakup with his fiancé. Alan was a pleasant, unthreatening distraction from my monotonous days: days that melded into each other until I existed in one long, endless cycle of light and darkness. Our outings became a regular ritual, and somehow my distraction morphed into a boyfriend.

We had been dating for about six months before I allowed him to look at me. I had been dreading intimacy throughout our entire courtship, petrified of my vulnerability outside the protection of my clothes. If the scars lining my leg didn't do it, then surely the remaining burn marks on my upper chest would render him impotent. The doctors managed to work with my face to the extent that I was able to hide the leftover scarring under my chin and hairline with makeup–though there was no hiding my sunken cheek or widened nose–but my chest was another matter. Though now significantly faded, the altered skin was evident, a rippled epidermic blanket covering my broken heart. I knew I should be thankful he was a doctor and wouldn't gawk like people do when accidentally offered a glimpse of my skin. With his line of work, he would have been callous to these imperfections. I wasn't his patient, however; I was his girlfriend, and should have been flawless–an escape from his everyday travails.

On that fateful night, kissing in his bedroom, I was reluctant to disrobe. He began to unbutton my blouse, and I backed away.

"What's wrong?"

"I…I can do it."

"Okay." He whispered and sat on the bed.

I stood before him and slowly unbuttoned my blouse until the sides hung open over me. His wordless gaze held mine as I pulled down my jeans, stepped out of them and waited. Waited for him to stare at the scars, to react–anything. His eyes stayed glued to mine, wanting me to understand he was looking at me and not my body. At that moment, I knew Alan would take care of me and never make me feel like less than a woman. This knowledge brought me some comfort.

I closed my eyes and dropped my shirt, unclasped my bra and slipped off my panties. For the first time in my new body, I stood before a man wearing nothing but my vulnerability. I shuddered and waited while my oratory sense prickled in preparation for sounds of disgust, disappointment, rejection. I remember being aware of Joni Mitchell's sad, beautiful voice singing *Both Sides Now* in the background.

Without a word, he pulled me toward him. "Open your eyes." He whispered. When I did, his radiated kindness and understanding. We held each other, and the tender way his fingers skimmed my back assured me I would be safe. His movements were gentle and slow. When he entered me, he held my head in his hands as I bit my lip to keep from crying.

Afterwards, I lie fitted to his frame, like spoons, and he ran his fingers through my hair. I couldn't fight the tears. With my back to him, I tried but couldn't push away the memories of my nights with Daniel: the way my body anticipated what he would do before he did, the completeness I felt while we were one for those treasured moments until we finally, reluctantly pulled apart.

I revealed little of my past to Alan. I was a different person. I'd even changed my name. Alan is not aware of my relationship with Daniel. No one, outside of my parents, really knows who I am. My past is too painful to revisit.

Wrapped in Alan's arms, after making love, I should have felt connected, happy–or at least *relieved*. Instead, I was consumed with an emptiness that unraveled me. Little did I know how contradictory my feelings turned out to be; that was the night I got pregnant with Stacy.

Tonight, as he climbs on top, Alan looks down into my eyes, and I see him fight to prolong his orgasm. He is a good husband, a good man, and deserves more than what I give him. When he comes, I smile and hug him before he pulls himself from me and rolls over.

Unlike the first few times, we don't hold each other afterward. How can I hold this man when I dream of someone else? Ours never followed the normal path of a relationship, where lovers first can't get enough of one another before eventually settling into a comfortable, fulfilling routine. Alan and I seem to grow closer with each passing year, a direct correlation to my letting go of Daniel. As my heart rebuilds itself, it invites Alan in. I can't deny my husband the intimacy he needs and deserves. I only hope that one day I'll enjoy it, too.

When I step into the bathroom, I catch my reflection over the sink. My thoughts are always the same. *You ungrateful woman.* I climb into bed and remind myself to call Noreen tomorrow.

* * *

"Mommy, Nikki's here!" Stacy sprints from the living room window to the front door, leaving behind a small circle made by her breath on the glass, surrounded by icy condensation. The light dusting of snow in the frigid January air, gives the lawn a sparkling effect in the sun. I never tire of winter's beautiful landscape.

In the kitchen, I put the finishing touches on the crumb cake and stand back in satisfaction. My most sought-after recipe is borrowed from Mrs. Klein, next door. The elderly widow showed up with this delectable treat when we moved in, and it has graced my table regularly ever since. I place the dessert on the counter and walk into the den to greet my friend.

The girls hug each other and scamper off to Stacy's room, leaving Nikki's coat lying in a heap in the foyer.

"Well, she feels comfortable." Noreen says, picking it up before slipping off her own coat. Sounds of their conversation drift into the kitchen, where Noreen sits watching me scoop coffee into the filter.

"I have two hours before Devin gets under my mother-in-law's skin, and I'm going to enjoy every minute. She saved me today. If he was here, we'd have no chance to talk. I owe her one. She'll make me pay, too. But it's worth it." Noreen stands to look around. "Your house is beautiful. So big!"

"Oh, thanks." We moved into this Brookfield colonial after Alan started his practice. He loved the house more than I did, and since his exuberance outweighed my indifference, we made an offer. I hid for two years decorating the space, trying to create a homey, welcoming environment.

Noreen walks toward the den connected to the kitchen. She takes her time looking at the pictures on the mantle.

"Your husband?" She points to a picture of Alan with his arm around my shoulder, standing behind Stacy. My dad took the shot right after we filled four bushels of apples at Lewin's farm near my parents' house two Octobers ago. Stacy beams as she holds a small bucket amid a rich fall hue of red and blood orange foliage. It's one of the only pictures I like that includes me.

"Yes."

"How did you meet?"

I walk to the kitchen table and position the coffee cake between the two place settings.

"He's the son of a family friend."

Noreen lifts the frame from the mantle to inspect the photo. Her silence compels me to speak–to recapture her attention.

"You know, Mom worried I was letting too much time go by finding a husband, so she thought she'd move me along for fear I would be eternally single. She orchestrated our meeting. I was reluctant at first, of course; but Mom wore me down. It turned out we were compatible. We dated for six months. I got pregnant. We got married."

"Ah, the typical Cinderella story." Noreen winks at me and returns to the picture. "Hmmm. He seems...nice." She carefully places the frame back and continues around the room, her fingertips touching the spine of a book, a lamp, a table. "Dutch and I met on a blind date. Would you believe it? I'm a cliché."

I smile and pour coffee into her mug, hot water into mine.

"He was reserved, but I loved him immediately. It took me three years to convince him he loved me, too. He's not Nicole's dad. She had just turned one. My first husband was an ass, and we split right before I found out I was pregnant. The only thing I offered him was her last name. We barely talk, and he's a sucky father. Anyway, Dutch fell for Nicole at first sight, but took his time falling in love with me."

I wait while Noreen pokes around the attached rooms, chatting tirelessly before meeting me back in the kitchen. We sit down and

I cut two generous slices of cake. "We should get our families together."

"Definitely. But summer's better. Dutch travels a lot, now."

"What does your husband do?" I ask, watching Noreen ignore her fork and lift the cake to her mouth with her hand, taking a bite.

"Oh my God! This is the best crumb cake I've ever tasted!" She takes another quick bite, licking her fingers in bliss, and I swell with pride.

"I stole the recipe from my neighbor." I confess. "It's easy. You can have it."

I wait for her to finish her piece and smile as her cheeks puff out like a chipmunk storing food while she works on swallowing the mass, a wonderful compliment. I suspect she'll hit the gym tomorrow—hard. There's not much room for cake in that body.

"I have a better idea. Why don't you just make it whenever I come over? I hate to bake, so this works out. I prepare elaborate meals and cheapen them by throwing an Entenmann's on the table."

"Perfect. You cook and I'll bake. We'll make a great team."

I stand to refill Noreen's coffee mug, with a cheerfulness that I haven't experienced in many years. I work to ignore the bittersweet pang at the thought of Nan, grateful for Noreen's chatter.

"I'm glad the girls get along so well. We moved here over the summer, and Nikki knew no one. She couldn't sleep for three nights before the start of school," Noreen says.

I nod. Neither could I.

"Where did you move from?" I ask.

"We lived in Westchester until Dutch's business took us here. It was hard to leave our friends and my job at the law firm, but the money wasn't coming in. I had Nik, and when we found out we were pregnant with Devin, my working days were numbered. Now, we're here. I wasn't happy at first, but I'm starting to feel like I belong. That's, in part, because of you; so thanks."

"We got here when Stacy turned two, but I still feel an outsider. My neighbors are all old, and there are no children on the block. Maybe I haven't tried hard enough. I was preoccupied, and Stacy is so shy."

Noreen watches me an extra beat from her seat, and I wonder if she can see right through me. For how long can I hide behind my daughter?

Finally she smiles and holds out her plate. "Well, friend, I'd love another piece."

∽

Chapter 6

Noreen

Devin is asleep when I pick him up from Dutch's mom. My only consolation for her surprise move to Lebanon last year is free sitting. The half-hour ride home is quiet as his head bobs against his car seat cushion while he dreams and Nicole stares out the window, a contemplative expression on her small face. She's probably wondering how her friend has that huge room in that huge house, while hers holds little more than her bed and dresser. Or maybe that's just my hang-up. I must make sure not to impose my insecurities onto my daughter. She can get them all by herself. Either way, it should come as no surprise that their house is huge. Beth certainly stepped in it. How did I not know until today that she's a doctor's wife, if even just a dermatologist?

When I saw a picture of Alan earlier, the question of who Stacy looks like remained a mystery. Where does this little girl come from? She exudes an aura of otherworldly grace, an angel in a six-year-old body. Her blond hair shimmers as if reflecting the Sun's rays. Her smile could melt an iceberg. I assumed her prominent cheekbones and slightly upward-sloping nose would be indicative of her father. In short, I had expected Mr. Butler to be drop dead gorgeous.

It was now clear that Stacy had not inherited the physical genes of the man smiling back at me from the mantle. Alan is average-looking; thinning light brown hair, squinty but friendly eyes, and pale complexion. A good match for Beth. He does not possess any of the distinguishable features of his daughter.

No wedding photos were displayed. I thought that odd and was going to ask, but got the impression Beth didn't want to dwell on the pictures. After getting over the surprise of Alan, I took in my surroundings. Her house is tastefully done, bringing in traditional style mixed with a contemporary flair; plaid chairs alongside a cream-colored leather sectional in the den. Must have cost her a fortune to decorate the place. In the formal dining room, my feet tingled with the shock of standing on the authentic Oriental rug, so I quickly stepped back into the more comfortable den, not wanting to interrupt the perfect design with my footprint.

Having only known Beth for a few months, I expected an easy-going, messy, cluttered space and was thrilled–and disappointed–by what I saw instead. The woman severely contradicts her surroundings. As we were leaving, Beth's mother, Teresa, stopped over, and I understood immediately the source of Stacy's genetic perfection. Mystery solved. My initial theory that Beth had some sort of unfortunate accident came to mind. Teresa is striking and poised, and in her company, one stands a tad straighter in order to meet her clear, disapproving gaze. She reeked of Chanel, covered herself with a cashmere pashmina and carried her belongings in a Salvatore Ferragamo bag.

I pull into our driveway just as Devin starts to grumble. My peaceful afternoon has come to an end. Carrying him inside, I try to formulate acceptable excuses not to reciprocate Beth's kind invitation.

∽

Chapter 7

Beth

Today, Dad and I pull into the parking lot at the same time. Looking back, I should have suspected something was amiss. He walks across the lot to where I stand by my car, parked right in front of the restaurant. The mild April air is welcome after a harsh winter, and he is wearing a lined barn jacket that makes him appear younger than his sixty-five years. Patrick Adler is a handsome man, and pride fills me.

Dad holds me an extra beat before pulling back.

"Are you okay?" Up close, I can't help but note his wan complexion.

"I'm perfect," he answers, casually dropping an arm around my shoulder. We head in and settle at our booth.

Candy fills our glasses with water, and we chat briefly before she leaves us. Dad seems preoccupied.

"No stories today. Are you disappointed?"

He smiles and shakes his head. "I couldn't come up with anything, so this works out well."

I sip my water and raise my hand to Candy. After ordering two iced teas, I find out what's on his mind.

"Your mother's noon showing cancelled today." Teresa decided to get her realtor's license when I turned twelve and it was clear that Dad had hit a pay ceiling with his job. Her spending habits needed additional support. She turned out to be a formidable saleswoman, and her salary now exceeds her husband's.

"Dad." My peaceful lunch has quickly turned into a chore, and a wave of disappointment washes over me. I glance toward the door.

"I didn't invite her," he says, interrupting me. "Not that she would have come."

"No. Her perfect granddaughter isn't here."

"Elizabeth." One word; but heavy in its delivery.

"Sorry."

A group walks into the restaurant, shattering the silence with laughter and loud conversation. There were about ten women in it, each talking over one another, similar to my group at Mayfair Elementary; perhaps they are coming from a PTA meeting. I watch them wait to be seated, a welcome distraction from my guilt.

"I wish you wouldn't be so hard on her." Dad says.

"Hey, I'm deflecting."

We both sit back, our cackles raised. Dad and I are usually on the same page; but when it comes to Teresa, we can't find common ground.

"She doesn't get me."

"She's your mother."

"Are you sure? We look nothing alike."

The pained expression on his face burns the backs of my eyes, but I push away the tears. No more.

"I'm sorry." I whisper.

He reaches across the table and takes my hand. His warmth soothes my chilled soul. I was Teresa's trophy, a proud display of her genetic capabilities, until my accident. My childhood was spent in front of a camera, every stage of my unflawed development recorded and shared. Now, I'm relegated to holding the consolation prize of being Stacy's mother. Teresa points the lens only at her granddaughter.

"It's just her way." He says, as if that exonerates her for all of the pain she's caused me. Dad appears tired today, so I acquiesce and nod in agreement.

"I know. I'll try, Daddy. I really will."

He smiles and pats my hand before letting go. Does my mother realize how lucky she is?

* * *

The gift of forewarning isn't mine. If it were, I would have stayed home that night twelve years ago, instead of heading to Peter Spidaro's party, and the course of my life wouldn't have been altered by a one-hundred-eighty-degree turn. I would answer to Mrs. Daniel Fergusan, mother of a brood of children and employed as an environmental scientist, perhaps even by the government. Instead, my life floats about on chance, and I merely react to occurrences around me.

The day after my lunch date with Dad, I walk into my home after putting Stacy on her school bus and am greeted by the shrill ringing of the telephone. For some eerie reason, this doesn't surprise me.

"Your father's had a heart attack," my mother says without preamble. Though I half-expected them, her words suck the breath from my lungs, and I bend over, gasping before clawing my way to the kitchen table to drop onto a seat.

"Oh, God, Mom! Is he...?"

"He's in intensive care. He may not be strong enough. Elizabeth. Come."

The dial tone drones in my ear, while spasms of nausea clutch my gut. *Daddy. No.*

I don't know why I thought my mother would be waiting for me in the lobby of the hospital. I can't remember how we ended our phone conversation earlier, and just assumed she'd be there, for me. The receptionist at St. Agnes Medical Center feels my distress. She finally writes down directions to the I.C.U. on a ripped piece of telephone message paper after I ask, for the third time, whether to make a right or left following the second set of elevators.

The I.C.U. is cordoned off by large, automatic glass doors. Inside, I walk to the center island, where a nurse points me in the direction of my father. Hidden behind the partially open curtain, I see Teresa sitting by the bed, leaning forward in her peach pantsuit, her hair tucked behind her ears. In those few moments before she notices me, her face droops, her moist eyes blink incessantly and her mouth moves in silent prayer. I struggle with the desire to go to her side, embrace her, so she knows she's not alone.

When I pull the curtain aside, Teresa sees me and her wall is back in place, her vulnerability once again hidden behind a veneer of perfection. My desire to hold her dissolves like sugar in water.

I am wholly unprepared for the sight of Dad lying attached to tubes and wires in the bed. Not a strapping man to begin with, he appears shrunken, and I start to cry. His veined hand is cool in mine. Opposite my mother, I stare at the man who gave me everything and pray over and over, *Please don't take him.*

Nurses are in and out all morning, checking machines, drips, charts, as we sit, muted in worry. Alan finally arrives at noon from work, and the three of us stay with Dad the entire afternoon, saying very little. The doctor shows up at six in the evening and tries to prepare us for the inevitable.

"His heart is weak. It took a beating this morning. I'm sorry. It's touch and go. If he makes it tonight, then we have a better chance. I would call anyone who might need to be here."

I send Alan home at seven, to relieve his mother, who is staying with Stacy. Since there is no one else to call within driving distance, my mother and I stay with Dad and keep vigil. An only child, the responsibility of keeping my father company is mine alone. This gives me some respite, as I could not imagine giving up a single moment with him to another being.

The constant sounds of the I.C.U. are somehow softened by night. The nurses' low chatter blends with the beeps, whirs and even phones, melding into a background din that eventually I can't even hear. My mother gazes at her husband. Surrounded by the unnatural iridescence of the overhead lights, there is a peacefulness about her that I envy. I want to scream and cry and pound the walls in frustration; but Teresa sits still, staring at my father so intensely, I wonder if she is trying to telepathically penetrate his mind and find out if he knows what his fate is.

Does she accept this? The idea unnerves me.

"Mom, are you okay?" I whisper. We are on either side of Dad.

"No." Her words betray her actions as she sits calmly across the bed.

"I don't understand. Why are you taking this so well?"

Teresa pulls her gaze from my father toward me–wincing, as if the gesture pains her. "What goes through my mind is how fortunate I am to have this man to myself. Me. I found and shared my life with the best person." She sighs as her eyes swoop back to him. "We had thirty-eight years together, full of love. How many people can say that?"

She is a peach and blond blur through my tears.

"I want more, and if God listens and I find myself back here in ten years, I'll want ten more. The wanting will never end. Crying and carrying on won't change anything. I'll wait to see if he'll stay with me. I'll wait however long it takes."

Just after midnight, she forces me to go home with a promise to call me with any change. I don't argue, knowing Teresa's resolution, when it comes to her husband, is indomitable. Part of me does not want to be here, anyway, watching the man I've loved most in the world take his last breath. I cowardly agree there's no room in this hospital for both of us to stay overnight. She leaves the room to give me a moment alone with Dad. She'll be back before long.

I stand close to his pillow, so my face is above my father's. I hold his hand in mine and cup his soft cheek in the other. My thumb gently rubs his bristled skin. The pain deep inside of me is nauseating. How do people do this? How can we keep saying goodbye? I take in the man who gave me everything; who was so full of love, he overflowed. Thin rivulets of tears slide down my cheeks as I watch his eyes move beneath his waxy lids.

Are you scared? I am.

My nose is running, but I don't want to let go. Not until I've said what I need to say.

Anyone can be a hero when things go well, but true character shines when tested. I came out of my coma, unaware of where I was, or what had happened to me. My father was my comfort. Dad had the strength to tell me about Nan. I realize now I wouldn't have accepted the news from anyone else. When doctors warned me I may never walk without a crutch, or have children, or look the same, he offered no pity. Dad reminded me of everything I had when everyone else around me reminded me of what I had lost. He was my anchor and my light–the reason I eventually picked myself up and started over.

"I love you, Daddy," I whisper. "Thank you."

Teresa returns, and I brush her cheek with my lips. She seems relieved to see me go. She wants to be alone with him.

Driving on the road, I replay our conversation and wonder what would go through my mind sitting vigil by Alan's bedside, death hovering over him. Would her words be mine? Peace and love, with no regrets? I maneuver the car through my tears, astonished that there is any moisture left in my body.

Unlike my mother, I did not marry the man of my dreams; I fight the resulting rage that spirals up inside of me constantly. This rage is most often directed at my mother, whom I place at fault for my decision years ago. It may not be just, but it's how I've felt since the letter left my fingers and changed my life. Adding insult to injury, while depriving me of the opportunity to share my life with a man I love with all of my heart, she has openly enjoyed that very privilege. The accident added to the chasm between us, which I don't think will ever be crossed.

I am racked with guilt over how unfair I've been to Alan as I pull into my driveway.

At six o'clock the following morning, Teresa wakes me to tell me that my father passed away, in his sleep.

* * *

Sitting on the bed in a fog, I hear Alan letting someone into the house, followed by quiet murmurs downstairs. There is a soft knock on my door before Noreen pokes her head in; "Hey, Beth. I'm here," she whispers.

I stand as she steps into the room and comes to me. She wears a snug charcoal, silk wrap dress, her hair in a smooth bun at the base of her neck, and minimal makeup. Even in the throes of desolation, I am inconsequential next to her, in plain black pants, nondescript beige blouse and a blazer. Her hug warms me, and I relish her closeness. Then Noreen takes my hands in hers, and guides me back to the bed. I sit dumbly; together, we stare at the wall where my wedding picture is displayed, next to the closet.

"It's pretty," she says.

Alan hung the picture, against my wishes, giving me the choice of here or downstairs in the living room. I chose the sanctity of our bedroom, hidden from all but him and me. And now, Noreen. I love to stare at the sky in the photo, framed by the delicate gold, laced with leaves. The gray clouds were muted and beautiful, as if protecting us from imminent weather only for the hour. I don't often look at the bride, a stranger to me then, but at her surroundings, trying not to remember the terrified feeling of being pregnant and beginning a life with a man she hardly knew. Sometimes I still can't believe the person in the picture is me. Now, the sentiment only overtakes me occasionally. I started to forget Lizzie, as if she were simply a figment of my imagination.

"You ready for this?" Noreen asks, breaking the silence.

We had held a wake service for two days, during which the funeral home was consistently packed with people who loved my father: our meager family, his fellow teachers, and an unending parade of former students. They all waited on line to tell me things we already knew: he was compassionate, funny, endearing, and bright. He was beautiful. Teresa, in true character, remained calm throughout the entire process, receiving guests and performing her duties as strong widow to perfection.

I fear the wake had been the easy part. Dad had still been in the room with us. Today, he will be gone.

"No."

"I didn't think so. You focus on your mother. She's going to need support. I'm here if you need me."

"Thank you."

"Stop."

At the funeral, Noreen sits behind me and eases my pain somewhat with her presence. The strength of our bond anchors me, and thoughts of Nan flit through my mind. We host a gathering at our house following the burial, for those who remain with us. At ten o'clock, when the last guest drives away, Teresa asks Alan to take her home. My arguments for her to stay with us are tossed to the wayside, like trash. This was another one I wouldn't win.

"I want to go home, Elizabeth. I want to lie in our bed and dream of my husband. Allow me that. I am not an invalid. I'll call you tomorrow. I promise." She offers me a quick, hard hug and walks out.

Stacy and Nikki are asleep upstairs, so Noreen and I are left alone. She finds me in the living room and offers me one of the two glasses of wine in her hands, which I readily accept. She settles down beside me on the couch and tucks her feet under her.

"She's a tough cookie. You must be like your dad, because I don't see a lot of her in you," Noreen says.

"She means well; she's just not demonstrative."

I rest my head against the cushion and close my eyes. This is one of the hardest days I've had to endure–more so than the day I lost Nancy. Noreen's presence, her friendship guiding me throughout the whole process, is immeasurable. "How can I thank you?"

"Don't. Listen, I'm sorry again about Dutch not being here. He couldn't get back in time from the trade show."

"It's okay." I'm not in the right mindset to meet anyone at this point, and relieved to avoid the expected formalities of dealing with someone new. I remember Alan's suspicion announced earlier that day, that Noreen isn't really married. He calls Dutch "The Phantom."

I'm spent; my mind cannot process or accept what happened. "I can't believe he's gone. I mean, you know it's going to happen, but when it does, it's…surreal," I say.

Noreen picks at her manicured nail. "My dad died when I was sixteen. I didn't go to his funeral. I blamed him, because he smoked. I was angry. And rebellious."

Noreen focuses on her nails. We know so little about each other. Dad took me to New York City for my sixteenth birthday, to see Man of La Mancha at the Vivian Beaumont Theater, followed by dinner at the new restaurant, The Jackson Hole Burger. We talked about the play (which we both loved), and anything else on our minds. I don't remember anymore what we discussed, but we never ran out of things to say to each other. It was a date I've always cherished. For years after, when we heard Impossible Dream, we'd share a smile at the memory–one of countless we've shared. For the first time, I pity Noreen. What would my life have been without this man?

"What will I do without him?"

Noreen takes my hand and we sit on the couch–connected, but lost in our thoughts. She doesn't try to fill the air with ineffective words. How many times must I hear I'm sorry? Or, it was his time, or, he's in a better place?

"Life sucks sometimes." She says.

When Alan returns, Noreen takes her leave without Nicole, after I convince her to allow the girls to stay together tonight. Silently, we both undress and climb into bed. On our pillows, we look to each other and wordlessly, he turns toward me, on his side.

I turn away and shimmy over to him until my back is fitted to his frame, and he wraps his arms around me. Our breaths find their rhythm, and we inhale and exhale in unison.

Eventually, Alan's hold on me slackens as he drifts into slumber, and I move back to my side of the bed. I am exhausted, but can't sleep. My father no longer shares my world, and the thought bars me from any chance of rest. I slip out of bed, climb into sweats and sit in the living room, watching the moon's light play along the wall. At midnight, Alan's snores drift from our bedroom, and I am overcome with the desire to leave the house.

In the car, I keep the radio silenced and coast through the night, embracing the blackness around me. I try not to think of what it will feel like to call home and not have Dad there anymore. My five-year-old daughter will eventually forget her grandfather, and the idea fills me with pity for her. I have wonderful memories of the man–memories I can now only share with my mother, with whom I share so little.

Alan had swept me away from my parents' home early on in our courtship, so his relationship with them is built on holidays and birthday visits, and the occasional barbeque that he managed to attend when not working. He cannot share with me the countless small, quiet moments that occur between people who live together and whose depth of love cannot be plumbed.

The only other person who knew him well while I was growing up is also gone. How many nights did Nan and I sit at our kitchen table, playing board games with Dad, enjoying his attention? His warm, entertaining humor? His love? This realization fills me with an overwhelming sense of loneliness.

I have no plan or destination, and am surprised when I find myself on the highway, an exit from my parents' home. Maybe my mom is awake, and we can talk. The desire to be with her feels as unnatural to me as my glued-on fingernails, hastily acquired so as to temporarily conceal my latest bad habit. I cut the headlights when I approach her driveway, on the off-chance she is lucky enough to find slumber.

I climb out of the car and walk the brick path to the front stoop. Through the warbled glass on the side panel of the door, I can see a soft light given off by one of the table lamps in the living room. My parents used to leave this light on to greet me when I was out. On how many nights did that light welcome me home?

Nan's parents moved not long after the accident. Too many memories, they told us. To this day, I don't drive past her house.

If my mother were sleeping, the light would be out. I lift my hand to the knocker, but pause when I hear an odd noise. It is unfamiliar, and my initial thought is that Teresa has a guest. Eventually, I am able to identify the sound as the deep, guttural sob of a woman in anguish. The noise cuts through me like a razor; I lean against the door with my palm against it, sharing the moment with my mother, wanting my wails to combine with hers and bring him back. Tears blur my vision as I make my way back to the car and out of the driveway.

❦

Chapter 8

Noreen

At home, it's too quiet and I can't sleep. It's so rare I have the house to myself, I'm not sure if I love or hate the silence. I almost want to get Devin from Dutch's mom; but then realize I have wine. I pour a glass and bring it to the den. I feel like a shitty friend for being filled with envy rather than sympathy at Beth's father's funeral. She was distraught, and all I could think of is how the tears I had shed for my own father were not born of love, but of regret.

The television does little to distract me. I kick away the papers strewn on the coffee table, and see Nicole's recent graded project from school. She was so proud getting off that bus, holding it out to me as she walked up the driveway. I promised I'd leave it out for Dutch to see when he got home. I know he'll praise her. It's what a father is supposed to do, what Beth's father did; not mine.

"Dad, look! I got 100."

I had waited hours for him to get home from work to show him my test grade. No more drawings or macaroni art. I was in second grade now. This was the big time.

In the kitchen, I pass him the sheet, smiling, while my mother heats up his dinner.

Sitting at the table, he grabs the paper from me, glances at it while loosening his tie, a cigarette teetering from the corner of his downturned mouth.

"Spelling, huh?"

He hands me back the sheet as his plate is put in front of him.

"It's a good thing you're smart."

He turns to my mother. "Maybe she should learn to spell 'diet'.
What do you think?" He chuckles.

"Stan, stop."

"Well come on, Jean. Look at her. Maybe if you'd stop feeding her
so much, she wouldn't look like that. She'd have some friends."

I slink out of the room, pulling my shirt down over my exposed
belly, and rip up the test in shame, crying myself to sleep.

Sometimes, I want to reach up to the heavens (or down to Hell,
more likely) and show him what I've become. *Look at me, Dad. I'm*
thin, and beautiful—and I have a husband! I did everything you said
I wouldn't do!

Take that, you miserable shit.

Chapter 9

Beth

Two months later, on a Friday in mid-June, Noreen invites us for a barbeque. Stacy, intoxicated by thoughts of the fast-approaching summer vacation and a full afternoon with her best friend, pirouettes around the kitchen, while I sprinkle warm crumbs over my cake, specially requested by Noreen for her husband.

Packed into the car, I guide Alan along the route to her house using the directions Noreen had given me. We crawl through the small town, past the library, barber, hardware store, nail spa, and gym, to the other side of Main Street. I stare out of the window and watch as the properties become smaller the further away from our neighborhood we travel. The houses are close together, and though the street is quiet, I envision children bicycling or rollerblading up and down the block. A slight twinge of regret runs through me as I compare this to our own, secluded street.

When we pull into the Whites' driveway, I already love the house. The modest Victorian is charming and oozes with character. Below crimson peaks that reach for the sky, window boxes overflow with bright red geraniums. Multicolored pansies line the stone walkway to the front porch. It is a storybook home.

Outside the car, Alan walks to where I stand. "Cute."

I ignore him, taking it in, until Noreen pokes her head over the side fence.

"Yoo-hoo! Hey you guys, we're back here. Come on." She pulls the latch and opens the picket door, laughing as Stacy darts past her without warning, in search of her friend.

Alan chuckles. "And to think she was shy."

"Not any more, she's not." Noreen laughs with him. She holds out her hand when he reaches her. "Hi, Alan. Nice to see you again."

She winks at me as she gives Alan a quick hug before moving to me. Her thick, black hair is pulled back in a ponytail, revealing her catlike eyes and reminding me of Audrey Hepburn. I want to squeeze her fiercely, I am so happy to be here. I was looking forward to this as much as Stacy, and would have danced around the house too, if my legs would have cooperated. Noreen leads us into the backyard.

We follow a similar path as in front: stones laid in grass, lined with pansies. When we reach the yard, Alan lets out a whistle. We are greeted by an incredible palette of color. Clumps of fuchsia azaleas anchor the space. Around a small square of vivid green grass is another border of mixed wildflowers. Full, blooming white rosebushes cover the sharp corners of a brick patio. An oval, above-ground pool stands to the left, lined with thick coral impatiens, where Nicole bobs on a black tire tube and Devin holds onto the side in Bert and Ernie arm floats.

Stacy pulls her terry cover-up over her head and throws it to me as she runs across the grass to the ladder. She looks over her shoulder, back at us.

"Mommy, can I?" she asks.

"Go ahead, sweetheart. But please, no jumping." I look to Noreen. "Your house is stunning! I had no idea you were such a gardener. You never mentioned. The flowers…they're…."

Noreen smiles. "Well, it's not quite your mansion, but it's home. This…" she gazes around her, "…is all my husband. I wouldn't dare get dirt under these babies." Her impeccable manicure appears before us, and I laugh while handing her the cake, which she holds to her nose, taking a deep whiff.

"Alan, do you know how lucky you are to have a woman who can bake like this? I've never in my life tasted anything so yummy!"

Alan puts an arm around my shoulder. "Oh, I'm lucky, all right. I try to keep some control, though it's not easy." He pats his stomach, which, as he nears thirty-eight, has just developed a slight bulge.

"Let me go put this inside and see what's holding up Dutch. Please make yourself comfortable. Do you mind keeping an eye on our little swimmers? Be right back." She walks quickly to the screen door off of the patio.

We turn in the direction of the pool to find the children playing Marco Polo. I lean to Alan and whisper, "I guess we'll meet our first phantom."

He raises his eyebrows and whispers back, "He's not here yet."

I smile and elbow him in the side, and he chuckles. The weather turned out to be warm and wonderful, and watching my daughter playing so happily makes me grateful for Noreen and our friendship. Caught up in the noise and splashing, we don't hear someone walk up behind us until he speaks.

"So, this is the famous Beth."

The caramel voice surprises me with its familiarity. The hair on my neck stands up, and fear prevents me from turning around for several beats. When I do, I am caught in the unwavering stare of indescribable green eyes that once took my breath away—and apparently, still do.

I gasp and sway, causing Alan to take hold of my arm. "Beth?" he whispers.

"Good to meet you," Dutch says.

He holds out his hand.

My body flinches; my whole being hiccups, and my insides threaten to hurtle out of mouth.

"Hi! We didn't hear you walk up. I'm sorry. Alan Butler." My husband eyes me warily as, still holding my arm, he reaches out his other hand to relieve the hanging gesture.

"Daniel Fergusan. Pleasure. Thanks for coming."

"We appreciate your having us," Alan says.

The men look at me. My brain replays the last time I saw Daniel, walking away from me down the jetway, with his hand over his heart, mouthing *I love you.*

"Beth?" Alan says. To Daniel, "She's mesmerized with your yard and the kids and all."

Move! I tell myself. *For the love of God, get out of here!* My body is stone while my mind races frantically.

I'm not sure how much time passes before I muster the courage to reach out and smile.

"Pleasure," I think I slur, as if I'm on my third cosmo.

Daniel takes my hand and covers it with his. He gazes at me an extra beat, and his eyes squint just barely; but I notice. I don't miss the quizzical stare, and hope Alan does. "So, you're the person who Noreen can't stop talking about. The pleasure's mine, Beth," Daniel says.

I nod like a mute and pull my hand away. Alan supports my lower back and whispers, "Hon, you okay? You're pale."

"I need the rest room."

Daniel points toward the house to the screen door Noreen had disappeared behind minutes ago. I pass Noreen, who steps out carrying a Pyrex dish with marinated meat on it. "Dutch, have you met Alan and Beth, my new best friend?" She winks at me again; I try, but can't smile back.

"We did. What's your poison, Alan?"

"Oh, beer would be fine."

"You're sure? I think I'm going for the strong stuff today," Daniel says, as I close the door and find escape inside.

In the bathroom, I take deep breaths over the toilet and try to control my shaking. What just happened? I move to the mirror to find a scared, ghostly woman gazing back.

He had hesitated; I noticed. *Does he recognize me?* My own mother still gets confused. I inspect my reflection, turning my head side to side. No. No one who knew me before would believe I am the same woman. In addition to my complete change of hairstyle and color, my nose is wider than the one my parents passed down to me. If that wasn't enough to throw someone off, the most drastic change to my face is my left cheek, which is flatter than my right-the mask I can never take off: my permanent Halloween costume.

My eyes. They are still mine. And my heart, which until this moment I hadn't realized is still broken.

In my wildest imagination, I never saw it coming. He always wanted to settle in New York. Then I remember Noreen telling me that they had—until his business slowed down. Why, in this state, in this suburb, fifty miles away from where we started, in this school district, do we both have to live? What were the chances of my befriending his wife—my first, real, close friend after Nancy?

Their last names don't coincide. With some thought, brief nuggets of conversation float about my mind. During Noreen's initial visit, she had mentioned that Nikki kept her father's last name after their divorce. Noreen must have kept it, too.

Inhale. He is not your Daniel. He was Lizzie's Daniel, the girl who died in a car accident with Nancy. Exhale. Outside stands the man Lizzie said goodbye to twelve years ago, the man I worked for years to forget; years of pushing him from my daily thoughts until a day could pass in which he wasn't speaking to me, invading my dreams, refusing to leave. He was with me when Alan and I first met, and on my wedding night. I carried him in my heart until mercifully, his memory was chipped away by the tide of time. When my days and nights were free from his hold, I could finally focus on rebuilding my life. Now, here he is, in all of his beautiful glory. I forgot how mesmerizing he was. Those green eyes…

A soft knock has me gasp.

"Beth, you okay? Can I do anything for you?" Noreen's sweet voice filters through the door.

Tears spring to my eyes. Noreen is the best thing to happen to me, outside of my daughter, since I lost Nancy. She fills a void that Alan can't; an unfiltered sounding board, fellow mother, and the only one to make me believe I can enjoy a close friendship again. Often I'm hit with unexpected pangs of guilt when caught in unbridled laughter. I was the one responsible for Nancy's death and still I go on, laughing, living. Noreen made it feel okay to laugh again.

Another knock, this time louder. "Beth? You're making me nervous."

I stand straight and wipe my eyes.

"I'm fine. I'll be out in a minute. My stomach…" My voice is shaky, and I wait for Noreen to say something.

"Oh, okay. You know, once I was stuck on the bowl for half an hour after two strong cups of coffee. Crazy. Of course, I refused to blame the martinis. Well, I'll leave you to it. Gotta head back outside. I'm sure the guys are not paying much attention to our offspring. They're like big kids themselves, aren't they?" Noreen sounds relieved, and walks away without suspicion.

Of all the people I could meet and befriend, I had to find the one woman who married this man? *He was mine first!* I want to scream like a prepubescent at the dinner table. Envy fills me whenever they touch, or when Noreen tenderly wipes the corner of his mouth with her finger. I take in the scene as if catching them at a most intimate act, and despise myself for my thoughts.

By dessert, I gain some control and even manage to participate in conversation around the table. Noreen entertains the group with a story of our botched holiday party last December.

"And I started passing out the green paper for the placemats when Mrs. Walsh pulled me aside and told me we weren't allowed to do anything that mentioned Christmas at school. We were to do a 'general' themed craft so as not to offend anyone." Noreen glances at me and smiles before going on. "We just looked at each other like 'What the hell do we do now?!' and laughs as she shakes her head.

Daniel stares at me as his wife holds court. He leans forward, resting his elbows in front of his plate. "You seem very familiar..."

I flush, uneasy, and start to gather plates, not even mindful that they're Styrofoam, (the worst possible material), as I would have cracked ceramics with my trembling hands. I shake my head and stand. "Noreen, are you finished?"

When I extend my arm across the table, Noreen pulls her plate out of my reach.

"No rest for the weary, I guess. Beth, we don't have to get up tomorrow. Please stop cleaning. I'll do it later."

"Oh, that's okay. I like to stand after I eat. Helps me digest. I ate enough for an army. The food was delicious. Wasn't it, honey?" Stacy is happily oblivious to my discomfort.

"Yeah. Momma? Can me and Nikki play some more?"

My daughter and Nicole sit across from Alan and me, while Noreen and Daniel occupy the ends. Around the table, all eyes are on me.

Stacy sniffs and I lean over to see her eyes are red from the chlorine, or maybe the pollen. Thank God.

"Honey, I think you've had enough. Let's go home."

Chapter 10

Noreen

Dutch brings the kids up to bathe and get ready for bed as I linger downstairs, cleaning the kitchen. Did the Butler's enjoy themselves? I always feel like I have to pass some unwritten test when first getting together with people. Dutch hates that about me. *What do you care what people think of you, Noreen? You've got to relax!*

I look around the rooms from where I stand near the sink, trying to envision what it must look like to someone who lives in a house twice this size. Beth doesn't make me feel judged; but I don't know Alan. We didn't talk much during the funeral; he wouldn't leave Beth's side for long. Tonight, he seemed like a real down-to-earth guy, considering he drives a BMW. I thought of how Beth described her courtship with Alan: hardly the Cinderella story I joked about. If she only knew about my first date with Dutch.

He walked into the restaurant with an air of disinterest. I watched him as he spoke to the maître d', who pointed in my direction. He headed toward me, resigned. *This is a chore*, his demeanor screamed.

I remember thinking, *Perfect, he already doesn't like me.*

"Noreen." He said, holding out his hand. "Daniel."

I was seated and sipping my wine (he was thirty minutes late), so I left his hand hanging. To his credit, he left it out there, until he was sure I wouldn't take it before sitting across from me.

"I'm sorry I'm late. I was trying to come up with a pliable excuse to get out of this."

The harsh truth of his statement relieved me. He'd made up his mind not to want to be here–without even seeing me. He could have walked right past the table and I wouldn't have known. My hopes lifted.

"Ah, the truth. How refreshing."

At this, his glass facade cracked into a smile.

"My buddy, Robert thinks I need to settle down. He's on a match-making rampage. I'm sorry. I don't want to waste your time. I'll understand if you get up and leave right now. You can even throw a glass of wine at me, you know, to save face."

I considered his proposal, feeling a twinge of regret that I put so much effort into looking this good for someone who clearly didn't want to be here. He waited for me, with calm detachment– expecting, I'm sure, that I would get up and go. I took in his face (rugged, chiseled, gorgeous) and made my decision.

"And if I stay? Would you be terribly disappointed?"

He rested his elbows on the table and leaned toward me. My insides went aflutter.

"Well, why don't we find out?" He glanced up toward the bar, where a small group of wait-staff stood watching the dining room, and raised his head. A waitress walked over and he ordered Jack Daniels straight.

I was a fresh divorcee, with a one-year-old–and, at this point, nothing to lose. I've been treated worse. This guy can't do anything to me that hasn't been done already. The fact that he didn't want to be there, but somehow was, secured one thought in my mind, which played over and over: This might be fun.

Ours didn't follow the typical first date protocol. He didn't try to charm me or inquire about my past or plans. Instead, we treaded the surface of the newly introduced, keeping to the jaunty circle of *let's not give too much of ourselves away just yet*. His intention, his actions told me, was to get through the night and part ways. No leading me on, no making empty promises; he wasn't that guy. We made small, superficial talk while we waited for our pasta. I drank a bottle of red, and I'm not sure how many times Sheila (our waitress) returned to the table with a fresh drink for my very uninterested, but incredibly hot date.

He wore a button-down, Ralph Lauren shirt and crisp jeans, even though it was Saturday night. I'm not sure if he noticed my dress; I practically poured myself into it.

So why did I invite him to my apartment and sleep with him after knowing him for all of four hours? He was beautiful–he still is–and his eyes spoke volumes. Someone did a real bang-up job on him.

I figured, *Hell, this may be the last time I see this guy, or God willing, we have a future.* If I was a betting woman, I'd choose the former; so I went for it. I was glad I did. Where we fell short in conversation, clothed, we more than made up for in the bedroom. He was rough and commanding, but not in any way that hurt or made me feel small. This was a guy who made love to strangers: no small talk, or tentative undressing, no question of what was going to happen.

In the bathroom, flushed and sated, I looked at myself in the mirror over the sink. *Don't get attached. He's not into you. He's probably climbed into his jeans and slunk out while you stand here, talking to yourself in the mirror.*

Well, good riddance, then. Thanks for the memory.

I went back into the bedroom and, sure enough, it was empty. I fought disappointment. *Didn't we just have this conversation in the bathroom, you stupid woman? Why do you expect them to stay?* Under my sheets, still warm and fragrant, I stared at the ceiling taking deep breaths.

"Noreen?"

I sat up and saw him standing by my bedroom door, in boxers, and that body. I reminded myself to thank Dana, again, for taking my daughter for the night.

"You still here? Look, I won't marry you, if that's what you're thinking."

His arms leaned across the door frame, like muscled wings taking flight, and he let loose a wide smile. I dropped back down so he couldn't see my reaction (pure joy) and heard him walk toward me. He sat on the bed.

"Do you want me to make you something to eat? I checked out your fridge. You've got to be hungry after the Olympic stunt we just pulled off."

I smiled. "I was particularly impressed with your dismount. That one took practice, no?"

He chuckled and brushed my hair back along the pillow. "You're funny. I'm glad you stayed at dinner."

Me, too.

∽✦

Chapter 11

Beth

I roll over in the darkness and trail the outline of my sleeping husband with my eyes. *How did this happen?* As moonlight's shadow moves along the ceiling, I listen to the soft snore of Alan's breath. I stare at him until I can hold myself no more. I slip off of the bed, and out of the room.

In the basement, I relax my movements, knowing that the insulated ceiling will mute any sounds I make. I turn on the light over the large walk-in closet near the stairs. The perimeter is lined with shelves holding bins labeled by holiday, along with all the scrapbooking paraphernalia I've accumulated over the years. Alan built this room for me. When I picked up scrapping, he had an island built in the center, and I would lose myself for hours, making photo books of Stacy in every stage of her life, thanks to Teresa and her expensive Nikon.

I walk the length of shelves, my fingers lightly brushing over the labels: Christmas, Easter, Thanksgiving, Fourth of July, until I come to the bottom corner. I lower myself to the floor and pull the Valentine's Day bin out. I lean in, trying not to place too much pressure on my clipped leg, and reach back until my hands touch the hard cardboard tucked against the wall.

The island supports a butcher-block top, where the box now rests while I breathe heavily, more from nerves than from exertion. This box has not been opened in a decade. It was sealed two years after my accident, after the surgeries and therapies–after my first and last letter to Daniel, ending our relationship. The whole of our courtship in a neat, cardboard box.

I lift the cover, thick with dust, and put it aside. Lying on top is a photo of me when I was Stacy's age. We look so similar, it's frightening: long blond hair, a perfect up-sloped nose, smooth complexion, posing in the front yard on a tricycle. I turn it over to see my mother's meticulous handwriting: *Lizzie, age 5, June 1962*.

Lizzie. I close my eyes and whisper the name. After the accident, as my face was being patched together, I began to look like someone else, someone I couldn't recognize—and for a long time, someone I didn't like. In my bedroom mirror, on the eve of my final plastic surgery, I decided to say good bye to Lizzie forever, and from that moment on, answered only to Beth.

A smattering of pictures lies about the box. Teresa must have the rest. I push them aside without looking at them. I don't want to see that girl anymore. It still hurts to know she existed, and that I have taken her place. Beneath the photos I spot some old memorabilia: my old cheering skirt, high school graduation cap and yearbook, science medals. My acceptance letter to Juniata's coveted internship program at Rayston Field, an Environmental Field semester: the bridge that would have brought me closer to my dream of becoming an environmental scientist. I had devoted four years to obtaining that letter, in pursuit of that dream, only to give up my spot so as to endure my metamorphosis.

I bypass all of this stuff, reaching along the bottom of the box until I feel what I am looking for. I pull out a small pile of letters and clutch it to my breast, while my fingers play with the frayed pink ribbon holding it together. Though I know every word by heart, I slide the ribbon from the letters and, through my tears, proceed to read them, one by one.

June 5, 1978

Dear Lizzie,

It seems hard to believe that I'm 3,500 miles apart from you. Just know that leaving you was the hardest thing I ever had to do but I need to be here much more than I realized.

My grandmother met me at the airport and it was gut wrenching to see her so forlorn. She wrings her hands, is easily distracted and becoming forgetful — but I could tell she was glad to see me, as if I was going to make everything better the way they used to be.

My grandfather was a complete shock! I had no idea how devastating a stroke could be. This once robust, powerful man is just a shell of what he used to be. His left face droops and his voice is almost unintelligible — he can't move his left arm but he is able to walk with my assistance. I don't know how Grammy dresses him and I'm sure this sudden dependence has made him terribly depressed as he thinks on what used to be. I take him to therapy and they are very sweet and encouraging but behind their smiles I see the truth.

I'm sorry, I don't want to be any more depressing to you but you deserve the truth. I'd give anything to be back in your arms but this is where I have to be and I hope you understand that. Say a prayer that things here will improve so that I can return to you with no lingering cares.

72 more days until I can see your beautiful face. They'll be the longest days of my life.

With all my love,

Daniel

June 20, 1978

My Lizzie,

As the days pass, I find it more difficult to be without you. You're in my every thought, with me as I help Gramps dress, walk, eat, and I lose myself in memories of us. As I wait to hear from you, I recall every moment we spent together. I don't think I ever told you how I felt the first time we met. I watched you in the lobby of the library, amused as you shook the snow off your clothes, stomped your boots and jumped up and down. Then you unwrapped your scarf to reveal the most beautiful face I'd ever seen and I stopped smiling. But that wasn't when I fell in love with you. It was during our first date at Café Diem, you pointed out a crumb I had hanging on my lip. When I asked where, you leaned over and with the lightest touch kissed it. My heart stopped beating for me and at that exact moment, was yours.

57 more days, Lizzie, and I will take you in my arms and make up for all of this lost time.

July 1, 1978

Dear Lizzie,

…I have a recurring dream. You are waiting for me at our place as we planned. I walk through the door and there you are. You run into my arms, every time, and I hold you. I will hold you forever Lizzie. It's all I want to do.

In 46 days, my dream will be our reality. This thought keeps me going.

July 14, 1978

Lizzie,

The days are endless here without you. Every face I pass in town is yours. Every voice I hear is your voice. I miss you more than I can write in words. I can't wait to come home and take you in my arms. I promise, I'll never let you go.

33 days…

July 26, 1978

Lizzie,

Why haven't you written…

21 days can't pass by fast enough.

August 4, 1978

…So, in closing, I leave you with this; I love you more than life itself and more than I love myself -you are my everything…

In 12 days, I will kiss every perfect inch of you, and in-between each kiss, I will promise my undying love.

August 11, 1978

…I should have never left you.

At dawn, I climb back into bed, eyes red-rimmed and burning, laden with the heavy guilt of my emotional betrayal. As Alan stood at the altar and watched me move toward him, comfortably hidden under a protective veil, I imagined for those precious few moments, that the man who waited for me was the one true love of my life. After the ceremony and party, on our wedding night, I had invited Daniel into my mind, pretending he was the man to whom I made love. There, I was beautiful and happy.

My tears won't stop. Alan is a good man; he accepts me, and provides a comfortable life for the three of us. The odds of becoming pregnant had been stacked against me after the accident; when we found ourselves expecting, still in the throes of our courtship, I refused to believe something so wonderful could happen to me until I held her in my disbelieving, undeserving arms. I tried again, tempting fate, asking for more; though I was trying not for my sake but for our daughter-so that she could enjoy the company of a sibling, as I had never done.

I give in to the pain of remembering our failed attempts. After Stacy, I miscarried in my third month–three times. Stacy was our miracle child.

I find some semblance of resolve. *I will do nothing to jeopardize my family's happiness.* Daniel is a piece of my past. We've both moved on, and only one of us is aware that our paths have crossed again. No one will ever find out. I never want to hurt Noreen. It is clear to me now that I made the right decision in letting Daniel go. Noreen is stunning; I am, by contrast, an ugly duckling with a twisted foot.

The scenario that has plagued my imagination for years now seeps into my head, uninvited.

August, 1978: Daniel is home from London, and shows up at Café Diem, as planned. In a sentimental romantic gesture, we chose the location of our first date as our reunion backdrop. He stands at the door, canvassing the room, overlooking the woman with the mangled face, and screwed-in, gimp leg; trying to find the one he left in May, and not seeing her.

In my mind, he keeps scoping out the restaurant, wondering where I am, until finally, I stand–the only one–and he is forced to really see me. His eyes will give him away: *Who are you? Where is my Lizzie?* He'll mask his disappointment, of course, because in his heart, he is kind. He will come to me, take me to him and tell me he missed me. This is where the truth ends; from then on, I would never know if what he says is real.

In all the similar scenarios played out in my mind through the years, each one ends the same. He would have left me anyway–if not physically, emotionally. I would have never recovered.

I fall back to sleep as the sun begins to rise. I awake sometime later, holding onto Alan.

Chapter 12

Beth

"Hey, good morning!" Noreen is chipper and her mood is contagious. I smile into the receiver.

"Noreen, thank you for such a wonderful time yesterday."

"Oh, please. Don't thank me! We had fun. Dutch couldn't stop talking about you!"

"Well, tell him I only have room for one friend."

Noreen's deep, throaty chuckle echoes into my ear. "I already did. Listen, I gotta go do the mother-in-law thing. I'll call you afterwards. We'll make plans. Oh, you left some stuff here; Stacy's flips and her cover-up. Nikki loves it so much, I'll have to sneak it out. I'll drop them off before dinner."

"Okay. Thanks, Noreen."

"Oh please! Stop. Mwah!"

Hours later, the doorbell rings twice before I can pull away from cleaning the toilet. Peeling off my stained, yellow gloves, I glance in the mirror and balk. In baggy sweats, a bleached tee and no makeup, I am a sight for a Saturday afternoon–for any afternoon. I try to push back the loose strands running amok from my stunted ponytail, but my efforts are futile. I walk through the house, praying it's Noreen and not Mrs. Klein, who always appears put together no matter the hour; or worse yet, Theresa, who easily puts Mrs. Klein to shame.

Upon opening the door, I find that my unexpected visitor is none of the above. The last person I would have ever expected to ring my bell greets me; but then, nothing should surprise me at this point.

On my porch stands Daniel, with a smile and a plastic bag. My hand immediately goes back to my hair. I am mortified.

"Hi, Beth."

Through the screen, I stand like a mute. My mouth is open, but no sound comes out.

"Are you okay?" Daniel asks. This is the second time he's asked me this question on the two occasions I've seen him. *Pull yourself together, Beth!*

"Oh, hi. Sorry. I wasn't expecting you, obviously. Sorry." I sputter like a school girl, feel my face grow hot, and drop my shoulders. I can't look into those eyes.

Daniel, to his credit, says nothing and smiles. He wears his hair a bit shorter than he did a dozen years ago, but it's still thick and dark and covers his neck. Oh, I want to twine my fingers in those curls. He is in tan cargo shorts and worn, blue tee. He always could wear the hell out of a tee shirt.

A full minute passes before I can gather the strength to invite him in and he accepts, stepping into my foyer. Someone somewhere really has it out for me. If I could have been doing anything other than cleaning my toilet…

"Your place is beautiful. Noreen didn't do it justice."

"Thank you." Small gifts. I had just cleaned the foyer and adjoining living room. *Please God, don't ask to use the bathroom.*

"She pushed back on having you guys over, and now I understand why."

"Oh, she's ridiculous. Your house is lovely!"

Daniel says nothing. I am embarrassed by my good fortune, and hope my response doesn't come off as condescending. In truth, I find their house much more welcoming than my own. We stand awkwardly, until he holds up the plastic bag in his hands.

"You left these at our house last night."

I take the bag. "Oh, right. I forgot. I thought Noreen would bring them by."

"I offered. This is a great neighborhood. I've never been in this area before."

"Thanks." I manage again. If there was an award for exuding the least personality, I'd be a shoe-in.

Daniel nods, saying nothing. I feel my entire body start to shake standing so close to him. I want to touch him. I'd give anything to know what is going on in his gorgeous head. The phone pierces the silence and I jump, which makes him smile again. Oh Lord, that smile.

With a raised hand and an accommodating nod from my guest, I move as fast as my limp will allow to the kitchen to answer.

"Is he still there?" Noreen asks.

"Who?"

"The Hulk. My husband, silly. Did he drop off your stuff yet?"

"Yes. He's here." I lean into to the entrance of the living room and point to Daniel and back to the phone. He understands and shrugs.

"Perfect. Listen, can I borrow three or four cloves of garlic? I'm completely out and my linguine with garlic and oil will be linguine with oil if I don't get some quick. Do you mind?"

"Not at all."

"Oh, you're my savior. If I had to send that man to a store, we'd never eat tonight. Do me a favor, push him along, will you?"

"Sure. Talk to you later."

I turn to Daniel, who stands where I left him.

"What does Her Majesty want?" He asks.

I step onto the porch behind Daniel and hand him a small garlic-filled baggie.

"You must go now. Orders." I say.

"Well, it was certainly so nice to finally meet you both. I hope we can do it again soon. We enjoyed your company."

"Nice to meet you, too." I keep focus just over his shoulder to avoid those eyes. My behavior is odd, I know; but I am powerless to change it. If I look at him, really look, I fear I'll lose control and say or do something I'll regret.

I'm surprised he hasn't spun on his heels and left already.

I can't ignore his quizzical stare, and retreat behind my screen door. Daniel takes a step back, but his focus stays on me.

"I'm sorry. This sounds strange, but you seem so familiar to me. We've never met? Maybe in passing?"

"No. I just have that common face people think they've seen before. Happens all the time."

What am I saying? There is nothing common about this face. *Stop looking at me!* I take a step further back into my house. Finally, he shrugs.

"Okay. Sorry. I'm usually pretty good about that sort of thing. Well, take care, Beth." His warm smile and half-wave are needles in my heart. After over a decade, he can do that.

Closing the door, I wonder how I am going to manage a friendship with Noreen without going crazy. Back in the bathroom, I attack the porcelain with ardent fervor.

Chapter 13

Noreen

Dutch returns, finally, with the small baggie holding the garlic. "How did she act?" I ask, following him into the kitchen.

"What do you mean, how did she act? She was fine." He says.

"I'm telling you Dutch, she seemed weird to me Friday night. Do you think I did something to upset her? Did she say anything that might give you an idea?"

My husband shuts the refrigerator door and turns to me, sighing. "Listen, babe. I have no idea what you're talking about. She was fine. She seemed to hold no ill will toward me or you. Other than the fact that I probably embarrassed her, she was normal. Whatever that is. I only met her once."

"Oh, God. How did you embarrass her? What did you say, Dutch?" *Shit. Did he ask her if she had a problem with me? Please say no.*

He stares at me, silent. He's annoyed; still, I need to know what he did.

"I didn't do anything. I think she was embarrassed because she was in the middle of cleaning. I could smell the bleach from her foyer. Her hair was messy, and she was wearing crappy clothes. That's all. She seemed uncomfortable. Jesus Nor, stop being paranoid."

Shaking his head, Dutch goes outside, leaving me alone with my thoughts.

I definitely offended Beth somehow. Her whole disposition changed at my house. I thought we were getting close, but she really pulled away Friday night. Something is definitely amiss.

Through the window over the sink, my husband is tending to his beloved flowers, his sanctuary. If the yard didn't look so beautiful, I would bitch about all the time he spends out there. He's angry with me. I can see it. It's written all over his face.

∽

Chapter 14

Beth

"Let's go to the new water park. I'll swing by and get you."

Noreen's voice is full of enthusiasm, and can bring me out of any funk—usually.

"I can't. I promised my mother we would spend the day with her shopping, Stacy wants some new school clothes." I gnaw at my thumbnail, letting the silence between us linger. The heat of the sun through my kitchen window is making me uncomfortable.

"Oh. I thought the girls were planning to go together. Okay. Another time." Noreen says.

I am thankful for the privacy of the phone, a coward hiding from Noreen's clear disappointment. This is her fourth attempt to make plans with me since that night at her place, and so far I've managed to derail each one. I wonder when she will give up.

I thought I could do it. I really did; but when Daniel showed up at my door two weeks ago, my resolve was weakened to the point of near collapse. I need to talk to someone, and can't even enjoy the irony that Noreen, his wife, is my someone. Knowing that I am the only one aware of what is going on brings me such loneliness that I am sometimes engulfed entirely, not rising from my bed until prodded by my daughter or questioned by Alan. This occurred to the point that I ultimately found it easier to go through the motions than invent a reason for my behavior.

I miss Noreen. She makes me laugh, and I need her in my life-almost as much as I need to breathe. *Why did Daniel volunteer to come to my house?* This question plagues me. Am I making too much of a simple gesture? I'm sure he's crazy in love with his wife, and will do everything and anything for her. Why do I insist on making something out of nothing?

When I hear the dial tone, I choke up. Stacy scampers into the kitchen in her pink shorts and Hello Kitty tee shirt, oblivious to my mood.

"Mama, can I see Nikki today?"

I have to clear my throat before words will come out. "No, honey. Remember, we're going shopping with Grams. We promised her."

Stacy stamps her foot. "I haven't seen Nikki in a long time! Why can't we play? Mama, why?"

"How about we invite Jordan over again?"

She crosses her arms and her sweet face morphs into creases and frowns. I want to smooth them, to make it all better; but I know she won't allow me the luxury. She is angry and frustrated, and the only thing that will placate her is seeing her best friend. I can relate.

"She's too bossy. I don't like her." Stacy says before skulking off to her room, leaving me alone to wonder what the hell I am doing. Why am I jeopardizing her closest friendship? Oh God, I need help. Which would be harder, ultimately: living with Daniel back in my life, or living without Noreen in it?

Alan said something at dinner last night.

"You seem sad. What's going on, Beth?" He gazed at me across the dining table, over his skirt steak and potatoes.

"What are you talking about?" I threw on a smile and returned his gaze with as much vigor as I could muster. After seven years of marriage, Alan can see through my charade. Do I even try hard to hide my moods anymore? Maybe I *want* him to notice. Without Noreen, I have no one to confide in; now, looking at my husband, I realize I cannot confide in him any more than I could my best friend.

"You've been different; distracted. Do you need to tell me anything?"

I put my fork down and wiped my mouth with my napkin while deciding how to respond. I looked at Alan long and hard, wondering what he would do if he knew what was swirling about in my mind, and feeling thankful that he didn't. Finally, I forced myself to appear relaxed, and smiled.

"No, honey. Nothing to tell. I'm just not feeling myself lately. Maybe I'm coming down with something. I promise. Nothing is wrong."

Satisfied, he shrugged and returned to his dish while Stacy's eyes flitted between us. Her fork held midair, she stayed on me until I winked and nodded for her to eat.

I passed the rest of the meal in silence, beside the two individuals with whom I share most of my waking hours, who I have vowed to love and care for; with whom I share every meal, every experience, year after year.

They really know so little about me.

* * *

At the mall, Stacy waves to us from her perch on the shiny stallion, frozen in a cantor with his head down and mane cascading over his eye. I wave back and wait until the music begins, signifying the start of the ride, to confide in my mother.

"I have a problem." We are standing along the metal fence surrounding the carousel between Macy's and Lord & Taylor.

Teresa slips her lipstick back in her bag. At sixty-five, she is still a striking woman, someone I used to resemble very closely.

"Is it Alan?"

"Well, yes. No."

"What is it, yes or no?"

"It's Daniel."

Her face is blank.

"Daniel who?"

"Mom, come on. Daniel. Fergusan. From Juniata."

"Oh. Well, how am I supposed to know? That's such a common name. Don't snap at me."

"Sorry."

Teresa runs her manicured fingers through her short, blond hair. "So? What about him? Why bring him up after all these years?"

"He's Noreen's husband."

My news registers right away. "Nicole's mother?"

I nod.

She stares ahead; my guess is she's thinking back to the days of my recovery. Eventually, she turns to me. "Hmmf. Small world. What were the chances?"

"Exactly."

The carousel whisks the children around to the music. I wave to Stacy as she passes.

"So, what's the problem?"

I gawk at my mother as if she'd just told me Michael Jackson called her this morning.

"Are you kidding me? Mom, I was in love with this man. Now he's married to a close friend. I have to see him. We do things together, with his family. Noreen's always inviting us over."

Teresa sighs and shakes her head.

"Elizabeth, you were with this boy, what, ten, twelve years ago? You were both young, had a few months together. You hardly knew each other. The relationship is always rose-colored at the beginning, and yours never had the chance to go bad. Your memory is skewed. Trust me." She turns to face me. "You're married to a wonderful man, with a beautiful daughter. Stop dwelling on what might have been and focus on what is yours now."

I pick at my nails and avoid Teresa's glare. In minutes she had managed to invalidate any inner turmoil I'd been experiencing. I am ashamed—a common emotion evoked from this woman. In this case, she may have a point.

"Does he recognize you?"

I shake my head.

"Well, sounds to me like you're making the problem. Let it go. He doesn't even know it's you. He's obviously moved on. He has a family. Leave him be."

I stare out, past the carousel, lost in my thoughts. My mother watches her granddaughter.

"You have another choice."

"What's that?"

"You can end your friendship. Cut all ties. If this is going to be a problem, end it."

"I couldn't. Nicole is Stacy's best friend. She needs her."

Teresa gives me a knowing look.

"Are you sure you're talking about Stacy?"

The music stops and the controller walks through the horses, un-looping belts, freeing small passengers. We make our way with the crowd toward the exit.

"What does Daniel do?" Teresa asks.

"He's in construction."

Her tiny, self-satisfied smile makes me simmer. "Well. Sometimes things work out, don't they? You did well for yourself. You're a doctor's wife. You're a lucky girl, Beth. Don't ever forget it."

Later in the evening, I lie in the dark, beside Alan who is blissfully lost in slumber, replaying Teresa's words over and over. The meaning behind them is undeniable. She thinks I'm lucky to have married a doctor, of all people, in my condition.

I recall a conversation we had after the accident, the one that ultimately made up my mind.

She walked into my room holding Daniel's latest letter, to find me in my usual spot, hidden in bed.

"Have you decided what to do?" She said

I shook my head from the depths of the blankets.

She stood at the window, gazing outside, rubbing her fingers over the smooth paper. "A lot changed since you've seen each other."

"Yes." I mumbled. "You keep reminding me."

"And" she continued, ignoring me. "You won't be returning to school this year. You have months of therapies and surgeries ahead of you. You need to focus on yourself and your recovery. You don't need a distraction right now." She turned from the window. "Think of him. What's he going to do? Commute back and forth four hours every weekend to see you? How will that help him finish his studies?"

The sun shone brightly; her face was lit by the rays, giving her an unnatural, angelic aura.

Her voice softened as she pulled my blanket back. "You were only together a few months. How well do you really know each other? What if he doesn't stay?" She sighed and stood back. "Elizabeth, you may think this is the end of the world, but you're only twenty-one. You're so young. Your life is before you. There will be another."

"I love him."

She stared at me for a long time. The unspoken question passed between us. *Who does he love?*

In the heavy silence, Teresa sat on my bed and stroked my hair—a gesture I used to pine for, but which now sent chills down my spine.

"What if he wants children?" She whispered.

She placed the letter on the side table and left me. At the door, she turned. "Please consider what you're doing. Your father and I don't want to see you get hurt."

Her words hung in the air like a pestilent fog. My hand shook. He wanted to hear from me. Anything, his last letter pleaded. What would I say to Daniel? My body was broken. My face had been mutilated by glass and plastic, and would never look the same. He would be repulsed by me.

I thought of my friend Jamie, my first visitor; followed by Peter Spidaro, awkwardly holding flowers. I remember their responses at first sight of me weeks ago; Jamie's hand involuntarily flying to her mouth, Peter's waxen expression. The shock registered on his face, and that slight flinch—as if she'd been slapped—still resonated inside me. I couldn't accept a similar reaction from the man I loved.

Teresa's words were daggers in my heart: not because they were cruel or even because they were true, but because they fell from my own mother's lips. Shouldn't she try to convince me he'd love me the same way, no matter what? Isn't that what a mother is supposed to tell her child?

Hurt as I was, I still recognized the truth in her words. I would never know if Daniel stayed for the right reasons, and I questioned the unfairness of strapping him down for the rest of his life with someone like me. A small part of me wondered if he would leave. Either scenario would break my heart.

I got up shortly after she left, and wrote him the letter.

Tonight, lying next to Alan, I succumb to the familiar pangs of resentment starting in my toes, moving through my body. The woman never fails to humble me, reminding me at every chance that I am not beautiful and deserving of true love. As if I could forget; a one-hundred-eighty-degree turn from my childhood, when all she wanted was to enter me into beauty contests.

"Oh, don't be so damn dramatic!" Teresa snapped when I expressed these thoughts at the mall. "Don't be ungrateful. Look at all you have. Get over yourself and your childish fantasies. Now. Before someone gets hurt."

Stacy, who had been window-shopping at the candy store near the carousel, skipped over to us, clipping our conversation short. With a huff, Teresa took her hand and I followed them, stung.

As much as it pains me to heed my mother's advice, I call Noreen Friday morning. It takes three tries for me to dial the phone with a shaky finger. She is cool when she hears my voice, but her reluctant acceptance to my invitation to get together fills me with relief. We make plans to meet in the afternoon, at the community park the girls love. The promised water section is open, with various stations of sprinklers and small geysers, and their patience is rewarded.

Later, Nikki and Stacy run and shriek from station to station while we monitor under the protective cover of an oversized oak.

"Do you even remember when you could scamper around in your bathing suit without being horrified?" Noreen asks as she watches them.

Oh yes, I do.

"Is anything bothering you?" She says.

I shake my head emphatically. Too much? "No. Nothing's wrong. Everything's fine."

Noreen turns away from me, back to the children.

"I worried maybe I'd done or said something. You were so quiet at my house, and we haven't gotten together since. I thought something might be wrong." She sighs. "We've only known each other a year, but I've grown close to you. I don't want to do or say anything to offend you. I can be offensive." She gives a small smile.

Oh, it's nothing. I was just in love with your husband a lifetime ago and if I didn't go and get into an accident, he would be my husband instead of yours. I wonder how offensive she'd find that.

"I'm sorry. The days got away from me. That's all." My eyes well under my sunglasses. "I feel the same way about you, too. It's like the girls brought us together. I've clicked with you more easily than with anyone else since I moved here."

Noreen nods in agreement, and relief washes over her face.

"You're my best friend." I add.

We sit in silence as the children run amok through the park until Noreen says, "Should we kiss or head into the sunset?"

We look at each other and burst into laughter. I wipe away tears that fall for so many reasons.

Chapter 15

Noreen

We've taken to calling each other every morning. I don't know how it happened, but here we are, talking at 8 o'clock, over coffee, trying to make a plan. Beth is two people: a shrunken, mouselike public persona and a chatterbox behind closed doors.

Devin is already on my nerves. He woke up in a mood, and I am tempted to spike my second cup of coffee. Thankfully, I have a reprieve–*Sesame Street* just started. The hour is mine.

"Want to go shopping?" I ask Beth between sips. A good day in the department stores usually re-invigorates me–and it's more socially acceptable than drinking before nine am.

"Again?"

"What do you mean 'Again?' When's the last time we went shopping?"

"It seems like we just went."

I roll my eyes–a habit I need to break, but in this case, is completely warranted. The woman has more money than God and she hates to shop, preferring to wear loose pants and some variation of a crewneck sweater for eternity. She may have some face and walking issues, but she's thin and can wear anything.

"Beth, we went back in June. We're due." I've been three times since, but there's no need for her to know that. There's a sale at Macy's I have to take advantage of: I need some new lingerie. Daniel's been working late again, and I want to make sure his mind is not on that bimbo in his office; not that he's into blondes with fake boobs–I hope.

Her soft chuckle through the line answers my question. Not going to happen. She hates to say no to me, so she always skirts her rejection this way.

"Noreen, I don't need anything and I already bought Stacy her school clothes. I want to take her to the park today. I can take Dev and Nicole if you want to go."

I hear Elmo's grating voice carry through the house and dump the remaining coffee into the sink as a warm breeze blows through the window. She's right. It's too nice to be inside. I can get some sun instead.

"Fine. I'll meet you. See you later."

I put the phone down and turn around to see Dutch waiting for me. He is dressed in cargo shorts and faded red tee, and looks *delicious*.

"You have plans?"

I walk to him, still in my nightie, and wrap my arms around his waist. How much time do we have left of my hour, I wonder?

"I told Beth I'd meet her at the park. Why?"

"I took the day off since school starts tomorrow. Patti will take care of things today."

Ah, yes–blonde, big boobed Patti.

I lean my head against his chest. "Why couldn't you have hired a frumpy, old maid to run your office?"

Dutch sighs and puts one arm around my back. "Stop it, Nor. I can do things around the house today. Go have fun with Beth."

"Come with me." I say. Beth and I don't spend enough time together with our husbands. Alan's work schedule puts even Dutch's to shame. Since the debacle at our barbeque in June, it's been awkward between Beth and Dutch. It would be so easy if they got along. This could be the perfect opportunity to get their relationship going. Dutch couldn't stand Bridget, or Dana. He thought they were too superficial–and their husbands, too 'low class'. As a result, we were often excluded from group dinners.

I was that chubby middle-school outcast again.

I smile up to my husband, using my powers of coercion (with my hands), to get him to acquiesce. It doesn't take much convincing. With a lingering kiss and a gentle tug, I pull him to our bedroom and shimmy out of my nightie, relishing the idea of a quickie before spending the day outside together. Suddenly, a blood-curdling scream invades our space.

Chapter 16

Beth

"Stacy, time to get up, honey." I whisper into her ear. Her cherubic face is peaceful, and I lose myself in her beauty and innocence, relishing this quiet moment before she awakens–before she starts to talk, demand, and exploit her forming personality, which is strong and warm and, occasionally, trying.

I love watching my daughter's eyes flicker every morning. It is one of my favorite things to do; to rub her small back as she is gently coerced into consciousness. This is our routine, one I will strive to keep for as long as I can. Stacy rolls over and rubs her eyes.

"What, Mama?" She croaks.

"Time to get up. It's the last day of summer vacation. I thought we'd do something together!"

I leave out the small detail of wanting Stacy on a better sleep schedule. I've been negligent. If she sleeps in this morning, she'll never fall asleep tonight, and the school year will start off groggy.

Alan is at work, leaving us free. Stacy looks at me and frowns.

"School tomorrow?"

"Mmm hmmm. I can't believe my baby is starting first grade!"

She covers her eyes, but cannot conceal a smile.

"And Nicole's in my class!" She points out.

"That's right."

Against my better judgment, I agreed when Noreen suggested we request the girls be together one more year. Mrs. Mendelson admitted she would have placed them together, anyway. They were good for each other, she'd said. They bring out the best in one another.

"I thought we'd go to the park with the pond today. Just you and me. How does that sound?"

"Can Nikki come?"

"Not today. Devin is in trouble, and Noreen is keeping him home. So Nikki will stay with them. Her mom has something nice planned for her, she said. Anyway, you'll see her tomorrow."

A flicker of disappointment prompts me to throw in the clincher. "I'll take you to Frosty's after we feed the ducks."

At the mention of her favorite ice cream shop, Stacy sits up, tosses her thin blanket aside and hops out of bed.

It is a glorious afternoon. The air is warm, but the low humidity allows me comfort in my long, cotton skirt. We meander slowly along the path surrounding the pond. The area is empty, and I imagine people are out shopping for school. I never find myself in this predicament, never leave anything for the last minute; I'm always organized, scheduled, boring. Stacy's backpack was filled and ready in July. With a sigh, I gaze around me and appreciate the solitude. The peaceful calm is broken only by the soft rippling of water in the wake of gliding ducks and the occasional chatter of my daughter.

We choose a bench under a large elm, sit down and eat sandwiches and strawberries. I pull a thermos from the sack and give it to Stacy. No plastic bottles allowed in my house; I am working to teach Stacy to leave a small carbon footprint, to understand the important role we each play in protecting our environment. "Earth will be here long after we're gone", I remind her. Since giving up on my dream of environmental work, I've focused on my tiny corner of the world, and the difference I can make within my family.

Once finished, Stacy grabs the bag of grapes, corn and barley and walks to the pond. She sets the bag down and reaches in with her tiny hand.

"A little at a time, honey. Remember."

Stretching my legs, I watch the swans in their ethereal beauty move effortlessly on the water. I envy them their gracefulness, their existence among the natural, rich landscape of their surroundings. I close my eyes to increase my oratory senses, and enjoy the undulation of gentle ripples against rock, and the birds' mating songs–until the shrieking of my own child disrupts my reverie.

"Mama! Look!" She turns to yell back to me before sprinting in the direction of two figures making their way along the path. The smaller figure takes notice of Stacy and lets out a similar shriek of her own before running to her friend. Nicole and Stacy embrace, both talking at once. Daniel–Dutch (still not sure what to call him)–watches from several feet away before looking at me. I struggle with what to do, and note that my hesitation is making him uncomfortable. I finally offer a small wave, and he seems to consider my greeting before deciding to walk over to the bench and sit beside me.

We have not seen each other since his surprise visit to my house weeks ago. I have managed to avoid outings with the four of us while keeping in close contact with Noreen. It's not such a challenge with Alan's overextended work schedule, and Dutch has been busy with new contracts. Two months have passed, and yet once again I am near breathless at the sight of him.

"We're to be having bonding time." Daniel says as he sits, and I wonder if he means with Nicole or me. Noreen can be unpredictable, and I don't think my silent question is without basis; but I hold my tongue. What does it matter?

"Noreen's idea?"

"Well, her suggestion." He admits with a shrug. "She decided it's not fair to keep Nik inside just because Devin's horns came out. Her words, not mine. My son is perfect. Hers is questionable." He adds, using quote marks in the air.

I smile. Devin is tough.

Daniel leans forward and squints his eyes toward the girls. "What are they feeding the ducks?"

"Sliced grapes, corn and barley." When he turns his head to me in question, I feel the need to explain. "Bread is unhealthy, has no nutritional value, and birds get lazy and rely on handouts. They can get sick. So, I did a little research and found the best alternative to their natural diet. Duck feed from the local farm is most appropriate, but I didn't want to trek ten miles out of my way today. The supermarket was closer."

Daniel stares at me for several beats while I hold my breath. Finally, he turns back to the pond.

"We used to feed them old bread. Times have changed."

We watch the girls toss the food into the air, giggling in euphoric glee as the ducks swarm around them, diving for each morsel. I try not to focus on the tingling sensation of my body. The desire to hold him hurts. When we were together, we couldn't keep our hands off of each other; a part of us was always attached–fingers intertwined, or in hair, or scratching a back, lingering on a thigh...

I cross my legs and arms as if to protect myself from my own desire, surprised I still feel this away after all of these years. I struggle for something to say, but my mind comes up empty. Everything sounds trite in my head. Daniel speaks first.

"So, tell me about yourself, Beth. You're quiet. I understand why Noreen likes you." He smiles.

Oh, no. Please don't ask me about myself. The less you know, the safer I am.

"What's to tell? I'm married, have one daughter and your wife has become my closest friend." It's odd to be speaking with him this way, ignorant of to whom he is speaking. Odd, and sad.

Daniel leans back against the bench and crosses his legs. "Okay. So you were born a married woman. Interesting."

I concede a smile. "I'm not interesting. There's nothing to tell."

He looks at me squarely and for a flicker of a moment, I believe he knows it's me. "There's always something to tell. Don't sell yourself short."

I clear my throat. "How about telling me about you, instead? I'm a better listener than I am a talker."

"Well, that would be a first." He smiles and shrugs. Noreen does manage to dominate most conversations; but she's interesting.

"Now's your chance. Quick, get it all out." I say.

We share a laugh, and my heart moans. He hasn't changed much in a decade. I follow his jawbone and try not to recall his soft lips, or how I loved to nibble at the dimple in his chin. I could stare at him for hours, uninterrupted.

Without effort, a vision pops into my head. It was the afternoon I ran to his house off campus, after learning of my acceptance into the exclusive intern program at Rayston Field. It was perfect May weather, balmy and sunny, and I wore a white eyelet dress that barely covered my mid-thighs. I was so free, holding my future in my youthful clutches. As I ran up his front steps with my letter,

Daniel opened the door with a wide smile. *You made it, he said. I knew you would, baby.* He took me easily into his arms and carried me inside.

I am brought back by his voice. "Well, I migrated from New York. Went to Juniata College." At the mention of our school, I stiffen, but say nothing. "It's small, in the middle of nowhere. Studied architecture and construction. After graduation, I travelled, a lot, and eventually settled back in New York. Work slowed down, and we left. My best years were here, and I wanted to come back."

He stares out at the pond while he talks, and I lose myself in his profile. I wait for him to bring up our relationship. I'm not sure why he would, to a complete stranger; but as I've learned, anything can happen. He says nothing more, and I realize I am expecting too much. It is a forgotten period in his life.

"So, how did you and Noreen meet?"

"Didn't she tell you this already? Isn't this something you girls volunteer the first or second time you get together?"

I grin. "Yes. I want your version."

"Okay. My version. Let's see. I was abysmally single and a buddy of mine, Robert, couldn't stand to see me so unhappy. So, he introduced me to his newly divorced friend. And that, as they say, is that."

"Love at first sight?" I say. Why am I fishing? Noreen told me it wasn't. Maybe I need to hear it from him.

Daniel shakes his head slowly. I don't realize I am holding my breath until he turns away, and I exhale. He leans over, rests his hands on his knees, and we listen to the girls as they quietly sit together, flicking food to the gathered gaggle.

"The truth is, I didn't want to like her. Until Noreen, I had managed to avoid any serious relationships."

I know I shouldn't, but I can't help myself. "Why?"

Daniel stares, past the girls, who have now abandoned their task and chatter nonstop while making their way to the path. What do I want to hear? I follow his gaze, and immediately regret the question. No answer would be welcome.

"You know what? Forget it. I'm being nosy. I'm sorry." I stand and face the girls as they move away, and head towards them. He follows in silence.

We walk the path back toward the parking lot. The girls frolic ahead and occasionally glance behind them to make sure we are still there. The sky is a perfect blue and the clouds could be drawn from a book.

"I can see why Noreen enjoys you. You're easy to be with," Daniel says.

"So is she." I say. "We've become close in a short time."

"Yes. She talks about you a lot. Well, when we talk. Lately the house is filled with riotous tantrums, so there's not much conversation happening. I don't know what we're going to do with that child."

"Is he that bad? Maybe the second is harder, like they say. Maybe he has to prove something. Noreen tells me stories I'm not sure I can believe."

"Well, believe them. Trust me."

The girls decide to sit on the path in wait. Their heads are together, whispering conspiratorially. Occasional giggles drift along the still air and reach us. Stacy is a different child since meeting Nikki; more outgoing and confident. A woman walks up to them, bends over and says something. She's too far away for me to identify, but she seems familiar. Their heads turn up to her, and then they point back to Daniel and me. She watches us for several beats, putting her hand over her eyes to make us out, and I am uncomfortable. As I am about to say something, she leaves– probably satisfied they're not alone, unsupervised.

I have fallen several feet behind Daniel. My left leg, filled with rods, scars and screws, will never work properly again. I'm thirty-four years old and walk like I'm riddled with arthritis; even my hip is out of alignment. I look like a broken doll from the Island of Misfit Toys.

Daniel glances back, and stops to wait. When I catch up, we continue together.

"Do you mind if I ask what happened?"

I pause, and he stops. "Too personal?"

I shake my head, recalling my own question minutes ago. "No. It's fine. I got into an accident a hundred years ago. Crushed my leg, among other things. I sometimes worry its glaringly obvious. Then I forget I have it."

"Sorry. I tend to be direct. One of my many flaws. Must have been a pretty bad accident."

I nod and continue walking.

"How long were you in the hospital?"

"Five weeks. Six days in a coma."

He whistles. "Wow. Surgery?"

"I had twelve, overall."

Daniel stops to digest this, and I fear I've said too much. I don't want to go into my trauma, yet I love talking with him. He shakes his head and moves again. I think he's shocked into silence. We take several wordless steps.

"How does the name Daniel become Dutch?" I ask.

His lip curves up as he considers my question. "Noreen prefers it over Daniel."

"Why?"

"Because my mother hates it."

I smile as he continues. "The first few times we went out, she insisted on paying her own way. Trying to prove her independence or whatever. I guess she wanted to feel in control after her divorce. I don't know. Soon it became a joke. I'd pick her up and she'd say, "Where to, Dutch?" I guess it just stuck."

As we near the cars, the girls stand with their arms around each others' shoulders. "Can Nikki come to Frosty's with us, mama?"

I look at Daniel and shrug. He nods. "How can we not get ice cream on our last day of summer vacation?"

The girls scream and hug, and I shake my head with a grin. I open the door and Daniel peers at me over the roof of my car. "A hundred years ago, huh? I think Noreen's rubbing off on you." He smiles before walking away.

That evening, I peek into Stacy's room to see she is fast asleep, full on a family dinner and a movie. Alan sits in bed, reading a medical journal, and our roles are reversed; this time, I walk into the bedroom late. Silently, I pull off my pajama pants, letting them fall to the floor. I keep my tee shirt on as I've been inclined to do after our first time together. Rarely do I lie with Alan fully naked. My husband looks at me, uncertain of what to do. The forgotten journal lies flat on his lap. I step to his side of the bed and he quickly puts the book down on his nightstand and lifts the covers. Without a word, I go to him.

∽

Chapter 17

Noreen

The mirror wants to be my friend. On the surface, she shows me a flawless woman, who is shapely, smooth and whole. *Look at you,* she says, enticing me to believe her. What she doesn't know is I still see the awkward, overweight misfit lurking behind the woman, mocking me.

The clock is a few minutes fast, giving me some time before I have to get Devin. The towel falls to the floor in a thick, pink, terry heap, and I take in my reflection. My fingertips walk down my body, past my collarbone where I enjoy the feel of the bone through skin, to my breasts, barely grazing my nipples, relishing that familiar feeling of warmth that spreads through me as I think of Dutch and how he makes me feel when his hands are on me. Our lovemaking is intense, almost angry, and it's all that I want and need. I laugh at those over-sentimental made-for-TV movies where the coupling involves cherished gazing, interspersed with gentle kisses and murmurs of love. *Please!* We're so compatible in this way that everywhere else we are is just circumstance–someplace I have to endure before I can lie with him again.

My hands travel along my rib cage, past my navel, and down. When I get there, I close my eyes, feel the folds, smooth and silk. I look, loving the way it looks and feels, exposed, and unblemished.

I can't wait to show him what I've done.

In jeans and tee, I pick up Devin from his playgroup, and hit the butcher. I'm in the mood for something special tonight. Sensing my upbeat frame of mind, my three-year-old is agreeable, and we get in and out of the store with little hassle. At home, I set him up in front of *Sesame Street* and prep the spinach salad before starting on the balsamic glaze.

The squeal of the bus breaks at the corner near my house and I run to the door, where Burt can easily see me, and allows Nikki off. I wave goodbye and he continues his route as my daughter jaunts along the sidewalk, swinging her Hello Kitty lunchbox.

"Mom, can I play with Stacy today?"

I grab her in a bear hug before she sneaks into the house. "What? No Hello, Mom? I missed you?"

"Hello, Mom. Missed you." She says, peeling away from me. "Can I, huh?"

I head back to the kitchen, pour the child a glass of milk to wash down her Oreos, and hand her a napkin while she sits on the chair. Devin walks in, possessing that uncanny knack for knowing when snacks are available. He was two rooms away, in the den!

"Not today, Honey. Stacy is visiting with her grandma."

"She always is visiting her!"

True, because Beth is afraid to tell her mother she wants to do something else.

"That's not true. And it's nice if she visits with family."

"How come we don't see our grandma that much?"

Because you only have one left, and I don't like her.

"I'm not sure. I guess she's busier than Stacy's grandma. Now go inside. Mommy's making Daddy a special dinner."

"How come? It is his birthday? Are we having cake?"

"Cake! I wan cake!" The toddler comes to life, splaying his Oreos across the table.

"No, it's not his birthday. Sometimes it's nice to do things for someone just because you love them."

And today I got a Brazilian wax and your father is going to go ape shit on me and I can't think of anything else.

"So, go inside and play with your brother. Go ahead with her, Devin."

"No! I wan cake!"

Well, it was nice while it lasted.

"I'll find something for you later. Nikki, please, I beg you, take him into the other room. I can't afford to have a headache today."

The filet mignon is finished just as Dutch walks in from work. I couldn't have timed it better. I pour us each a glass of wine while I wait for him to change out of his work clothes. He returns looking disheveled and adorable in sweats and torn tee, filling the small kitchen with his solid, six-foot-two frame. He runs his fingers through his hair, a sign that he's stressed or trying to control himself.

"Rough day?"

"You could say that. The Triangle Group decided to go with someone else."

Shit. This is the second job he'd relied on to get us through this spring.

"What about Jared? Didn't he say he would connect you with someone?"

He swings his leg over the kitchen chair and sits. "Nor, I don't want to talk about it. Let's talk about something else. What did you do today?"

"Not much. Childcare. The usual." I keep my appointments to myself in light of the recent news. He doesn't need to know what I paid to Sonia's wax salon, or that I opted for the 90-minute deep tissue massage instead of my normal hour. After the past weekend with Devin, I was in need of some extra TLC from Ricardo.

"Any altercation with Devin today?"

"Actually, Ms. Pederson told me he and Robbie have come to some unspoken agreement. They spent a good portion of the two hours together."

When I drop Devin at playgroup three days a week, it's a crapshoot as to whether I'll have the full two hours to myself. I've been called many times to pick him up early. Mrs. Rose's Daycare has a no-tolerance policy against hitting, kicking, biting, or generally, any normal three-year-old behavior.

Dutch is preoccupied at dinner, and though the filet did come out amazing, it feels wasted. I stand to pour him another glass of wine and lean over his shoulder, to kiss him on his cheek.

"Hey," he says, rubbing my arm and leaning back. "Sorry. I'm with you. I'll shake it off."

"It's okay. I have a surprise for you." I mew in his ear. He tilts his head back to look up at me.

"You got a job?" He smiles but it quickly drops when he see my expression. "Babe, I'm kidding. Tell me. What's my surprise?"

The ambience I'm trying to set is tainted by what he says. I know he wants me to work, so he's not really kidding. I'm almost tempted to keep it to myself and end the night early; but then I lose, too–and I've been looking forward to this all day.

"Later. Go say goodnight to the kids first. They're bathed and ready."

I am waiting for Dutch on the bed, in my birthday suit, not a stitch of hair on me below my eyebrows. He walks in, looking exhausted from a combination of the long day and wine: but when he sees me, the corner of his lips raise and he is stripped out of his clothes before he even makes it to the bed.

༄

Chapter 18

Beth

In September of Stacy's second grade year, Noreen and I recognize the other women milling about as we enter the cafeteria. After signing in, the PTA meeting is under way. Meredith will hold her presidency for one more year, having beaten out Stella Rubin—her only opposition—by a narrow margin.

She walks importantly to the podium, and Noreen raises her eyebrows at me as we wait for her to adjust the microphone to reach her mouth. I stifle a giggle at our inside joke that if there was ever someone who doesn't need to amplify her voice, it is Meredith. After some unnecessary pomp and circumstance, she is ready.

"Welcome back, ladies. We're excited to embark on another successful year! I am pleased to hold my position as PTA President of Mayfair Elementary School for one more term. For those joining us for the first time, allow me to introduce the board…"

While introductions are made, Noreen entertains me with a whispered comment on each member. *You'll notice Brenda wears a snap-down shirt which can be taken off without effort when she works the pole at night…And Lorna is having an affair with our hot principal, a soon-to-be-not-happily married Mr. Tortelli….*

Her imagination is on overdrive today, and I'm sure we come across as rude and distracting. I try to shush her, but she's having too much fun. Our immature antics almost cause us to miss the first, official announcement.

"We need someone to take over the fund-raising this year. We lost Linda to middle school, and I need a volunteer to head the committee. Do I hear any takers?" Meredith asks, looking around the room.

The women shift in their seats, turn their heads away from Meredith, murmur and ignore the request. Noreen elbows me. "Why don't you do it?"

I give her a look that I hope she interprets as *Are you kidding me?* She might have suggested I run for town mayor. Noreen shrugs, not to be deterred.

"Why not?" She whispers. "You're organized, and you were the one who ran the art sales again last year. We made a bunch of money doing that. Come on, you're perfect! I'll help."

I roll my eyes, about to squash her suggestion, when a thought occurs to me. Maybe I can do it. What else am I doing all day? Stacy is in school full-time. I raise my hand, and Noreen preens. Meredith looks over with a wide smile.

"Okay, ladies, we have a taker! Mrs. Butler is head of fundraising this year. Congratulations, Mrs. Butler!"

"I want to incorporate a recycling program into the school. I would like to start by getting the students at Mayfair Elementary to bring in a re-usable bottle in place of plastic bottles every day. If we can raise two-fifty per child, we can buy each student a metal container, BPA free. This way, no one can give the excuses that they forgot to buy one or they don't want to spend the money."

I look at Alan. "How did that sound?"

He glances up from his Sunday paper, peeks at me over his reading glasses. "Hmmm? Sounds great."

I review the notes again, satisfied with my message. I got the idea to recycle when I walked into the cafeteria to bring Stacy her lunch, and saw garbage pails overflowing with half-full plastic bottles. We've been conscientious at home, and I am confident I can bring a program to the school. For the first time in years, I am energized with a sense of purpose.

At home, I had started planning a proposal to introduce at the next meeting. Noreen loved the idea, and we spent the entire weekend organizing our thoughts, researching various companies for the best price for metal bottles.

Alan folds the paper, and sets it down.

"What time are 'The Whites' due over?" He asks.

"They're not 'The Whites.' They're 'The Fergusans.' They'll be here in half an hour."

"I wonder why she kept her old married name? It's not like she would be a Robinowskowitz or something. Fergusan's easy."

Had Noreen introduced herself as Mrs. Daniel Fergusan, I would have run the other way and missed the joy of our friendship. I'm glad she didn't.

Stacy and Alan give my world much of its color, but Noreen adds the deep indigo to my life's rainbow. After our unplanned meeting at the park, and our pursuant conversations, my confidence in a platonic relationship with Daniel (Dutch–I must to stop doing that!) grows. I am working to consider him simply the husband of my friend.

We decided to eat dinner together after spending the entire afternoon working on the proposal. We agreed on pizza, and Noreen went home to get Dutch and the kids. When the doorbell rings, I feel a happy anxiety course through me.

Later, as I am clearing the table while Alan and our guests relax with wine, loud shrieks emerge from the den. Alan and Noreen jump up and run inside, leaving me standing mid-way to the sink, still holding dishes.

Dutch sits at the table, still holding his wine glass. Reluctantly, he stands.

"No use joining them. Too many cooks, and all that. Where do you want these?" He holds up the salt and pepper shakers.

"I'll take them. Thanks."

He walks to me and waits, while I place the dishes in the sink.

"I like your idea for the recycling program. Noreen's excited."

"Oh, thanks. I figured it's a good start for the district. You know, to try to be environmentally conscious." I lean down to put the salt and pepper shakers onto the lazy Susan. When I stand, Daniel is watching me.

"What?"

He pauses for a moment before shaking his head. "No. Nothing. It's nothing." He sits back at the table, and I try not to look at him while he swirls his wine in thought.

Noreen returns with Alan behind her. "Dutch, please tell Devin to stop beating on the girls. He had them both by their hair.

Ugh! This child is exasperating!" She throws her hands up. "Beth, where's my wine?"

"And so, I'd like to propose a bake sale at the Fall Fair, where the proceeds go to buy each child, in all grades, a metal water container."

I end my speech and gaze around the cafeteria. I'd hoped more parents would attend the monthly PTA meeting, but would have to settle for word of mouth and hand-outs. More wasted paper to reach those who can't spare an hour to find out what is happening at their child's school. I know many parents work, but hundreds don't. Looking at the women (it is always women who show), I count twenty-six in attendance. Always the same people, meeting after meeting, year after year—a feeble representation of the district.

I glance over at Noreen, who gives me an enthusiastic thumbs-up and smiles.

Meredith clears her throat and springs up from her chair, indicating to me to take a seat. The PTA president moves to the podium and again, adjusts that microphone.

"Thank you, Beth." Meredith begins. She glances at her board, sitting surreptitiously along the table, beside the podium, before returning her gaze to the PTA members—avoiding me.

"While a very nice, well thought out proposal, I must express my concerns. The fund-raisers we hold here at Mayfair are to raise money for educational programs and for extracurricular school needs, such as cultural arts plans—like the children's author brought in last spring—and updated playground equipment. To hold a fund raiser specifically for water bottles is not in direct correlation with its purpose. I speak for the board when I say this won't work. Okay, next on our agenda is school banking. Lorna Dorsen, you're up."

Noreen wears an expression of complete and utter disbelief that mirrors my own. How could she squelch a proposal, without even consideration or a vote? Isn't that illegal?

I am fuming. The woman didn't even have the audacity to look at me while she spoke!

I cannot hear a word Lorna says about banking. My other senses shut down, and all I see is red. Frantically, I try to collect my thoughts, taking deep breaths. Before I realize what's happening,

Noreen stands up, and faces the board. Lorna stops speaking mid-sentence, and freezes.

"Excuse me." Noreen starts. "Meredith. I was under the impression all proposals go to vote at PTA meetings."

Meredith sits in her seat and accepts the microphone from Lorna, like a royal.

"Mrs. White. I didn't bring it to vote because the rules of fund raising are to bring in monies for the…"

I put my arm on Noreen's, and motion for her to sit. This is my fight. I stand in her place, and continue my argument.

"I understand the rules. You just went over them–again. I think a recycling program is necessary for our children. If they don't learn at a young age how to protect the Earth, then we're not doing our jobs as teachers and parents."

"I hardly think metal cans are going to save the Earth, Beth. I think you're putting a bit too much emphasis on nothing."

"I disagree. We have to start somewhere. Let's make an example for the rest of the district. Children *want* to help. They *do* care, and we should take advantage of their openness and adaptability now. We can start with lowering the volume of garbage we produce, and take it from there. I have plenty of ideas. This is only the beginning…"

"Okay. Enough. Enough." Meredith holds up her hand. "Fine. Let's take a vote. All who agree with the proposed fund raiser for recyclable metal water bottles, raise your hand."

Noreen's hand shoots up into the air and she mouths the words, *Nice job!* I am shaking; my body courses with adrenaline as I peer around the room, imploring my fellow parents with my eyes to raise their hands. Slowly, hands rise into the air. I count to myself as Meredith counts aloud. Four, five, six, seven, eight, nine, ten, eleven…

"All those who oppose, raise your hands."

Three, four, five, six! The entire board has its hands raised in support of its beloved president: brainwashed soldiers mimicking their tightly wound dictator. Are they afraid of her? What are they thinking? Still, the vote is in my favor. I've won my first battle in PTA. Maybe not a large achievement, but I have to start somewhere.

Meredith's eyes reach mine, and I cannot see what's hidden behind them. Her face is a mask. I don't smile or smirk, though I want so badly to stick my tongue out and *nah nah nah nah nah,* her. I remain steadfast, until she knocks me down with her closing statement on this subject.

"Ok, folks. Your votes. Your choice."

No *Congratulations.* No *We're looking forward to a great fund-raiser.* Just a cold, *Okay folks. Your votes. Your choice.*

"What a bitch." Noreen sighs on the way home. "I can't believe we put her in charge of our PTA for another year."

"Actually, I didn't vote for her. I thought Stella Rubin would be a better fit for the position. Don't you remember? I don't think you even voted last year. Anyway, who cares? Her reign ends in June, and someone new will take over. We still have four more years here. We've just begun."

I pull into Noreen's driveway and put the car into park, as I glimpse someone peeking out the front, bay window. The way my heart flutters, I know it can only be Daniel. I wonder if Noreen reacts the same way when near him. I assure myself that she does; that he has this effect on everyone. She told me earlier that he was home this morning. He starts a big project tomorrow, so they'll spend the afternoon together. I can't remember the last time Alan took a day off from work to stay home with me.

"Thanks for sticking with me. I appreciate it."

"Are you kidding? You were awesome! I almost cheered out loud when we counted the votes. You were calm and collected up there, my friend. I think you missed your calling."

I focus on my lap, trying to hide my disappointment. I did miss my calling. After my accident, I gave up my internship at Rayston Field. Noreen has no idea. I share little about my past dreams with her, for obvious reasons. There can be no link between me and Juniata, knowing they would put it together at once. I am on egg shells when Alan is present, wondering when pieces of my past will surface and shatter my very existence. My husband knows nothing about my past relationship with Daniel, but he does know where I went to college. For some reason, the details of my education have not come up in conversation with Noreen and Daniel; and I pray that now, having passed that initial questioning period of where we came from, they never will. I am grateful that Alan is not much of a talker.

"You know, it felt great speaking my mind–especially about something I care for this much. I hope I'm not on Meredith's shit list."

"Oh, please! What can that woman possibly do to you?"

Chapter 19

Beth

My lips touch the rim of the steamy mug as I lounge, lazy in pajamas, when Daniel calls me at home on a Wednesday. This is the first time he has called the house, and his voice is more effective than any cup of tea on this cold, cloudy February morning.

"I want to throw a surprise party for Noreen, for her fortieth. I need your assistance."

I flush, settling on the living room couch, near the bay window. "I'd love to help."

"Great." The relief in his voice makes me smile. "I have some ideas, but I'd really like your input. Do you think we can get together? I'm at a job site, and it's not easy for me to talk now."

We decide to meet the following night at a diner outside of town, to avoid any familiar faces. Noreen drives the girls to dance class this week, giving us an hour and a half alone. When we hang up the phone, I lean back on the cushion cupping my steamy mug, a comfort against the bleak sky overhead, and try to ignore the butterflies that have taken flight inside of me.

Daniel is waiting at the diner when I arrive. He stands, and kisses my cheek before sitting back down in the booth near the window, where a cup tea sits in front of him. I ask the waitress for the same, and settle myself across from him, pushing my coat behind me.

"I hope I didn't put you out by asking you to come here. I figured it would be hard to explain why I was at your house, or you at mine, without giving anything away. I don't know what I'm doing, and I need you." Daniel says.

"Of course. I'm happy to help."

"Well, you're much more capable than me to put something together. Noreen says you're organized. Now, I want to run some ideas by you…"

He reaches into the leather portfolio on the table, and sorts through pamphlets. I wait and watch, unable to believe I am sitting across from the man I once thought would share my life. *Do you ever think of me?* I want to ask. *Do you miss me at all? Or am I a remote piece of your past?* My fondness for Noreen does not soften the jagged pain in my core as I sit across from Daniel, alone, without being able to touch him, to express myself.

"Here we are." He says, laying three menus on the table to face me. "I was thinking of maybe having the party at one of these places. What are your thoughts?"

I study the brochures, under the heat of his gaze. "Um, I think we can rule out The Grille. Noreen once mentioned she went to something there, and was unimpressed with the food." I push the menu aside. "Hmm, I like Thurston's, with that beautiful room in the back, which resembles a big tent. I heard the food was excellent. Of course, I can't say for sure. I've never been."

I look up, and his eyes are on mine. He smiles, and my insides alight. "Okay. I liked Thurston's, too. I was impressed with the room when I stopped in for the menu. I'm glad you agree. I think we should sample their food first."

"How do you plan to do that?"

"Well, why don't you call Noreen and suggest we try it? You know, the four of us. Alan will be in on the surprise, so it will seem like we're just going out to eat. We've been to Luigi's three times already in the past two months, and I'm getting bored."

We get together often with Noreen and Daniel–and, somehow, always end up at Luigi's. It seems to be our place, but Daniel is right. Noreen would never think there was an ulterior motive. It is time for a change, anyway.

"Or," he says, "you and I could go for lunch and discuss the choices."

I lean back against the booth in thought. I wonder if I can share a meal with this man alone without saying something I'd regret. Right now, sitting at this diner, I am expending enormous energy focusing on the task at hand, when what I really want to do is tell him who I am, and that I never stopped loving him.

"What are you thinking?" Daniel says. His head rests on his hands, and he is gazing intently at me.

I blush. "I was just wondering what etiquette says about dining with a married man."

He closes his eyes and nods. "You might be right. I don't usually think that way. I would never…"

"Nor would I…It was silly. I mean, we're trying to throw a party for your wife. What would be the harm? How about the four of us go out and you and I can discuss our thoughts afterward. Maybe Noreen will help us out, by offering her opinion on the food."

"*Maybe* she would give her opinion? Do you know her *not* to offer her thoughts on anything?"

We laugh, and fall into silence. The waitress stops at our table to refill our mugs, and Daniel orders a piece of lemon meringue pie for both of us, ignoring my protests.

"I shouldn't," I admit, patting my stomach. "Doesn't come off easily."

"You have nothing to worry about. You look great."

His lie hurts.

When I turned thirty-five last year, I begged Alan not to throw me a party. He obliged, probably grateful. I've so few friends and little family, the invite list would have been pitiful. Instead we went to the Cape with Stacy and enjoyed the weekend. Afterward, Noreen took me out for a private "girls-only" celebration. It was perfect.

When the pie is served, Daniel smiles at me. Against my better judgment, my fork finds its way into my mouth.

"See? Everyone needs pie in their life, now and then. Life's too short to go without."

"I have to starve myself for the next two days for this."

"Why don't you go to yoga with Noreen? She tells me you don't belong to the gym with her. I thought you two did everything together."

I dab the napkin to the corners of my mouth, and back across my lap. I am embarrassed by my body; but for some reason, I want to share with him.

"I can't work out. My left leg is an inch and a half shorter than my right. I'm afraid to try yoga. You need balance."

Daniel holds me in his gaze for several beats. My heart pounds in my chest, as I feel him looking into me. I reacted the same way when he first surprised me at the library, the day we met, the day he stood at the counter and asked me to help him find The Power of Microeconomics, Book Two, Volume One; the day my whole life changed.

How does he do that with those eyes? Time for me has melted away. I am a twenty-one-year-old school girl again.

"Was anyone else with you in the car?" I know he is referring to my accident. His interest in the event is at once unnerving, and endearing.

"My girlfriend. She died before help arrived."

"Oh, God. I'm sorry, Beth. Must have been so hard for you."

"It was. It is. I still think of her."

Daniel shakes his head. His fork plays with the remains of the pie. His silence indicates his thoughts to me.

"I know. I'm a lucky girl. You can say it; everyone does."

He leans over the table to me, and a rush of adrenaline rises from the soles of my feet. "I wasn't going to say that, Beth. I was going to suggest you try something else at the gym instead of yoga. Like weights. You sit to use most of the machines. I go a couple of nights a week, if you ever want to try. Noreen refuses them. Maybe she'd reconsider if you joined."

"Thank you. I don't think so."

Daniel pays the bill, and we walk outside to the parking lot. The chill forces me to wrap my coat around me, hugging myself. He escorts me to my car, where we stand in awkward silence, our frosted breath mingling, until I glance at my watch and realize the girls' dance class is almost over. Reluctantly, I climb into my front seat, start the car, and wait for the heat to kick on. Through my rearview mirror, I gaze at Daniel with longing as he crosses the parking lot to his car. The vision of him walking backward from me at the airport is crystal clear, and tears well.

As I pull out, I pass an idling minivan parked a few spaces down, and peek into the window. Meredith? When I check my rearview mirror, there's no one in the driver's seat. My mind is playing tricks on me.

∽

Chapter 20

Noreen

Devin is screaming bloody murder again, so I take this opportunity to sneak outside and fetch my mail. Still able to hear his high-pitched shrieking from the curb, I glance to my right and left and, satisfied that I am safe from the threat of social services for now, decide to brave the chilly air and stand here for a respite. As I sift through our credit card and bank statements–dangerously similar–I find myself under a cloud of helplessness. Dutch's business is just not growing at a fast enough pace to keep up with our expenses.

My mental checklist of luxuries I should give up is long. I decide my monthly bikini wax, weekly mani/pedis, hair color and cut, and gym expense, are essential to my well-being. Sure, we'd have more money; but Dutch would be married to a gray-haired, bushy mongrel. I wonder, which is worse.

Maybe we should cancel our dinner date with Beth and Alan.

Mrs. Neilson pulls into her driveway across the street, so I make a hasty retreat to my house, for the joint purposes of avoiding long-winded, nonsensical chatter and silencing my rowdy child.

Inside, his screams have not diminished an iota, and I have to admit, I am impressed with Devin's stubborn fortitude.

I drop my mail onto the table, grab my son–roughly–and drag his writhing little body from the den to his room, shutting the door on him. I didn't think it possible, but his tantrum gains additional fervor

As his screams follow me down the hall, I know I will never cancel dinner. Going out with friends is the very foundation of my sanity.

Back in the kitchen, I make a cup of coffee and resume the chore of sifting through the mail when I come across a piece of what I refer to as "fun mail." This constitutes anything wrapped in an envelope without a clear window. In this case, the encasing is pink -no return address -and I rip through it like a child on her birthday, to see who wrote me a letter.

With Devin's shrieking in the background, the plethora of bills scattered atop the table, I read the contents, and my blood goes cold.

I knock the chair over as I run to the bathroom to vomit up breakfast.

* * *

Dutch and I are already seated at Thurston's drinking our wine, when Alan and Beth are escorted to the dining room. Beth wears a wide grin, watching us. She's not paying attention to where she is going, so she doesn't see the chair in her way, and nearly stumbles when her foot catches a leg. Alan quickly grabs her arm to support her, saving her from total embarrassment. Dutch stands immediately upon seeing them and steps around me, shoving my chair in, so he can kiss Beth and shake Alan's hand.

While the three of them work their way into conversation with initial pleasantries: *Have you been waiting long? What route did you take?*, I watch my husband and Beth closely, trying to get my head wrapped around the accusations of the letter. There were no names mentioned, but the sender did specify 'husband and friend' and who else would come to mind but Beth? Between sips of wine, I mentally challenge myself on how that could happen. A man cheats on his wife if he is unsatisfied, right? Isn't that what Vogue says? No, there is no way. No one has more sex than us. I love Beth, but Dutch would never be attracted to her -not when I am home, waiting for him. There's no comparison between us.

If Dutch could read my mind, he'd leave me without a second glance back. I look to Beth, who is uncharacteristically animated this evening. Maybe she's sort of pretty, in her way. Her smile, though crooked, is appealing and comforting, telling the receiver, *You can trust me; If I smile at you, I am genuinely happy.*

I would have pegged him for the bombshell at his office. Maybe I misunderstood. I'll bet it's her. It definitely cannot be Beth. There's no way.

"Noreen." It's Alan, whispering to me across the table. "You okay?"

Beth hears her husband and looks to me. "Noreen, what is it?" She appears concerned, her brows furrowed, and all conversation stops. How long have I been zoning out? Relax, Noreen. It's a mistake.

"I'm just...I have a headache."

"Oh!" Beth rifles through her purse, pulling out a travel-size metal container. She takes two pills and hands them to me.

"Here. This'll fix you up. Make sure you wash it down with wine." She winks and the waiter arrives to take our orders.

Despite my ambivalence on coming here, I'll apologize later to Dutch for giving him such a hard time earlier, dinner is delicious. I order the sea bass, which is rich with flavor and juicy, while Dutch orders the pasta special. I try Beth's Chicken Piccata–it's to die for– and even poke around Alan's skirt steak. While we wait for dessert, I slip from my chair and go to the bathroom. Washing my hands, I decide to forget about the letter for now, take a deep, cleansing breath, and head back out.

I step out of the restroom corridor and view our table across the dining room. The men are both leaning in to listen to Beth, who looks to be in the middle of quite an interesting story. What has gotten into her? To my right, two busboys stand talking and an idea pops into my head. I check my purse and feel a sense of victory as my hand wraps around my disposable camera, left half-filled from my mother-in-law's seventy-fifth birthday brunch last month. I step over to the boys and discreetly ask one of them to take our picture.

Dutch is quiet on the ride home. The radio plays softly, Anita Baker, and I lean my head back.

"Nice place." I say. He stares at the road and I watch him, his beautiful profile, the way his hair flips over his collar. He is inside of himself.

What are you thinking, husband? Am I enough for you?

∽

Chapter 21

Beth

A few weeks later, we decide to have a Friday girls' movie night–child-free, at Noreen's. To my surprise, she chooses *Love Story*, a heartbreaker.

"What happened to *A Fish Called Wanda?*"

My answer–a dismissive shrug.

"*Planes, Trains and Automobiles?*"

Nothing.

As she sets up the movie, and I settle onto the recliner, I joke about how we should really re-think our future "fun" nights without kids. She is unresponsive. Did she roll her eyes?

We watch the movie in silence, and cry into our wine. While the credits roll, Noreen lounges on the couch, holding her glass. I stay on the recliner.

"This is perfect, isn't it?" She says.

"What?"

"The quiet, just us, no screaming, bratty kids, no husbands, Ryan O'Neal... all of it."

I smile. It is nice. And I'm relieved she's talking.

"We should do this once a month. Treat ourselves to a girls' night." I say.

"Agreed."

Noreen wipes her eyes, the last residue of tears. "I don't care how many times I see it. I just love that movie. What a love story. Don't you think?"

"It was a great book, too."

"Please! Why would I read the book when there's a movie?"

I smile at my friend. "You should try it sometime. You work all of your other muscles. Why not the large one between your ears?"

"What's wrong with my brain? Hey, I was smart enough to land Dutch, wasn't I? Can't be that stupid. I mean, he's no doctor…"

I turn crimson at her remark. If she only knew of my dreams to be a builder's wife. This builder's wife, that is.

Noreen sets her glass down, and puts her hands behind her head. "I know I'm not being realistic, but sometimes I wish Dutch felt about me the way these actors portray in the movies."

"What do you mean?"

"Oh, I don't know. He's not free with the 'I love you's' and all things romantic. Never has been; but lately, he seems especially frugal."

I keep my mouth shut. During our time together, it was all we could do not to profess our love to each other. I think of his letters, tucked in the corner of my basement. Perhaps that would have changed over time. I think of Alan and I, how little we express these thoughts, and it makes me sad.

"I wonder if he'd take care of me if I got sick." Noreen says, breaking the silence.

"Bite your tongue!"

"No, really. What if something were to happen to me? How can I be sure Dutch would take care of me?"

I pull up my recliner to sit straight, and look at Noreen. Fragments of my conversation with my mother so many years ago ricochet through my mind. Hadn't Teresa posed a similar question? Does anyone really know?

Noreen watches me, waiting.

I think of Daniel; the man I knew fifteen years ago, and the one I know now. The answer is as clear to me at this moment–as it should have been, then.

"He would. I know it. Noreen, he loves you. He'll always take care of you."

She stares at me closely for what seems a long minute, and I wonder what is going through her mind. She seems standoffish tonight, and I hold my tongue, instead of asking her what's wrong, as I should.

I exhale when, finally, she relaxes into a smile. "Yeah, maybe. And if all else fails, I have you."

"Yes. You have me."

"Well, thankfully, I'm still young and vivacious. Okay, not young–but fairly active."

"If you're not young, then neither am I. I'm only a few years behind you!"

"Please. Stop reminding me."

Chapter 22

Noreen

I don't know what to do. I came so close to showing Beth the letter, but lost my nerve at the last moment. I couldn't detect any guilt exuding from her. She was as relaxed for girls' night as she's ever been with me, and I can't understand how someone can sleep with my husband and still sit with me for a movie and conversation without remorse. I don't know what upsets me more; the fact that I seriously doubt the character of my best friend, or the idea of Dutch having an affair. With my best friend.

Beth was so certain of his love for me when I expressed doubt, that I convinced myself the letter was meant for someone else, and somehow ended up in my mailbox. I felt foolish and put the whole idea behind me–until I ran into Meredith at Hannaford's two weeks later. We were in the frozen food aisle, and I was politely ignoring her even as she bounced up next to me, hair bob and all. I stared straight at the peas, as if the answers to life's questions were stored there, until I felt her elbow in my side.

"Oh, hello Meredith."

"Well, funny meeting you here." She said, with a satisfied sigh.

Is it? I didn't think so. Everyone has to shop for food at some point.

"I almost didn't recognize you without your buddy. Where is she today?"

Two sentences, and I was already annoyed with this woman. I think it's a new record.

"Really, Meredith? How should I know? I'm not her keeper." I still focused on those damn peas, but she would not go away.

"Hmmf. Perhaps you should be."

I forgot about the peas and turned to give this woman my full attention. "What the hell are you talking about?"

"Oh, nothing." She shrugged and stared past me, into the case. "Now where are those string beans? Oh! There they are. Right under my nose." She pulled a bag from the freezer and turned back to me. "They always seem to be, don't they?"

I felt the color drain from my face. I couldn't speak, but I don't think she seemed to notice because her pie-hole kept moving.

"You know, I don't see how you two work. I mean, you're beautiful and outgoing and she's….Well, you'd think…." Then she paused and looked at me for a full beat, before shaking her head. "Never mind. Well, good seeing you." With that, Meredith practically skipped away.

It took me a few seconds to catch my breath before I went to find her. She was in the organic aisle; I knew not to look near the bread. I stepped in between her and the granola and put my face close to hers.

"Listen to me and listen good, because I'm only going to say this once. If you ever insult my friend, or even talk about her in my presence, I swear, it will be the last thing you do." I shook, and it took every ounce of control I had not to hit her.

Meredith looked sufficiently horrified and shocked. She leaned back slightly, her mouth agape.

"Beth is my closest friend. You do not fall near that category, and don't think you do. Whatever it is you're trying to say, I'll pretend it never happened. Butt out of my business."

I left my full cart and stormed to the door. I swore I wouldn't let that woman get to me; but over my silent denouncement of her accusation, the very next night, I found myself following Dutch's truck, with Devin in the car, after I dropped the girls off at dance. Even as I kept a safe distance behind him, I felt like an intruder; one of those lame jealous housewives exploited on those corny Hallmark movies. I had no idea what to expect, and found no solace as he pulled into a remote diner on Route 11. We were miles from town, and my puzzlement grew as he walked in, and settled into a booth by the window.

"What are we doing, Mama?" Devin squeaked from his car seat behind me.

"Mommy just wants to rest the car for a minute. Here." I reached back and handed my six-year-old a bag of M& M's, buying myself ten minutes. He happily munched, oblivious to his loony mother's shenanigans. I watched as a gray-haired, friendly-looking waitress chatted briefly with Dutch, while placing a cup on his table. When she walked away, he appeared to be reading something; a newspaper? Building plans? I knew it wasn't a book. My husband has not read one cover to cover since we've been married.

After fifteen minutes of sitting in the corner of the parking lot, I realized what an ass I was and started up the car. The man wants to have a cup of coffee here; who's to say no? I was giddy with relief as I pulled out of the lot, and would have just missed it, had I turned around a second later.

My heart rose to my throat, and I gagged with disbelief as my suspicions came to fruition.

Beth's car turned into the parking lot and pulled up to the handicapped spot under the diner's window.

I went straight home, brought Devin into the house, and called my neighbor, Gertrude, who I knew would be available. It was Thursday --her only free day --as I'd learned the hard way over the past two years. In fifteen minutes, she appeared at my door, and I promised to be home within the hour.

I could not control the shaking, and willed myself to keep it together. I knew where I was going, but had no definitive plan of execution once I reached my destination.

Minutes later, I knocked on the door and forced a smile when Alan let me in.

Chapter 23

Beth

Stacy's happy chatter greets me when I return home from the diner. She is in the middle of telling Alan a story about the latest drama of her dance class. I step into the kitchen at the end of her anecdote, punctuated with an exasperated eye-roll and deep sigh at her disappointment in Jessica, her schoolmate and the daughter of her beloved dance teacher, Miss Jenny.

"She just doesn't listen, Daddy! Me and Nikki are getting sick of it!"

With that, and after offering me a quick wave and wide smile, she jaunts off to her room.

"So, another typical day for our fair friend." I say, putting down my notebook and purse.

"I just can't get over the details she includes. The child has an elephant's memory." Alan adds.

As I sit at the table, he stands and takes the dessert plates to the sink. With his back to me, he inquires about my meeting with Daniel. I give him a quick synopsis of our progress, as I watch him diligently scrub the two small dishes.

"Are you mad at them?" I smile.

His shoulders are hunched, and at my light retort they ease down.

"Alan, are you okay?"

He straightens up, places the dishes into the drying bin, and looks out of the window. I wait, wondering what could be bothering him this evening. Immediately, I am guilty for meeting Daniel; but cannot figure out why this would upset Alan. He knew where I was going, and why. Could he possibly detect my inner thoughts? Am I transparent? Oh God.

"Alan…"

"It's nothing." He says, cutting me off. "I had a rough day at work. Two cases of melanoma, back to back. They've been on my mind, that's all."

I keep to my seat, to see if he needs to talk about it. To see if this is really what is bothering him. I wait until he turns around to me, gives me his smile and a kiss, and walks to our bedroom.

I don't hear from Noreen all week, which is odd. Her surprise party is Saturday night, and I finally call her on Thursday to check in; but the conversation is stilted. Finally, I ask about her plans for the upcoming weekend.

"Dutch wants to take me out Saturday night. For my birthday," Noreen says.

I stand in my kitchen, clutching the phone, ready with an excuse as to why we can't join them. Two months of planning have led to this moment. Daniel and I talked about it, and he decided it was easiest if he took Noreen to dinner for her birthday, knowing as well as I did that Noreen would want to invite us. She isn't one to need romantic dinners with her husband.

"That's nice," I say. It sounds lame to me, but I am afraid to utter another word, as I feel a thin veil of perspiration form on my brow. My excuse is foolproof. We are to be going to my mother's because it's my parents' anniversary, and we don't want her to spend it alone. This happens to be true, though we will be seeing Teresa on Sunday.

Instead, Noreen surprises me by not inviting us to join them. I am beside myself with worry. *Why wouldn't she invite us? Have we misjudged our plans? Does she suspect a party?* My mind is rattling with thoughts and in our silence, settles on one; she doesn't want me with her. She wants to be alone with her husband.

"Dutch wants to go to that Thurston's again. He seemed to really like it."

"Didn't you?"

"Well, sure. But you know me. I'm a Luigi's girl."

Oh no. Did we make a mistake? I close my eyes and say a silent prayer that this thing would turn out okay.

"You're a creature of habit. I enjoyed Thurston's. I thought you liked their food."

"I did. It'll be nice. Okay. I gotta go. I'm off to Pilates."

The evening of the party, I have just finished dressing, when Alan peeks into the bedroom. "Almost ready?"

"Almost." I stand before my cheval mirror, slipping my diamond-studded earrings through my lobes.

He steps behind me, puts his hands on my waist, and rests his head on my shoulder, so we're looking at each other in the mirror.

"You look beautiful, you know."

His eyes, so sincere, stay on mine. I smile. It is not enough, and I turn to him, placing my hand on his cheek. "Thank you." I say, and kiss him lightly on his lips.

He leaves the room, and I turn back to really see myself in the mirror–something I so rarely take the time to do. Beautiful? No; but I will admit, I do look nice. My hair is working for me today, looking shiny and full, grazing my shoulders. My conservative dress barely hides my imperfections, but I am sick of wearing practical pants and collared shirts when we go out. I slip on my shoes; low heels with the left sole an inch and a half thicker than the right, custom made for me last spring.

I turn from the looking glass, embarrassed. What would Alan think if he knew I got dressed tonight with someone else in mind?

Noreen and Daniel walk into the restaurant, greeted by the sound of a large crowd screaming *Surprise!* Noreen looks completely taken back. Daniel seeks me out of the crowd, where I lift my glass in a silent toast, and we share a triumphant smile. Fifty friends and family members wait their turn to personally offer the guest of honor birthday wishes. I don't fight the crowd to see Noreen, knowing we'll talk tomorrow and meticulously review every aspect of the evening. Instead, Alan and I enjoy conversation with mutual friends, hit the buffet, and watch partiers dance. I used to love to dance, but now refuse to try, and Alan claims he has no rhythm. We're the perfect wallflowers.

Late into the evening, I sit at the bar, to rest my aching legs and feet. I have been standing much of the night, something I am not used to doing, and my body is retaliating. I left Alan in deep conversation with an oncologist. Most likely, he won't notice my absence for some time. Daniel finds me a few minutes later, and takes the seat beside me. The bartender puts a drink in front of him wordlessly; Daniel smiles, and nods his appreciation.

"Well done," I say, turning on my stool to face him.

"Couldn't have done it without you." He says, lifting his glass to clink mine.

I shrug and sip my wine. I'm going to miss our secret meetings, but I don't dare verbalize this. So, he surprises me with what he says next.

"Now we have to plan something else. I enjoyed our diner chats." His smile is warm, and innocent.

I blush, and pray he doesn't look into my reaction as anything more than embarrassment. He has always voiced my thoughts. It's eerie. Even now.

"Well, Alan won't be fifty for several years, so…"

Daniel chuckles as Noreen walks to the bar. I watch her step to him, and marvel at her beauty. The dress she chose tonight clings to her flat belly and shapely legs. Her loose hair falls like silk to her mid back, and her face is flawless. I glance sideways to see Daniel watching her too. Again, I tell myself I've made the right decision. They're a beautiful couple. He deserves her.

Noreen has been drinking all evening, and her baby blues are glassy.

"I can't believe you pulled this off. No one ever surprises me." She slurs.

Daniel puts his arm around his wife, and nods to me. "I couldn't have done it without your other half. She was instrumental in this whole thing. We had to meet without you so you wouldn't suspect."

"Please. You're giving me too much credit." I say.

Noreen steps to me, and takes my face in her hands. I think she plans to kiss me right here. I smell the perfume and alcohol on her breath and, for a split-second, grow worried she'd really lean in.

"I knew it. I know my friend. Better than anyone. Better than any nasty, jealous bitch." Noreen says to me. She is not smiling, but her eyes shine. "I love you, Beth. Thank you."

She turns to Dutch, and kisses him deep and hard. I leave them at it, while I wonder what the hell she is talking about.

Noreen invites us for dinner the following weekend. She wants to thank us for helping to "lessen the blow into old age." She also has a surprise.

"I have something to tell you." She gushes over her empty dinner plate. Noreen looks across the table at Alan and me, and finally to Dutch, who nods for her to continue.

I sense Alan stiffen as he removes his hand from the back of my chair. I hold my breath, waiting for her to announce she is pregnant. What else can it be? Visions of our lives play in my imagination. I see a lot of cancelled girls' nights in my future.

"We're going to St. Lucia!" She spurts.

I let out a sigh of relief. As happy as I would have been to hear about a baby, I don't want to admit a new life would certainly impede the smooth road we are riding now, together. The girls are in fourth grade, and slowly becoming more independent. Even Devin is finally starting to come out from his heinous tempertantrum stage.

"That's wonderful! When do you leave?" I say.

"May 18th."

"Oh, I'm so happy for you. Will you be taking Nicole? Do you want us to watch her?" I look over to Alan, who I'm certain would be okay with Nicole spending time at our house. He plays with his napkin, and doesn't see me.

Noreen smiles, and leans back near Daniel.

"That will be kind of hard, since you're coming with us!"

"What?" I turn to my husband, who looks at her, incredulous.

"Please come." Noreen says.

I look over at Daniel, who watches me digest the news.

"It's my birthday present. Dutch is taking the four of us to St. Lucia–my favorite place! And now, I get to go with my favorite people!" Noreen says. She claps like a child.

"It's the least I can do for what you've done for me. Noreen's sick of being with me alone, anyway. You have to come. A guy at work has a timeshare, and is letting us use it." Daniel adds.

Alan and I wait until Stacy is asleep later that night before we get into a discussion about the Fergusans' wild invitation. He adamantly refuses to go to St. Lucia with them, listing various reasons–all riddled with holes, except for two: work and money.

How can he shut down his practice for a whole week? His patients rely on his stability, and how can Dutch afford to pay for the four of us on his modest salary? The plane fare alone costs a bundle. The first question can be answered simply. The man needs a vacation. I remind him, gently, that we have not been away together for any length of time alone since before Stacy was born. Nine years is a long time to go without recharging our batteries.

Alan's second concern is a valid one, to which I don't have a viable answer. I am not privy to Noreen and Daniel's financial situation, although Noreen has alluded once or twice in the past to "slow" months, where she has had to consider sacrificing a massage or pedicure. The time-share factor is definitely a help, but he'll still have to lay out money.

"I think it's a cyclical thing. You know, his job. He has been busy lately, which is why we've had to meet after work to plan for the party."

"I don't know, Beth. I am not comfortable allowing them to pay our way."

I look at Alan, and when he doesn't return my gaze, ask. "Is there another reason you don't want to go? Because Alan, I don't think your excuses hold water. I'm not sure I want to go. You know me and the sun…it's like pitting fire against ice. But if the man wants to take us away, will we insult him by refusing? Is there something else?"

I hold my breath, wondering what might come out, and if I can face it.

We are in the den, in the dark. The flickering light coming off of the television plays on our faces. Next to him on the couch, I lean over, and put my hand on his cheek. He looks up at me then, and smiles.

"No, there's nothing else. If you really want to go, we'll go."

I am ambivalent. The thought of being away at an all-inclusive resort for six whole days sounds positively enchanting; however, six days alone with Alan and Daniel nearly every hour of every day may be daunting. For me, that is; I know the rest of my group has no issues with this. I debate internally for two days until finally, Noreen calls and, using her well-honed skill of persuasion, convinces me to say yes.

Six weeks later, Teresa and Stacy stand at my parents' window, waving goodbye as we back out of the driveway. On the way to the airport, I try to relax. I have never left Stacy for more than a night since she was born. Now we'll be away from her for almost a week, and I say a silent prayer she'll be okay without us. Lord knows the damage that could be done under the temporary reign of my mother. Prior to leaving, I even checked the local papers, to ensure there were no pageants planned within a seventy-five-mile radius.

Chapter 24

Beth

The flight is uneventful, as is the taxi ride to the hotel and check-in. Noreen is giddy, and implores us to drop our bags, and meet them immediately by the pool. I push Alan to go ahead, claiming I need to freshen up. This will be the first time I will wear a bathing suit in front of anyone outside of my husband. While the Fergusan's and Alan are poolside on our first afternoon, I meander through the hotel, taking in the ostentatious lobby, spas, and restaurants and trying to appreciate its magnificence, reveling in its beauty. Only when I exhaust all my diversions do I reluctantly step to the back patio.

Outside, a gentle wind rustles the banana trees just enough to wiggle their large, deep green leaves overhead. I walk unevenly to the enormous pool, flanked by hundreds of teak chaises along the surrounding deck. In sandals, I feel more self-conscious about my limp than when I wear sneakers or shoes, and it slows me down further. The beach is just beyond the deck, looking exactly like every postcard I've seen. I am relieved to find my three travel companions near the deep end, relaxing, and not on the beach. I am certain the sand would prove too difficult to navigate. Noreen lounges with her eyes closed next to the men, looking gorgeous. The gym serves her well. Her legs are shapely, and tan, and her flat stomach disguises her history of two pregnancies.

"Hey hon, what took you? It's beautiful out here. Take a seat." Alan pats the empty lounge chair between him and Daniel.

I sit down, wishing for a cooler breeze. Keeping my cover-up on, I busy myself with a magazine. I feel Daniel's eyes on me, but refuse to meet them, and try to lose myself in an article about the efforts being taken to save the bears in the polar ice cap. An hour later, Noreen awakens from her relaxing slumber and looks around, stopping when she finds Alan cooling himself off in the pool. She stands and drops her sunglasses onto her People magazine. I avoid her stare, hoping she doesn't ask me to join her for a dip. She doesn't, and I watch her walk confidently to the water, envying her freedom and those killer legs. Daniel is still next to me, quiet.

"Having fun?" He asks.

"Oh. I thought you were sleeping."

"I'm not. Are you having a good time?"

"I am. Thank you, Dutch. It's magical. I don't know how we could show our appreciation for this."

"Forget it. If we can't take time to enjoy ourselves every now and then, then what do we have?"

I nod, and watch Alan tread water as he listens to Noreen talk. They appear to be in serious conversation. Every so often, he glances at us, and back to Noreen.

"You don't have to be embarrassed, Beth." Daniel says.

"Hmmm?" I look at him, unable to decipher where his eyes are through his dark glasses. As if reading my mind, he slips them off, and looks at me.

"You look uncomfortable. It's warm." He nods to my long dress.

"I'm okay. This is fine."

His eyes stay on mine an extra beat before pushing his glasses back on and reclining. "Suit yourself."

I watch the swimmers carelessly frolic in the pool, which is just as stunning as the hotel, with waterfalls flanking the north and south sides, and a swim-up bar in the middle. This is where I now find my husband with Noreen. Whatever they were discussing earlier seems to have morphed into a lighter dialogue. Alan smiles, and I watch them toast each other and sip from colorful glasses adorned with tiny umbrellas.

"I have scars." It comes out of my mouth without warning.

Daniel looks over to me.

I lift my cover-up to my waist, exposing an eight-inch-long, wide scar on my upper left thigh. "This is the worst one. But there are more."

Daniel leans over and tilts his glasses up to get a better look. "It's not bad."

"Yes, Dutch, it is. And it will be even more noticeable if I get color."

He looks into my eyes, and I have to turn away. I pull my skirt back down to my knees and lean back in resignation.

"Well, you're beautiful. Don't let anyone tell you otherwise." Daniel says.

Though uttered by my husband through the years, the words falling from Daniel's mouth sound as new to me as a sunrise, bringing tears to my eyes. I hide my emotions under my sunglasses, and into my magazine.

Later, as Alan and I walk back to our room, I smile to myself, feeling confident and pretty–a rarity–as Daniel's words reverberate in my mind. I raise my head and shake my hair behind me, and as I do, catch an unexpected glimpse of myself in the lobby mirror. The truth stares back at me, merciless. When I step into the shower minutes later, I can't control the anger I feel toward Daniel and his pity compliment. I never took him for a fake, and my disappointment in him grows exponentially, until I can hardly speak when dinner arrives at our table an hour later.

At one point, Alan asks if I am feeling alright, and I realize my anger has formed a halo around me, so I am all but ignored. Noreen is on her third drink, caught up in the band and doesn't appear concerned. Normally, she would nag the hell out of me until I blurted something out that would pacify her. I'm not up to fabricating a story right now. She goes to the ladies room and Alan takes his turn at the bar, leaving Daniel and I alone. Daniel takes this opportunity to sidle over to me. He has to put his head close to mine to be heard over the music. The smell of him upsets me more, and my ire turns inward.

"Something's bothering you." He says.

"Nothing is wrong, Dutch. I'm just tired from the sun."

He shakes his head and frowns. "No. You're not. Tell me. Maybe I can help."

I struggle with my thoughts and desires and anger. I am finding it difficult to be in close proximity to him for so long. He is blissfully unaware of my issues, and I feel my blood boiling, wanting to explode in a frenzy of truth. I don't want to be here. It hurts to be here, and I am sorry I let Noreen convince me to come.

"Beth, what?" He watches me, and I wish at the moment I knew what was painted on my face.

"Dutch. Please don't do this. Don't ask what's wrong. It's nothing that concerns you." It comes out cold, but it's what I need to do.

He looks hurt and moves back to his seat across from me. Alan returns to the table with drinks, and sits down. I stand and whisper to him that I have a headache and I am going up to the room. I refuse his offer to come with me, imploring him to stay. I am almost safe in the elevator when right before the doors close, Daniel squeezes in with me.

"What are you doing?" I say.

"Noreen wants her wrap. I don't know why. Once she starts dancing she'll have no use for it. She's half in the bag already."

He presses the button to my floor, securing the doors shut and I feel the sensation of my stomach bottoming out as the box rises. I'm not sure it's the elevator making me feel this way. Seconds pass, and Daniel turns to me. "I'm sorry you're not feeling well."

I respond with a shrug and will the elevator to move faster. Before he turns back toward the door, he reaches his hand up to my face.

"You have something….." It's barely a whisper of a brush when his fingers touch the corner of my lips.

I bring my hand to my mouth and push his away. "Oh."

We ride the rest of the way looking ahead, while my mind whirls. The sound of his breathing fills the space and envelopes me. When the doors finally pull apart, I spill out, and with a quick glance back, wave goodnight.

In my room, on the bed, my chest heaves with loss all over again, and I am grateful for the empty room. I fall asleep to the vision of Daniel's face right before the elevator doors close between us.

Chapter 25

Noreen

I thought I had ruined my friendship forever. When I stepped into Alan's house the night I discovered our spouses at the diner, I'd had no plan. Anger is what drove me to his house: I was ready to tell him what I had discovered, and together we would devise our confrontation and see what course our actions took.

When he answered the door and I saw his pleasant, easy smile, all of my intentions dissolved. What was I doing? I could come up with no pliable excuse for my visit, so I dumbly told him I was looking for Beth. He let me in, telling me she was out shopping (poor guy), and I allowed him to pour me a drink while we waited.

He seemed on edge for some reason, and I quickly sucked down my martini. I declined a second, since I had to pick up the girls in less than an hour—as much as I really, *really* wanted another. He made himself a second drink, and I felt him begin to relax as we sat on the couch, trying to fill in pockets of silence, having little practice being alone together.

I thought devilishly of Beth's reaction if she walked in on us being here, waiting for her. What would be her response to our inquiry of her purchases this evening? Would her guilt give her away?

As I anxiously awaited her return, I took a good look at Alan, next to me. He wasn't attractive in the obvious way Dutch was. His light brown hair thinned at the top; his eyes, though friendly, are small and average brown. His body isn't particularly impressive. In fact, his chest appears concave, whereas Dutch has movie-star-thick hair, dreamy greens and boasts a healthy, sexy build: muscles enlarged just enough from hours spent outside, active.

But there was something sexy about Alan that I had not felt before. I took in his expensive suit and shoes, worn with the disinterest of someone comfortable with money. He was the antithesis of Dutch, who preferred flannel shirts bought at Target and refused new shoes until the bottoms of his old ones resembled Swiss cheese. Maybe it was Alan's quiet confidence that made me do what I did that night. Maybe it was the gin. Whatever it was, I did something I never in my wildest dreams would have thought possible when we first met.

His glass was empty as we drifted aimlessly in a lull of silence. I watched him stare down at the lone olive, wondering what he must be thinking. I succumbed to the urge of leaning into him, to be closer, to take in his smell, his breath. He looked at me as I did, and I took his face in my hands and kissed him. Our lips opened and his tongue felt wonderful on mine, tasting of ice and salt. I knew what I was doing, but could not stop myself any more than if someone had control of me with puppet strings.

It was Alan who pushed me back, gently—though not right away. He stood and walked to the mantle, to the picture of him and Beth smiling casually at us, unsuspecting.

"Noreen." Facing away, he exhaled and rubbed the back of his neck. I held my breath, feeling like a fourteen-year-old waiting to be admonished by her father for some adolescent wrong-doing– and knowing I was guilty and deserving of the consequences. I stared at my hands, struggled with what to say.

Finally, he turned to me. "You have to go," he said–and nothing more.

I stood, "Alan..."

"Please," he interrupted, holding up his hand.

Before I went to the door, with shaking, moist hands, I took the photo of the four of us at Thurston's two weeks earlier from my blazer pocket and placed it on the coffee table between us. *See for yourself*, I implored with my eyes. He glanced down at it and back to me, hurt and confused. When I stepped outside, the door closed quickly behind me.

I waited in the parking lot of the dance studio for the girls, trying fruitlessly to control my shaking. What had I done? What made my actions any more acceptable than Dutch's and Beth's?

I waited every day for an accusing, berating, insidious call from Beth; but it never came. She carried on our friendship as usual, and I knew that Alan had kept our visit to himself. Why, I wondered, would he protect me?

The reasons behind Dutch's and Beth's secret interludes became clear when I walked into Thurston's that Saturday night. Dutch happily explained how they'd met regularly to go over plans, to ensure everything was perfect for me. I tried to talk to Alan at the party, but he would have none of it. He was cool, and I accepted his reaction, though it brought to light just how important he was to me. I needed his approval almost as much as I needed Beth's.

That's why I orchestrated our getaway, manipulating Dutch into believing it was his idea. I needed to make things right. I was thrilled when Alan and Beth agreed to join us. Though we may still have a rocky road ahead, I really believe I made some headway into fixing mine and Alan's fractured relationship.

At the pool, Alan reluctantly accepted my apologies, and, to his credit, never mentioned the photo I gave him. I think at that moment, I found him the most attractive man. His unfaltering devotion to Beth makes him quite a prize. I wonder if she knows how lucky she is. Any other man would have taken advantage of me. I offered myself to this man, and he chose her.

Chapter 26

Beth

It's girls' night, but tonight Noreen doesn't want to stay home. She picks me up and we drive to Luigi's. It's a humid night in August. Nicole and Stacy are at a birthday party. Alan will pick them up for us, since Daniel is at a trade show for the weekend.

Over scallops and linguine, Noreen tells me she is going back to work. I can't hide my disappointment. What am I going to do without her all week? Who will I talk to?

"I have to, Beth. The staying at home is killing me. Devin starts second grade next month and Nikki's in fifth, so she can handle him for forty-five minutes until I get home. It's just fifteen minutes away. I'll be working for a law firm in Harrisburg. It's what I do. Don't make me feel bad."

I sip my wine, and listen to her argument. I know it can be tedious staying home all day while the rest of the family is a part of the world. When I'm not volunteering at the school, I spend much of my hours cleaning and preparing meals; but that isn't enough for some people. I push the thought away that I was once one of those ambitious souls who believed life is not life if you're not saving something, leaving a mark, reversing a wrong–or at least making money.

The funny thing is, from what I can tell, Noreen *loves* to be home. What is she going to do without her weekly visits to her salon, her massages, her daily gym classes? I pick at my food, while I wait for her to tell me the truth. It doesn't take long.

"And besides, Dutch's business is not exactly killing it right now. He's having a hard time, and I want to alleviate some of the pressure. He works so hard, and I want to help. Your husband is a doctor; you have no financial concerns. People will always need to see him, especially with the ozone problem. He's lucky–skin cancer is huge business."

Her dark humor makes me laugh, despite myself. Alan does well, and we will never have to worry about money. I can't imagine that stress; yet I am envious of Noreen. She has a career to fall back on; what do I have? Three and a half years of school. No diploma. No job. No career. Still in the throes of motherhood, the question of what I will do with my life when Stacy leaves is answered by my life choice: I am doing it. To think I once had dreams of helping the environment is unimaginable now. I have settled into a safe, monotonous existence, and I am comfortable in it.

The irony is that I *want* to be the person who has to juggle work, family and worry about bills; everything my mother fought against for me, and won. After all of these years, I just wouldn't know how to do it.

"We've been fighting." Noreen says.

"What do you mean?"

"Well, we're both on edge and we've been bickering. It's distressing. I rely on Dutch to be a rock. He puts up with a lot of my bullshit, and lately, he's been snapping at me. He mentioned last week that the house was a mess, so I wrote *Fuck You* in the dust on our dresser. He wouldn't talk to me for two days."

"Oh, Noreen. I'm sure he doesn't mean anything by it. It's just what you said, the pressure of work, that's all. It will be okay."

Noreen sighs. "I know. We sat down and talked, I mean, *really* talked, over the weekend, and that's when I told him I had contacted Schreiber and Schreiber for a job. He apologized for the way he'd been acting–said he's frustrated with his business, but he was relieved when I told him. That's when I knew I had done the right thing. Beth, I don't know what I'd do without this man. He's my life. I just don't know if I'm as important to him. He's been acting different lately, and I have to do something."

"What do you mean different?"

"I don't know. He's preoccupied. We don't make love as often as we used to."

"That happens to every married couple."

"I guess. I don't know. We'll see. I'll do whatever it takes to make it right. It's my last resort. I mean, I'm waxed, buffed, tanned, toned and polished. I have nothing else to work on. I wonder if I should get my lips done?"

I put down my fork and grin. "Why don't you start with not writing vulgar notes on your dresser?"

She shrugs, and we both giggle. "It was funny." She says.

"Evidently not." I lift my wine glass. "Okay then. Let's toast to you getting back into the world. Don't forget about me."

Noreen clinks her glass to mine. "Don't worry. It'll work out. We'll just do more of these. And there's always e-mail, if you need me."

∽

Chapter 27

Wednesday, September 22, 1995

> From: <meplus3@netmail.com>
> To: Beth
> Subj: New e-mail

Hi Beth,

This is my new home e-mail because I don't want to use my office address in case they decide to monitor me. Please save it and delete 'houseboundma' from your contact list. So far, job is fine. Two weeks have flown by, but I'm still learning my way around the office. Both Schreibers are nice enough. It takes all the strength I have not to break up when they're together. They share everything: clothes, spectacles (I swear, Milton's word, not mine—he's not even THAT old), even the perfect moon-shaped bald spots where their yarmulkes wore their hair out. Funny how family sticks together, isn't it? They each have their own office and both are equally demanding. I'll be working for Stan. There's another girl here, Meghan, who works for Milton. She's showing me the ropes, reluctantly. I still haven't decided if Meghan is friend or foe. She's attractive and dresses nice, which is two strikes against her. I hate to compete. My paralegal skills are rusty but coming back to me, thank God! Stan is going to start me on closing preps. Can't wait!

What are you doing Saturday? I need to go shopping to out-dress this woman. I want you to come with. How is your day going?

Love, Noreen

Wednesday, September 22, 1995

From: Beth
To: Noreen
Subj: New e-mail

Hi Noreen,

It's Wednesday and you know what that means, my weekly berating session with Teresa. She still insists we meet at Cosi, which is convenient for her. No matter how early I leave my house, I still manage to get stuck in some sort of traffic or unforeseen construction zone and show up late and sweating. Wednesday used to be a day I'd await with anticipation and is when I most miss my dad. The fact that Teresa tries to replace this time with her company since he's gone does give me hope that someday we'll get along. Unfortunately, I find she uses this opportunity to re-charge her negative battery at my expense. Today she applied her lipstick at the table while surreptitiously glancing at my naked face. Then she took me to the makeup counter at Macy's and bought me another bottle of cover up. You should have one in every purse.

I had a tasty sandwich though, so all was not wasted. I'm happy you're adjusting. I would love to go shopping with you. We have to out-do your competition. Let the games begin!

Call me later.

Beth

Monday, September 27, 1995

From: Beth
To: Noreen
Subj: Breasts

No matter how long I stare at them, they give me no direction. They just lie there, useless.

Beth

Monday, September 27, 1995

From: Noreen
To: Beth
Subj: Breasts

Wonderbra.

Just kidding. Why don't you bread them and throw them in the oven?

Nor

Monday, September 27, 1995

From: Beth
To: Noreen
Subj: Breasts

Boring. But I'll do it.

Monday, September 27, 1995

From: Noreen
To: Beth
Subj: Solution to Breast problem

I got it! Marinade in lime juice (with peel), chili powder, salt and pepper. Sauté bite size pieces, add peppers julienne and throw over spinach.

Hold your applause.

Nor

Tuesday, October 4, 1995

From: Beth
To: Noreen
Subj: Lazy

It's one o'clock in the afternoon. I have nothing to show for my free time today but the ingestion of two individual turkey pot pies and a handful of Mallomars. School is out in an hour and a half and my bathroom is still advertising mold.

I ran into Meredith yesterday at Kohl's. She tried to talk to me, you know, chew the fat, but I left clothes in the fitting room and ran out of there! Where is my friend??

Beth

Tuesday, October 4, 1995

From: Noreen
To: Beth
Subj: Lazy

Why don't you write little love notes in the dust throughout the house? I don't know why you don't get a cleaning lady. Why would anyone choose to clean their house if they don't have to? Get someone to tidy up that manse of yours....

I didn't realize Mallomars are in season! Thanks for the update.

By the way, I'm right here. Don't you dare replace me!

Nor

Chapter 28

Beth

It is a Friday in September, 1996, Alan is at work and Stacy, who got home from school an hour ago, is in her room, listening to some unrecognizable sound. She calls it music, but I can't really tell for sure. The windows on the ground floor are all open, letting out the acrid odor of bleach and Murphy's oil soap, while letting in the warm, Indian summer air. I feel good with my productive day behind me, and look forward to the weekend. I am just sitting down in front of the television when Noreen calls.

"What are you doing?"

"Watching Oprah. There's a woman on who has 20 personalities," I say.

"20? I have only two; bitchy and happy."

"Which one are you today?"

"Happy, I think."

"Good. I'm coming over."

"I'll chill the wine."

I bring Stacy with me, and she and Nicole disappear upstairs to Nik's room. Noreen and I drink half a bottle before the five o'clock news ends. Noreen has been working for a year already, and we have come to rely on these stolen snippets of time together. This afternoon she has me in tears with her stories about Devin:

"The child spends a good portion of each day regarding himself in the mirror and will not step foot out the door if one hair is out of place, though he'll give no thought whatsoever to knocking people down with his breath as his toothbrush remains dry and neglected in the bathroom. We had another knock down, dragged out fight about his

teeth this morning. I swear it'll take another kid to tell him he stinks before he'll listen to me!"

Daniel comes home and joins us for a drink, then convinces me to call Alan to come for dinner. The meal is casual and enjoyable, as usual. Everyone is in good spirits, and even Devin takes mercy on the girls.

I observe the interaction between Daniel and Noreen, but can detect no tension or unease and draw my conclusion that all is back to normal. Daniel is in a talkative mood, and laughs the entire night. When I mention this to Noreen in the kitchen, she dismisses it. "He's always happy when you and Alan are around. He loves you guys."

I disagree. He is attentive to Noreen, and…happy. I feel a sense of relief, and this gives me hope that I have accepted having him in this way in my life. When Noreen first let on that they were having trouble, I found the news disturbing. I rely so strongly on them as a couple, as part of our foursome, that I don't know what I would do if they split. Alan and I see few other friends, and spend much of our free time with Noreen and Daniel. Could I believe that Daniel is no longer a man I used to love, but a close friend that means more to me now than I believed possible when we'd met–again?

∽

Chapter 29

November, 1997
Beth

PTA meetings and school functions no longer fill my days. Noreen has been at her job for two years when my resolve to avoid exercise finally breaks down. I step into the gym and am greeted by high-decibel thumping and young, hard bodies scattered about the large room on various weight apparatus. The girl behind the counter smiles at me and waits until I walk across the lobby. I offer a small smile back at the flawlessly tanned, perky blond in a tank, thinking *What the hell am I doing here?*

Two hundred dollars later, I am a member of Total Workout World, and privy to a forty-five minute tour. The perky blonde spews snippets of instructions on differing weight machines, as foreign to me as the engine of a car; the steam room, locker, showers, etc. I graciously accept a current schedule of classes and dump it in the trash bin on the way to my car.

Alan had pushed me to join, tired of hearing me complain that my clothes are snug. He works out occasionally at the gym in his office building, which is inconvenient for me. I don't want to admit it, but it also gives me something to do. Stacy is in seventh grade and requires less and less of me at school.

Two days later, I work up the nerve to go back. Armed with my stretch pants, long tee shirt and metal water bottle, I meander around the room seeking a machine that might not scare me. I don't see Daniel until he taps on my shoulder from behind. Startled, I turn and sense the color bloom on my cheeks as I hastily kiss him on his.

"You made it!" He says.

"Yes. Finally. Although, I don't know what I'm doing. I'm a square peg trying to squeeze into a round hole."

Daniel smiles. "No, you're not. I'll help you. What part of the body do you want to work on?"

I look myself over and then up at Daniel, who laughs. "Okay, why don't we start with arms and move our way down so you can decide where you're comfortable. How does that sound?"

"Daniel, don't you have anything better to do than waste your time on me?"

It is a split shutter-fly second, but I don't miss his reaction. He is not at work but at the gym, with the unemployable, the young and a bunch of stay-at-home wives. I must be crimson, and want to crawl out of here. *Stupid woman! Why can't you keep your mouth shut?*

"I'm sorry. I didn't mean anything by it. I just meant…"

"It's okay. No harm done. I had early meetings, and my afternoon cancelled. So, I'm free. I'd be happy to waste my time with you."

I nod, feeling foolish and suddenly very uncomfortable. My vulnerability at not having my daughter or Noreen or a table to protect me from making a fool of myself has me on edge. Daniel senses this, because he gently guides me to a machine, sits down and carefully demonstrates what to do, explaining the part of the arm that benefits (triceps) before standing and motioning for me to sit.

When I lean my arms over the bar to lift the weight like he showed me, Daniel kneels in front of me. I am looking into green eyes that bore into mine.

"You called me Daniel. No one's called me that in a long time."

Shit.

"I'm sorry. I…don't know why I did that."

He shakes his head with a smile. "No, it's okay. I like it."

∽

Chapter 30

Thursday, November 30, 1997

From: Noreen
To: Beth
Subj: It's about time

Well, congratulations!! Dutch tells me you joined the gym.
I am so happy you finally decided to get there. I just wish
you would have done it while I was at home. Anyway,
how do you like it? He said he's been helping you with the
machines. I have one bit of advice. BE CAREFUL. Dutch
tears or pulls something weekly. Make sure he doesn't
overdue it in order to impress you.

Now I have to work on getting you to a night class with
me!

Oops–gotta go. I'm late for a meeting. Ta ta for now.

Nor

Thursday, November 30, 1997

From: Beth
To: Noreen
Subj: It's about time

Noreen,

Yes, I finally took the plunge and walked into a world
where I don't belong. Your husband has been very kind.

For the past week, he's been patiently showing me correct ways to use the machines. I'm almost ready to "do the circuit" on my own. I still won't go near the treadmill, though. No one needs to see a limp-a-long going nowhere. I stepped onto that horrible elliptical contraption and damn near killed myself. So, cardio is not in my future. Nor are night classes, as they will surely get in the way of my threesome (me, wine and couch). I'll stick with bulking myself up.

Are we still on for Sunday? My house this week. Kickoff is at one o'clock.

Beth

Thursday, November 30, 1997

From: Noreen
To: Beth
Subj: It's about time

He-woman,

Yes. We're on for Sunday. I'll bring my artichoke dip and chips. See you then.

Nor

I could hear the sleep in Noreen's voice even before her yawns interrupted her story. We were knee-deep in our weekly phone update, necessary to fill in the gaps around the mess of e-mails we send to each other while she's at work. Often innuendos are missed with the written word, and I like to hear her voice. She was going on about Meghan, her favorite nemesis; their relationship is congruent to my relationship with Meredith Sullivan, who even in middle school, still enjoys opposing most of my suggestions at school meetings (though she no longer holds any position or clout).

Noreen pauses to yawn again.

"Why are you so tired?"

"I don't know. Maybe it's because my bathroom door was open all night."

I smile into the phone. When Noreen goes to sleep, all doors in her room have to be closed or it throws off her feng-shui completely. She swore she never slept a full night until she made Daniel move their bed to the western wall. Until then, it had been facing the door, the ultimate Chinese no-no. So I am not surprised when she tells me she woke up angry with Daniel, who must have used the bathroom in the wee hours of the morning and forgot to shut the door. The poor guy was greeted with attitude when he woke up.

"When is he going to learn?" I ask.

"Please. He thinks it's all in my head. He's a beauty, but thick as a brick."

Chapter 31

Wednesday, December 19, 1998

From: Noreen
To: Beth
Subj: Aha!

Good Morning! I know it's early and you probably don't
even have your computer on yet, but I had to shoot
you a note. I've been here for over three years. Can you
believe it? Time moves at an incredibly quick pace when
you do the same thing day after day. I realize that being
at home is the only way to slow the clock. Leave the
house every morning at the same time and when you
turn around, Whammo!, forty months have whizzed by.
Well, the reason behind my "aha" moment stems from a
wonderful piece of news. There's a new company moving
in next door. Kevin from Frameworks filled me in last
week when they pulled out the last of their boxes. Today
the painters are in. And oh Lord, there's one in particular
that is Mmm mmmm! He is blond and cut and so good
looking, he's downright pretty. Brad Pitt who? We rode
the elevator together. I stood behind him undetected
and read his tattoos while enjoying his scent–something
familiar though for the life of me cannot remember it. It'll
come. Anyway, just stepped off of the elevator and while
his ode de hot still permeates my nostrils, I wanted to give
you my news. And I know what you're thinking. I know
your thoughts before you do. He's a pleasant distraction.
If you were here working eight hours a day with Stan and

Milton, you'd need a pleasant distraction too. Yes, even you. Perfectly happy married you. And I can't keep eating chocolate for fear Dutch will find more reasons to go away on business.

I'd ask how your morning is going, but it cannot compare with mine.

Nor

Wednesday, December 19, 1998

From: Beth
To: Noreen
Subj: Aha!

What happened, lost your taste for middle aged Jewish guys? What does Meghan think about your blond painter?

My day so far consists of a Meredith bashing PTA meeting followed by food shopping, your typical exciting day. These meetings are dreadful without you. I have to battle the hierarchy by myself. There's definitely safety in numbers. I still can't believe this woman has been harassing us since the girls were in Elementary school! It will most certainly be a bittersweet end to my PTA career when Stacy heads to high school next September. As much as I'll miss it, Meredith will finally be out of my life!

By the way, I know I told you already, but I just love your tree and decorations this year. You've inspired me to put away all things manufactured and stick with only Stacy's homemade ornaments I've accrued through the years. Of course, it still looks nothing like yours since I only have one child and therefore a handful of pieces to hang. I may start a new hobby. Are we still on for wrapping and wine tomorrow night?

I'll pick up Nikki later at five. It's my turn.

Beth

Friday, December 21, 1998

From: Noreen
To: Beth
Subj: Happy Friday!

Beth,

My blond painter said hello to me this morning. Accompanied by a nod. I almost peed my pants. He does see me! You asked about Meghan. I don't share anything with her. I am trying to keep my surprise treasure to myself for fear once she gets wind of my interest in him she will stop at nothing for his attention. Her boobs are bigger than mine. I wouldn't stand a chance. Fortunately, his schedule correlates with mine. Meghan starts half an hour before us. There is a God.

I'm sorry (again) for canceling on you last night, just fell into my bed after work. Stan must be working me too hard, though I can handle the workload with no problem. I'm going to finish all my wrapping tonight when they go to sleep.

Remember, I'll drive the girls next week.

Nor

Tuesday, January 8, 1999

From: Noreen
To: Beth
Subj: The King

Good morning. What do you say we rent *Roustabout* and *Viva Las Vegas* and stay in our pj's on Saturday with the kids to celebrate the King's birthday?

Nor

Tuesday, January 8, 1999

From: Beth
To: Noreen
Subj: The King

I would love to honor the King again with another
marathon, movie day wearing pajamas, but I am already
committed (and will be soon) to spending the day with
Teresa. She's joining some new ladies group and asked me
to walk in with her for the first time. Between Canasta
on Mondays, Mahjong on Wednesday's and book club on
Fridays, I don't know why she needs another group to join,
but I don't ask questions. I just do as I'm asked (told).

Sorry.

Beth

Monday, January 14, 1999

From: Noreen
To: Beth
Subj: Over-indulged

In yoga we learn balance. If you bend forward, then you
must bend back.

Yin-Yang.

This morning I enjoyed a breakfast of fruits and vegetables.

This afternoon I enjoyed a large, cheese calzone.

My yin feels great.

My yang can't move because it's too full.

How is your day going?

Noreen

Monday, January 14, 1999

> From: Beth
> To: Noreen
> Subj: Over-indulged

> This is why you should be home with me. I would make sure you eat healthy. Or, at least share the calzone with you.

> Now I'm hungry.

> See you later.

> Beth

Wednesday, January 16, 1999

> From: Noreen
> To: Beth
> Subj: You know who

> Beth,

> Well, at last the blond painter has returned to work after a too long vacation (if you ask me), looking better than before (as if that were possible) with a deep bronze tan that screams Barbados or St. Thomas. I found out, after subtle inquiry, that there was some snafu with the new construction and all work was stopped. Are you sitting down? You're not going to believe this. Today we had lunch together. Yes, you read that right. I was at my table in the basement cafeteria minding my own business, when who should appear but earth's answer to Zeus. He carried his tray and parked himself at the table directly next to mine. We sat for a full thirty minutes beside each other eating. I simply could not concentrate on my magazine and will now have to wait until tomorrow to find out if bell bottoms are back.

> Nor

Thursday, January 17, 1999

From: Beth
To: Noreen
Subj: you know who

Noreen, you are starting to worry me. How is it that an attractive married woman can convince herself that she dined with another man when in fact he simply chose an available table that happened to be next to hers? Have you lost all judgment? Did you even speak?

When you pass the salt, is when this becomes worthy of our attention.

By the way, Meredith called me today. I know, shocked me too. She wanted to know if I would be willing to run the Spring festival. Don't you think it's a little premature? There is still snow on the ground for cripes sake! I think she wants to plant seeds in my mind. Sadly, even though I no longer have a child in elementary school, I will most likely do it. I have no life.

I told her I'd think about it. Let her sweat it out a bit.

Beth

Friday, January 18, 1999

From: Noreen
To: Beth
Subj: you know who

Well, well, well....look who's turning into a be-atch. Am I rubbing off on you? Of course, you're perfect to run the festival. You're organizational skills are sickening (and I mean that in the nicest way). I would give her a week to sweat it out before you answer. Oh, I do miss the drama.

Speaking of drama, Blondie said hello to me today. We enjoyed a several sentence conversation. He'll be finished with the job in a week to my dismay. It turns out his name is Artie. To say I'm disappointed is to say I was sorry to hear the Backstreet boys broke up. I think I'll stick with our nickname.

I'll call you over the weekend to firm up plans for next week's Superbowl. I know you hosted last year, but do you think you'd mind doing it again? I don't know if I have it in me. I'll bring the chips and dip. I'll expect crumb cake.

Nor

~~

Chapter 32

Beth

Daniel and the kids walk into the house an hour before kickoff on Superbowl Sunday. He is armed with a bag of snacks and beer, but no Noreen.

"She's exhausted. I left her home, sleeping. When she gets up, she'll join us."

"She hasn't missed a game in years! Is she sick? Or are you working her too hard?" I smile, taking the bag from him. "She's been sleeping the past few times I called in the evening."

"I know. I told her she's doing too much. Between her work schedule and Devin's games, Nikki's dances... she can't be everything to everyone. She's such a control freak; I can't get her to put more on me. Even when I take Devin to his games, she shows up. Can't miss a thing."

I pat his back. "It's not that she doesn't want you to do it. She just wants to support the kids in their activities. She's a mom. They expect her to be there. We all do. Look at them, they're getting older, and it's going so fast. One day, the four of us are going to be staring at each other, looking for things to do."

Daniel smiles. "I can't wait."

Noreen never shows on Sunday. She calls at the end of the fourth quarter, just having woken up, pleads a headache and promises to call me tomorrow.

Noreen waits to phone me until after dinner on Monday.

"It's funny—I feel fine all day; but as soon as I get home, I feel like someone put two bricks on my eyes and I can't keep them open. I swear, I was at Dev's basketball game and feel like I missed it anyway. I can't focus. I zone out."

"Are you drinking too much coffee?"

"No more than usual. I've always had a low iron count. I'm sure that's it."

"Well, go eat some raisins and I'll call you on Wednesday. It's my turn to take the girls to dance this week."

"When will they be able to drive themselves?"

"Three years."

"Oh, good God. Now I really have a headache."

Two months later, on a clear March morning, Noreen leaves work early, not feeling well, and hits a guardrail with her car. Dutch gets the call on a site and immediately calls me to meet him at the hospital. I find him sitting at the admitting window just outside of the emergency room, distraught. Without thought, I sit in the empty chair beside him while he answers questions about insurance and Noreen's medical history. I take his hand in mine, remembering how comforted I felt when Noreen had done the same for me years earlier—on the morning of my dad's funeral.

When the paperwork is done, we head into the ER and wait. Forty-five minutes pass before a nurse calls Daniel to the door. We stand and he starts across the room.

"Dutch?"

He turns to me.

"I'll go get the girls and Devin from school. When Alan gets home, I'll be back here for you."

"Okay." He says, wrapping me in a hug before turning back to walk through the door behind the nurse.

Noreen is admitted six hours later, and I am allowed into her room that evening. She looks battered in the bed. There is a large gash above her eyes, covered by a huge bandage that hides half of her forehead. Dutch is seated beside her when I walk in. He stands to allow me his seat and leaves to get coffee.

"Where are the kids?" Noreen asks.

"With Alan. They had pizza and ice cream."

"Lucky bastards."

I smile, relieved to see some of my friend's personality peek through the tubes and bandages. The heat must have kicked on, because I get a strong whiff all of a sudden of the large floral bouquet resting on the heater by the window. The card was signed Schreiber & Schreiber.

"Smells like a funeral in here."

"Better than smelling like a hospital," I say. *If I never step foot into one of these disinfected rooms again, it will be too soon.*

Noreen shifts in the bed and winces from the pain.

"What happened?"

"I fell asleep on 322. Would you believe that crap? I could have killed someone, Beth."

I grimace inside, and she immediately puts her hand up. "I'm sorry. I didn't mean anything by it."

I lean over and gently wiped the lone tear from her bruised cheek.

"It's okay. You didn't, and that's all that matters. Let's focus on the positive. When can you leave?"

"I don't know. I hope by tomorrow. They want to do tests. I hate being here. I need to go home."

"Don't worry about the kids. I'll help Dutch. I'm here."

The doctor wants to find out why Noreen had fallen asleep at the wheel in the middle of the morning. She had not been drinking or taking any medication, and he feels there might be an underlying problem. Noreen tries to argue, but Dutch is adamant that they finally figure out the reason for her constant exhaustion. When I leave the hospital, Dutch is standing over her with his arms crossed and Noreen is fighting tears.

He arrives at my door hours later to pick up Nikki and Devin, and I convince him to stay for a bite. He looks a wreck. I heat up leftover dinner and, together, we sit at the table. The rest of the house is dark, save for the light over us. Alan has surgery early in the morning and had gone to bed, and the kids are in the den, watching a movie.

"I can't believe this happened," Daniel says, picking at the pasta.

I say nothing. What is there to say?

"She's been different for a long time. Tired, short-tempered, emotional."

"They'll give her tests. You'll finally have an answer, and you'll fix it."

Daniel lifts his head from his plate, and the look he gives me breaks my heart. It is filled with gratitude and love, and I work to push away the thought that he is beautiful. I put my hand on his, still holding his fork.

"I'm happy to have you. That Noreen has you. I feel... You make me feel…"

He stops speaking and pulls his hand away.

"Dutch, we've been friends for a long time. We've shared a lot of memories. Of course you feel close. I feel close to you, too."

He shakes his head as I speak. "No. I don't mean…Never mind."

We have been friends for a decade. I believe we share a closer bond than Alan and Noreen do, and now realize that he feels the same way. I have worked diligently to abandon any pangs of envy of Noreen or distress in the company of Daniel, allowing myself to simply enjoy the gift of having him back in my life, in whatever form that took.

I've even convinced myself that I made the right decision in letting him go. Noreen is a beautiful, successful woman who is a far better match for him than I turned out to be. He would never have found me attractive in the biblical sense, and I would have lost him altogether. He has become, instead, a wonderful part of my life.

Now, hearing his declaration again, I wonder how fair I've been. Daniel believed he was left by the woman he loved. Did I ever take that into consideration? He had alluded to his devastation in the past; but really, do I know anything about what he went through?

"I'm sorry. I have a bad habit of speaking my mind. I have to learn to keep things in. Noreen's always on my case about that."

"Dutch. I'm happy you feel close to me. I do, too. I want you to know I'm here for you, for Noreen, and the kids. You mean everything to me."

They hold Noreen for six days, and she is finally discharged on Tuesday, but asks that she have some time to be with her children before accepting visitors. So I wait until the following Monday to call and show up, as requested, with lobster bisque from Andy's Deli. When I get to her house, she is comfortable in sweats and, after letting me in, resumes her place on the couch, under a blanket. Dutch has returned to work and the kids are in school, so it is just us. Outside, the March air is chilly and damp, making it feel like spring is more than a mere month away.

Over soup, Noreen tells me that tests for fatigue illustrate to the doctors that she has iron deficiency anemia, and they prescribed her iron pills.

"Oh, thank God. You should have gone for a checkup long ago. You could have prevented all this," I say.

"Yes. I know, Mom." Noreen stirs her soup aimlessly. She doesn't appear as relieved as I feel.

"Why aren't you eating? Have you taken your pill today?"

She puts down her spoon and pulls the blanket up to her quivering chin.

"Noreen, what is it? What?" I move from the recliner to the couch to be closer to her.

"Oh Beth, they found something."

Alan knows something is wrong before I even step into the house. It is the pause on the doorstep, he'll tell me later. He heard me outside, waiting a full minute before I turned the knob. When I fling the door wide and stand in the foyer, he comes right to me.

I allow myself to collapse into his arms, and he holds me while I let go of everything I held in for the duration of my visit with Noreen. Deep, traumatized sobs rise from my bowels and erupt from me in loud waves of anguish. I don't know how long it takes before Alan can guide me to the couch.

In fragmented pieces, broken by tears, he patiently listens as I fill him in on details of my conversation with Noreen.

Along with tests, the doctor conducted a complete physical, and there was an inordinate amount of blood in Noreen's stool. He performed a colonoscopy on Friday, unknown to me or Alan, and found a large growth. A biopsy confirmed what the doctor had suspected upon finding the tumor. Further probing showed that she had an advanced stage of growth in her colon and evidence that it spread to her liver. This could have explained her fatigue.

Later, as I lay in bed waiting for sleep, my eyes puffy and my nose raw from tissues, I hear Alan go into the living room and pour himself something from the bar. I don't know how long he sits there by himself but he is still not back when I finally allow dreams to take me.

❦

Chapter 33

Noreen

I have to gather myself before I can see anyone. The news of my illness hovers over me, like a thunderous cloud, ominous and threatening; but I don't yet feel its fervor. Dutch and I decided not to tell the kids until necessary. I need them to keep their normal behavior and unaltered schedules, in order not to go crazy myself with the knowledge that this may be the last year I will know them. The thought threatens to paralyze me, but I work hard to keep it from taking over my mind.

Dutch is dealing with this his own way; working overtime and on weekends, immersing himself in the children's activities as never before. I leave him to his devices. At some point, we'll have to discuss plans.

Yesterday, I sat in the yard, wrapped in my wool coat, and watched the sun dip behind the trees, immersing my surroundings in rich oranges and red— something I never took the time to do. I didn't worry about what was for dinner, or if I would miss ER. Mr. Clooney would just have to make do with one less ogling mom. I just stopped everything.

I still feel like me. I cannot fathom the alien cells taking over my body. How, pray-tell, did I let them in? How in God's name did I allow it? My body is my temple. Who invited these killers into my temple??

∽

Chapter 34

Beth

When I call his office, I am told Daniel is on a job close to home. His assistant gives me the address, and I find it easily, arriving at four-thirty. Parked in the rear of the lot, I sit in my car and wait, not entirely sure what I am doing here. I only know that this is where I want to be right now.

Daniel had mentioned in the past, that quitting time on a site is most often determined by sunset. We don't change the clocks for another few weeks, so the days are still short. I figure I have less than half an hour to wait before dusk, so I try to relax, but soon realize it is impossible. I am a taut coil of nerves. When the first workers walk to the lot, I throw open my car door so fast, it swings back and hits me. *Breathe. Take it easy*, I tell myself.

Climbing carefully out of the car, I zip up my coat, and work my way to the cluster of cars and trucks. I need a head start because I am so slow, I'm afraid I'll miss him. I get halfway across the parking lot when I see Daniel. He doesn't notice me yet, so I wait. I still love to look at him, and now only allow myself the luxury of staring at the occasional odd moments, such as this. His hard hat is tilted to the side, and he trudges to his truck slowly, as if physically weighed down with his worries. His eyes follow the ground, and I lose myself in the picture of him, matured, slightly weathered and, if possible, even more beautiful than he ever was.

I am a few feet from his bumper, and he reaches for his handle when he finally lifts his head. He still doesn't notice me. When I left Noreen yesterday, Daniel had not returned home from work. Devin and Nicole walked into the house with their grandmother, and I took my leave quickly, allowing Noreen time with her children and mother-in-law. I haven't seen him since she got home from the hospital, and I am worried. This impulsive move is way out of character for me, but I am driven by concern. In all of the years of our friendship, I've never shown up at Daniel's work.

There is a twinge of regret as I stand dumbly, waiting. *What can I possibly do for this man? How presumptuous of me!* Before my self-doubt takes command, and I can turn around, he sees me. His tired eyes mirror the pain he holds back, while he continues to perform duties, as if his life hasn't been permanently altered. Still, I notice beyond the pain, a smile when he sees me, and I am certain it is not my imagination. He walks to me, and we embrace.

"Can you talk?" He says.

"That's why I'm here."

We climb into his truck, and he opens the windows a fraction. The cool, dank air mixes with the stale atmosphere of the cab, and feels good.

"How are you holding up?" I ask.

Daniel rests his head back. I follow a lone tear as it descends over his cheek, down to his square jaw, and disappears underneath his chin. I know at this moment I have done the right thing by coming here. This man will need just as much support as Noreen.

"You have to let me help you with the kids, as things get worse. I'm here for you. You be there for her."

Daniel nods, and reaches over the console to take my hand.

"I'll be okay—just need to digest this. It's so fresh. I don't know what to expect. I don't know what she'll need. We haven't told the kids yet."

"How much time are they saying?"

He looks at me. "They'll take out the tumor to relieve the blockage, and try chemo, but they can't promise a year."

Two weeks after she returns home from her surgery, Noreen decides to go back to work to give her notice, and help the Schreiber brothers, who already feel like family to her after only four and a half years, find her replacement.

"I'll go batty if I have to stay home and wait. Stan said no one else can find my replacement. He wants a replica. Sometimes I could kiss that man right on his sweet bald spot, I swear."

Monday, April 15, 1999

From: Noreen
To: Beth
Subj: Is this a joke?

I keep waiting for the camera crew to pop out of the bathroom or something, telling me this is all a joke. I don't have cancer and I don't have to leave a job I love.

It's odd to be here, trying to find my replacement. Like I'm moving out and trying to find a new roommate for Stan. The trouble is, I don't want to leave or be replaced. I'm perfect for this job, for Stan.

Okay, well I took enough of a break from my pity party to review thirty resumes and found three prospects so far. We start interviews next week.

Nor

Monday, April 15, 1999

From: Beth
To: Noreen
Subj: Is this a joke?

Noreen,

I know you love it there, but please hurry and find someone so we can resume our afternoon talks and our soul-cleansing bitching of our favorite subject…Meredith!

Beth

Monday, May 8, 1999

From: Noreen
To: Beth
Subj: Eureka!

Beth,

Well, after only six interviews, I think I finally made a decision. I went with Suzanne, who is a decade younger than our fair maiden, Meghan. This is not my reason for hiring her. I am a professional you know, but I would be less than truthful if I didn't admit it pleases me to no end that Suzanne is younger and prettier than my fine-haired friend. She has the chops this law firm needs. She's bright and sarcastic and we hit it off right away. It's a shame I'm leaving. I would have enjoyed working with her.

Nor

Monday, May 8, 1999
From: Beth
To: Noreen
Subj: Eureka!

Suzanne sounds like your twin, though I question her ability to match your levels of sarcasm. When is your last day? I want to have lunch with my unemployed friend. Tell that Meghan "adios" from me.

Beth

Tuesday, May 9, 1999
From: Noreen
To: Beth
Subj: Good Morning

To answer your question yesterday, I'll stick around long enough to get Suzanne fully indoctrinated to the office. I'm guessing it will take about a month. She's picking up quickly. I'm not sure if it's because she's as bright as I suspected or if I'm just that good. I'll opt for the latter. I am that good. Suzanne already gave me a going away present. Over lunch she confided in me she thought

Meghan was a beast! Oh, she'll have such fun. I'm envious! I told her so too.

Let's go out Friday. Screw Lunch. I want dinner. How about Thurston's? We'll bring the men.

Nor

∽

Chapter 35

Beth

Noreen left Schreiber Bros a month ago, and for the first time in years, we are both home together again. I missed our frequent visits, and used to (silently) hope their finances would strengthen, and allow her to quit her job so we may return to the way it was in the beginning. Now I would do anything in my power to have her back at work, healthy, and e-mailing me. Instead, I hold onto each afternoon we share like a precious glass souvenir, wrapping it carefully, and storing it in my memory.

The summer passes quickly, and as adults do, we frantically hold onto the green, floral days, cramming in lake visits and barbeques in August before the sun's warmth disappears for another six months. Noreen's tan covers her gray complexion, made worse by the chemo she endured over the past months, but since abandoned, complaining it was killing her faster than the disease. She hated the way it may her feel, taking precious time away from her kids and when the doctors told her it wasn't helping, she stopped.

"I won't listen to them." She tells me, as we watch Devin reach his arms out, trying to find the girls in the pool, screaming "Marco!" every few seconds. They're almost fifteen, heading into tenth grade, and still have no interest in tanning, for which we are thankful. We are lying on lounge chairs in Noreen's yard, and I can hear Daniel and Alan murmuring on the patio.

"Who?" I ask.

"Them. The doctors. They can't tell me when to die. What if I don't want to? What if I decide to beat this and stick around?"

I look to my friend, at her clenched jaw, as she keeps her focus forward, enjoying her children being children. She has tried several alternative treatments, the most recent being acupuncture. Her pantry is stocked with herbal vitamins, ointments, and creams made of plants and natural oils, which have replaced her typical staples of Doritos and Devil Dogs. She doesn't elaborate on her appointments, and I don't push, knowing that if she wanted to discuss them, she would. Maybe she feels hypocritical, having joked for years that chiropractors are not real doctors.

"Then don't. Don't do it. Stay with me." I say.

Noreen's eyes don't leave her children, but her hand reaches from her lap to mine, and she squeezes my fingers tightly.

The winter is brutal. Snow falls in record amounts in January, but I manage to make it to Noreen's three times a week. The kids are in school, and since Dutch picked up extra work driving snowplows for the town, I refuse to allow Noreen time alone. My company also dilutes weekly visits with her mother-in-law. Mrs. Fergusan tries hard, but it is clear she is not comfortable with the maternal care-giving of her daughter-in-law. Noreen blames her British genes. "They're a cold people, Beth. It's a miracle Dutch came out the way he did."

Noreen never met Dutch's father, who was Italian, and probably the reason for Dutch's warm heart. I remember how fondly he used to talk about his dad when we were together, and how devastated he was when, at eleven-years-old, he lost him to heart failure. That was when his maternal grandparents really stepped in and helped his mother raise him. She went to work full time, and sent Daniel to spend summers with them in England. They grew close. It was why he didn't hesitate to help his grandmother when his grandfather had his stroke. We were only supposed to be apart for seventy-nine days.

I realize Noreen has no idea how much I know.

Today, March third, a year after the accident, and subsequent discovery of her illness, we stand at Noreen's window, watching fat flakes drift to the ground. I sip my tea and smile.

"Remember how we used to stand here, and narrate the actions of the kids outside?" I stifle a giggle with my hand. "If those poor children only knew what we said, and how we laughed at their expense."

Noreen grins. "We weren't mean. It was funny as hell. They were oompah loompahs in those snowsuits, for God's sake! It took Devin what, ten minutes to get up from making a snow angel? I nearly peed my pants. I love free entertainment."

"What about the time we were driving home from the park, and realized there was a bee in the car…" I couldn't finish. I was laughing too hard. Noreen did it for me, which had me gasping for air.

"I pulled over, and we both jumped out screaming. The kids were in their car seats, wondering what the hell was going on. I can't believe they didn't get stung." She shakes her head. "We certainly weren't winning any parenting awards for that incident."

When we compose ourselves, Noreen moves from the window, and lowers herself onto the couch. Her smile cannot mask her fatigue. Her eyes, typically so bright, are taxed with dark rings. I follow, and settle myself on Daniel's recliner; the one I claimed at the onset of our friendship, when we saw *Love Story*, and discussed possible scenarios like this one. Who knew?

"You know, Dutch calls that Beth's chair."

"He should. It's mine."

Noreen smiles, and rests her eyes. Her blanket is pulled up to her chin. This is where I usually find her, lately.

"Do you think Tommy will ask Stacy to his Junior prom?" Noreen asks.

I nod. "They're already talking about it. Tommy mentioned it. She's ecstatic. And it's still, what, three months away?"

"I'll want them to come here after he picks Stacy up. This way I can see the four of them dressed. Nikki's convinced Rich will ask her. I hope she's right."

"You know, Rhonda says they usually go to the lake afterwards. Do you think you'd let Nikki go?"

Noreen opens her eyes.

"Would you?"

"I don't think so. She's only fifteen. I'd like her to come home."

Noreen nods, in thought. She lifts her head to look at me.

"I need you to keep an eye on her for me. Make sure Dutch doesn't overindulge her. He's not as strong as me when it comes to Nikki. Maybe because she's not his. I don't know. But she's tough. Has a hard head."

"Gee, I wonder where she gets it."

"Bitch."

"I'm just saying."

"Promise me, Beth, you'll take care of my family. They need you. Nikki will need you. Her boy problems haven't even started yet. Devin has Dutch, but Nikki…"

"Okay. I promise. Stop talking like that. I hate these conversations."

"Well I don't enjoy them either. But I can't sleep at night. I keep thinking of things that have to be said–to be taken care of. I won't be here in ten years, in five, in…"

"Stop it."

"Beth, the medicine is not working. Look at me. I'm atrocious. My body has gone to hell. It's given up on me." Before the holidays, Noreen admitted to finally breaking down her resolve of relying on "voodoo and witch doctors" and agreed to try a new, FDA-approved medicine. I can't deny the fact that she does look gaunt, but still hold desperately to hope that science will prevail.

"You're beautiful. You always were. You still are." I say.

Noreen leans over, puts her finger in her mouth, and makes gagging sounds.

I throw a crumpled napkin at her, eliciting a grin.

Chapter 36

Noreen

I open my eyes in bed, and look over at Dutch. For a sweet minute, I am healthy, and whole. I will make my children breakfast, send them off to school, spin a thousand calories from my thighs, and then lose myself in meditation, and stretches at the gym, followed by a deep tissue massage that will melt any anxiety that managed to survive my yoga class. I will expose myself to Sonia, expert wax technician, who will pull out every unwanted pubic hair, and make me smooth, and ready for my husband to take me at whim. I will prepare a masterful meal, and welcome my cherished beasts home, where we will fight, temporarily, over homework, before allowing our tensions to dissolve easily into play. I will do this because I am young, I am healthy; because I can.

I sigh, turn from my husband, and pull back the blankets, exposing my body—skin covering bones—and watch as the moment shatters, falling to pieces at my veined feet. Slowly, I work my way from the bed to the bathroom. I don't turn on the light anymore. I brush my teeth in the dark, and wrap myself in a thick robe before heading downstairs to the den. Nestled on the couch, I will remain here, or in the near vicinity, for much of the day, too worn out to explore beyond the confines of the first floor. I lean my head toward the picture window, and watch the spectacle of dawn as tears roll down my cheeks. What has become of me? How am I going to leave them?

Devin is the first to come down, as usual. He couldn't find me in bed, and looks forlorn until he spots me on the couch. Wordlessly, he climbs next to me, and I stroke his hair while he holds my other hand. I marvel at how tall he is getting, his feet reaching to my knees as we lay.

This child, who fought me at nearly every stage of his life, is now my shadow. We fall asleep together every night, and routinely, Dutch carries him, sleeping, to his room. We also find these quiet, stolen moments before school each morning. He stays beside me in the afternoons, while Nicole shuffles around the house picking up after him, admonishing him all the while. I can't help but fill with pride, catching glimpses of her in a maternal role. I have done well, and though I am not nearly finished, must figure out how to pass them on to Dutch, to carry out the job to fruition on his own. I love this man, but can he really do this himself?

When the children are off to school, Dutch brings me toast and orange juice. He sits with me while I choke down a bite or two, and we go over what needs to be done during the day. He has stopped forcing me to eat, tired of losing the argument, and now carries my plate with tight lips to the kitchen. With a quick kiss, he escapes to work, leaving me alone with 'Regis and Kelly.' By the second segment of 'The View,' I know Beth will let herself in, and stay with me until the kids come home. Aside from my morning time with Devin, this is the highlight of my day. Beth is my rock, my sounding board, and will be the one I rely on to get the rest of my wishes done.

On the phone yesterday, I asked for cream of broccoli soup, and Beth will stop at Andy's and pick up two containers. She does this, knowing I hardly eat anymore. She doesn't, either. Because she is my friend, she will put down her spoon when I do. I am awed by the woman who pushed aside her insecurities, overcame her inadequate physique, to become to me, one of the most beautiful women I have ever known. How did she do it? All of these years, I should have felt superior, because physically, I was: stronger, taller, firmer. I had two equal, working legs. Now, Beth shuffles through my house with a calm, soulful purpose, and I am the weak one, the crippled, the invalid. She gives to me what Dutch cannot: a sense of peace, and acceptance, and laughter.

For a few hours a day, three days a week, she is my angel.

Chapter 37

Beth

In spring, my visits continue, and I enter the house with a different meal each day. We move from soup to egg and chicken salad sandwiches, and Andy has two orders to go for me when I call. Conversations with Noreen lob between nostalgia, and talk of the future.

"Remember when I dropped that tray of lasagna all over the floor, and we just looked at each other without saying anything, and put it back in and served it to the men?"

"If I recall, they each had two servings."

"Make sure Devin gets a job when he turns sixteen. Don't let him drag his lazy ass around all summer. And please don't let Dutch force him to work with him. It can be dangerous. I already told Dutch, but I want you to hear it, too."

"Remember when we threw Dutch's nasty old sneakers in the chiminea without telling him? He searched for those damn things for days."

"Make sure Nikki's idiot father doesn't get drunk at her wedding."

"Will she even invite him? When did they last speak?" I ask.

"I'm not sure. I think he called two weeks ago. He feels bad about what's going on. Of course, not bad enough to call her more often. The creep. I can't believe I ever married him."

The conversations about Dutch are the toughest for me.

"After he has some time, make sure he gets out. I don't want him to be alone. He's too good to be alone. Find him someone like you. He's always had a thing for you."

"Please, Noreen. The sickness has gone to your head."

"I mean it. There's something about you. He's different when you're around. I'm not saying it's a bad thing. I'm not jealous. In fact, I'm glad he feels the way he does, though he would never admit to it. It made it easier for me. Outside of my family, Beth, you're the person I'm closest to."

On the quiet days, when the sandwiches are abandoned on the coffee table, she's lying on the couch and I'm sitting on the recliner, I watch Noreen, wondering what she must be thinking. Is she afraid? Of dying? Of leaving them? When I ask, she looks at me, sometimes for a long time, her gorgeous blue eyes, now a shade lighter than the sky, seem to see right through me and she doesn't answer.

Sometimes, in barely a whisper, she talks about how she'll miss the sight of Nicole's flushed face as Dutch walks her down the aisle, or share her pride as she holds her baby for the first time; revel in Devin's glow as he holds his diploma, or learns to drive, or experiences his first kiss. The tears roll down her hollow cheeks, rendering me mute.

Yes, she is afraid. So am I.

❧

Chapter 38

Beth

Daniel lets me into the house. It is dark, quiet, and warm, and I'm happy to leave the early October chill outside for a spell. Autumn has settled in; the leaves, in their brilliance, hold firm to their roots, awaiting the moment to finally let go, and allow the cool wind to guide them gently to the ground, to be covered in winter. They are waiting, I know, for Noreen. It is as if she is orchestrating the season to her death. In summer, she sat in the yard, willing the sun to warm her face, her weakened bones, her soul; and finally, two weeks after the children returned to school for a new year, decided she'd bid farewell to the sun for the last time, allowing it to move elsewhere, inviting the cool, the cold, death.

"How is she?" I whisper.

"Sleeping." He motions me to follow him into the kitchen.

I sit quietly while he takes the teapot off of the flame, and pours our tea. He sits across the table, and we sip. Eighteen months have passed since our talk in his truck. Noreen has surpassed doctors' predictions, as I suspected she would. She won't be told when to die.

"Where is Nikki?" I ask.

"With Rich. Movies, I think. I convinced her to go out. She needs to get out. Devin is over at Roger's. I wanted him to spend the night. He also needs a break, but he refuses and he's making Loretta bring him home. It's funny, how he and Noreen used to fight. He was so difficult. The yelling, my God–they made each other cry! But he hardly leaves her side after school. He lays with her, holding her, until he drifts off–and he fights that, doesn't want to miss any time with her. He cries in his sleep. I don't think he realizes it. Between the both of them, I'm back and forth all night."

I sip more of my tea, and reach for Daniel's hand. This has become our ritual. On Friday nights, I spend hours here, listening to him talk about the week, the kids, his job; everything and anything that comes to his head. It's his release, he tells me–his one request of me.

"Please, just once in a while, come over to talk. I don't have anyone to talk to that knows us as well as you."

It was an easy favor, I originally thought; but soon came to realize just how difficult it is listening to him speak of loss, endings, and insurmountable pain. I am not a professional, so I learn to listen, keeping my thoughts, opinions, my own angst and fear about losing my best friend, to myself. Twice in a lifetime, I will lose someone as close to me as a sister. With Nancy, I had no time to say goodbye. My heart was ripped from me: a page torn from my life, ravaged, leaving shredded pieces dangling, sharp daggers of pain to pierce the rest of my story when I least expect.

As Noreen walks slowly and deliberately into her next life, I will at least have closure. I can say goodbye, and voice thoughts I wasn't able to say to Nancy. I make sure not to waste the precious chance. Still keeping with my weekly visits to Noreen, to allow Daniel some time outside of the house to collect himself, I whisper for hours to her: neighborhood gossip, humorous anecdotes of Mrs. Neilson, such as her screaming at the kids in the street from her driveway while in her housedress and fuzzy slippers.

I fill her in on Teresa: her numerous clubs, and our continuous weekly lunch dates. She is getting older, but still a spitfire. I promise to watch over Devin, as he plows his way through puberty; to help Nicole shop for a wedding dress when the time comes, and throw her an elaborate baby shower. I even agree to watch Dutch, and make sure he keeps up with household chores, and keeps the place habitable for her children. I make sure to tell Noreen over and over how much I love her, how happy I have been with her in my life, and how Noreen had essentially saved me from a life of mediocrity.

What I don't tell her is, that in another lifetime, I have loved her husband; that I needed her friendship more than true love, and I don't regret my decision. This is the secret I keep from her. The only one.

At home, I immerse myself in the normalcy of my own routine; shopping, cooking and cleaning, focusing on Stacy's and Alan's needs, as if by doing so, I can push aside the horrific thoughts that plague me every day. Alan watches me closely, and I pretend not to notice. He doesn't ask about Noreen. He asks how I am doing, and I can only shrug as my eyes fill, while I continue with mindless work. I am closed off from my husband, keeping my fears, sorrow and worries to myself, and feel powerless to change my behavior.

Daniel, Nicole and Devin are at Noreen's bedside when she takes her last breath the first week of November. He calls after breakfast, and I sit for a long time while the dishes remain on the table. The syrup starts to harden, and I stare at the orange juice, knowing I need to put it back in the fridge, but unable to move. Alan walks in sometime later, dressed for work, and stands at the entrance, waiting for me to acknowledge him, which I eventually do. I look into his eyes, and without words, he knows, and comes to me, stands behind me, and hugs my back, resting his head on mine. I will tell Stacy when she gets home from school, though she will probably figure it out before that time because Nicole won't be there.

As Noreen had done for me when my father passed away, I take it upon myself to make all post funereal arrangements, including hosting visitors at The Fergusan's, handling the food and necessities–leaving Daniel and his family to focus on what they need to do to get through the days. Swarms of people from the community line up along the funeral home for one full day to see her family, and I finally meet Stan and Milton, who do resemble each other so closely you'd believe they were twins. Tears spring to my eyes as I remember Noreen's words and voice explaining them to me, making me laugh until I thought I'd choke. I try not to think about how much I miss her and about what my life is going to be like without her in it. The thoughts suffocate me, and every so often, I step outside to breathe in the crisp air, clearing my lungs of loss.

On the second Tuesday in November, on a gorgeous, clear, cool morning, my best friend is lowered into the ground, as I stand between Daniel and Alan at the gravesite. Noreen's children stand on Daniel's other side, and it is difficult to watch Nicole with Devin, who is inconsolable. When the priest is finished, the rest of the mourners slowly move away, leaving us alone with Noreen for the last time. I stare at the mound of dirt waiting to cover the coffin, and wonder what will happen to her insatiable, unquenchable soul. Where does it go? It is too rich and alive to be smothered under the dirt, and I look around me, praying it is somewhere else, drifting free.

I know I should walk away, allow Daniel his final goodbye to his wife; but my heart is breaking, and my feet won't move. Finally, Alan pulls me with him, and together with Stacy, we head to our car.

It is eleven o'clock at night when I finally unlock my door and turn on the lights from my foyer. I hate walking into a dark house, and feel welcomed by the illuminated rooms, pictures, furniture and other trappings waiting for me. Alan and Stacy are a few minutes behind, having stayed at the Fergusan's so Alan could help Daniel stack up the rented chairs, and put them in his garage, to be picked up in the morning.

After three long days, the whole funeral and wake process is over, and I feel like I can lie down and sleep, uninterrupted, for a week. I drop my coat and purse, kick off my shoes, and fall onto my couch. For a solitary moment, I close my eyes and take in the silence. I am drained–and relish the feeling, for I know tomorrow when I wake up, I will have to fight the urge to pick up the phone to hear Noreen's voice: her happy and infectious giggles, or entertaining banter. I will have to allow myself to be wrapped in loneliness; but tonight, I am empty and thankful.

The sound of the doorbell startles me awake, and I become immediately annoyed at Alan for disturbing me. *Why isn't he using his key?*

I open the door to find Meredith Sullivan standing on my front stoop with a bottle of wine, and an unnatural expression. Humility, I believe. I open the storm door and say nothing. With the throngs of people meandering through the funeral home at the wake, I failed to realize Meredith was one of the few from the school who was missing.

"Beth. Can I come in?"

Silently, I hold the door and allow Meredith to step in past me. At the edge of my living room we stand together, and I give her a minute to look around while she gathers herself to speak. I don't offer to take her coat, or the wine. I just stand there, and wait.

"I don't know what to say." She starts.

I raise my eyebrows. That's a first.

"I know we have never been friends, but I wanted to come here and tell you, away from the services or the wake, that I am so sorry for your loss. I know how close you were to Noreen."

I am unable to speak, so in Meredith fashion, she goes on.

"I thought maybe we can have lunch or go out next week. Linda and I play Bridge every third Thursday night. Chelsea is notoriously unreliable, and we don't put it past her to cheat, although Susan completely denies any possibility of it. Those two are always in cahoots. I'm sure we can use another…"

I listen to her ramble while I stare at the floor. When we first met Meredith, Noreen and I were at the beginning of our relationship, and I realize now how much of our bonding resulted from the antics of this woman. I imagine what Noreen would say if she could be privy to this conversation, to my predicament of being alone with Meredith in my home, and I start to giggle.

It's a rumble, low at first; but the more I try to contain it, the stronger the torrent becomes. Pushing aside thoughts of insensitivity, I allow myself to succumb, falling powerlessly into an uncontrolled hysteria.

Meredith watches me in horror, her lower jaw hanging open, while I hunch over, holding my stomach, as tears fall from my cheeks and drip to my carpet. I know it appears I am enjoying myself, and though partly true, what I feel as wave upon wave of laughter erupts, is a pain so intense, I cannot lift myself to standing until the feeling passes.

I'm not sure how long I am there; but when I finally manage to gather myself, I straighten to find my husband and daughter staring at me from the foyer. There is no sign of Meredith.

Without a word, my family walks past me to their bedrooms, and I am left alone in the living room. Drying my eyes, and calming my breath, I notice the bottle of wine sitting on the side table. Without thought, I grab the bottle, and go in search of a corkscrew.

Chapter 39

Daniel takes a month from work to focus on the children, who at eleven and fifteen are not children anymore, but young adults fully encompassed by their loss and still in need of their father's presence. When they finally return to school, after a somber Thanksgiving spent with his mother and stepfather, I respond to Daniel's pleas for help with the basic functions of the house, guiding him through a full course of laundry—tips for stain removal, reminding him to separate whites and colors.

Another visit has us talking about grocery lists and easy recipes he can handle for dinner. Noreen specifically asked me to ensure that he doesn't rely on fast food for nourishment. I have been bringing the family meals four nights a week, extensions of my own family's, and feel it is time to teach Daniel some basic dishes to get them through the rest of the week. We focus diligently on these mundane tasks, as if by devoting enough attention to minute details we might be able to push off the loneliness that waits to envelope us.

As we near mid-December, he knows the holiday will be a major hurdle to surmount with bitter hearts and moments of despair. It takes heavy doses of gentle coaxing to finally convince Daniel to buy a small tree. I return a few days later to find it still bare in the living room.

"They can't do it."

It wears only an angel on top. Its significance is so intense as to be almost cruel. I make Daniel take out ornaments and we quickly decorate it for the sake of the children.

When I offer to go shopping without him on a Saturday, Daniel reluctantly joins me. We struggle against the crowds and decide to stop after three hours, to eat lunch at the diner outside of the mall.

"I don't know why I'm even doing this. I just want the holiday to pass unnoticed." Daniel places his bags at his feet and shrugs off his coat.

"I know. But you know you can't ignore it. It's everywhere, shoved down our throats on TV, the stores—even in school. They're in pain, but they'll be even more forlorn without something to distract them—even for a short while. Spoil the hell out of them this year. It sounds materialistic and shallow, but so what? Try everything to bring even a small smile to their faces."

He sighs. "I don't know. I don't know the right thing to do. The school called me yesterday. Devin got into a fight. This is the second one in two weeks. I found out he was bullying a boy in a younger grade, and the boy finally hit him." Daniel looks at me, and his expression pains me. "Devin's never—in his *life*—ever bullied anyone. I don't know what to do. He won't talk to me."

"Well, what about a grief counselor? I overheard something when the hospice nurse was at your house. Have you thought about that? Nikki could probably use some counseling, too. Even if she seems like she's adjusting, she still needs a professional."

"I don't know."

"It doesn't make you a bad parent. Dutch, you've never been through something like this. How are you supposed to know how the kids will deal with it?"

The food arrives, and the waitress leaves us. Daniel picks at his sandwich.

"You know, I once lost someone close to me."

"Your dad?"

He shakes his head. "I did lose my dad young, and it was hard. As a result, I grew close to my grandparents—closer to them than I was to my parents. In fact, I spent every summer for ten years with them, in England. My last summer there changed my life. I should never have gone; but they were my two favorite people, and my grandfather needed me."

I stare at my salad with interest.

"I wasn't referring to my dad. I was in love once, before Noreen. I might have mentioned it in the past. But you don't know the full story. No one else does. We'd only known each other for a few months, but I was so sure she was it. As sure as I knew I would wake up the next day." He is still looking at me as he speaks, and my breath is shallow.

"We were perfect. I'd never been so happy."

Is he aware of my stiffened posture and silence? If so, he makes no mention.

"We had plans. We'd graduate and get married, but I left her to see my grandparents. I had no idea when we said goodbye, it would be the last time I would ever see her. I would never have gone if I'd known. Anyway, she seemed to accept it. We promised each other to meet again. I spent the summer in a delirious state. I could think of nothing but her. I wrote letters, every week. And I waited all summer for a word back."

Daniel stops, takes a sip of soda, and sits back, pushing his lunch away. I am mesmerized, listening to a story about someone else, in another lifetime. For twenty-two years, I've only known one side.

I should stop him now, but I can't. I need to know what he has to say almost as much as he needs to tell me.

"What happened?" I whisper.

"The first letter I received–the only letter–was two weeks before I was scheduled to fly home. She gave me some story about falling in love with someone else, and told me she never wanted to see me again. She just ended it. No explanation. No foreshadowing. It came out of nowhere. I was…"

Daniel stares past me, seeing himself a quarter of a century ago, while I hold my breath. The waitress stops at our table, and I look at her quickly, shaking my head. She steps away, knowingly.

"My grandparents didn't know what to do. I went to the airport the day I got her letter. I waited in the terminal for hours, trying to get on a flight. My grandmother met me there, sat with me, and eventually convinced me to come back home with her. I'm glad I did. I don't know what I would have done if I'd gotten on a flight that day. I wanted to show up at her house and demand an explanation. Something. Something to make me understand.

I had fourteen days to wait with myself. I must have been miserable company those last days. I spent a lot of time alone, taking long walks everywhere, remembering every single conversation we had. I couldn't figure it out. My grandfather tried to convince me the relationship was one-sided; that I had created this love in my mind. He said I'd obviously mistaken our time together as something more than she did. But I knew I didn't. What we had was very real and mutual. I mean, how could I be so wrong? Something had happened. It was killing me that I couldn't find out. She refused my calls.

When I got home, my mother had no idea what had transpired. I left two days later to return to school. I was hoping to find her there. I went to the place she was to do her internship. They told me she had given up her spot."

Daniel shakes his head and returns to the table, to me. I want to reach out and touch him, to comfort him. Instead, I clench my fists under the table.

"I never believed that she just left me like that. And I knew something must have been wrong for her to give up her dream. Not long after I got there, I left school, and found her house. I stood outside, watching it. I had no idea if she still lived there. I made it all the way, yet I couldn't bring myself to go to the door. So I waited for her to come out. Her mother made it clear on the phone that she didn't want to talk to me. She told me to respect her daughter's decision, and that she was truly, finally happy. With her words in mind, I still stood there waiting, hoping. I knew if I could just see her, just for a moment, I could have changed her mind.

I finally worked up the courage to cross the street, and had taken one step, when a car pulled into the driveway and a guy got out, holding flowers. He walked to the house with the familiarity of someone who'd been there before. That was probably the most painful moment of my life—even more so than when I got the letter. I scraped my heart off the ground and left."

I remember that day all too clearly—my visit with Jamie and Peter after the accident. Jamie was already with me when Peter Spidaro, feeling guilty that it was his party we'd been driving to, showed up. If Daniel would have stayed, he would have seen them leave together, half an hour later.

"The whole episode set me back."

"How?"

"I shut down: stopped going to classes, indulged in a drunken stupor for three months. It bordered on lunacy. One evening, I woke up and took a good look at what I'd become. My apartment was wretched; take-out boxes I don't remember ordering were all over the place, and a sickening odor had settled into the walls. I hated myself. So I stopped. Just like that. Picked myself up, wiped myself off, dove into my studies, and graduated in June—half a year past schedule.

You wouldn't have recognized me then. I turned myself completely off emotionally. After graduation, I went back to New York, went home with any woman who showed interest, and left them while the bed was still warm. I was a first class creep."

He stops and watches me. I stare back in disbelief.

"It took a few years to get that out of my system before I calmed down. I threw myself into my business, and was grateful for the long hours, the grueling work, trying to get it going. I never had another relationship until Noreen. Seven years. I didn't trust anyone. Found fault with everyone, when truthfully, the whole thing was my fault."

"Why do you think it was your fault?" I can't get my voice above a whisper.

He leans back and runs his fingers through his hair, leaving it messy and enticing. "I shouldn't have left. It's as simple as that."

Color rises to my cheeks, and my mouth is parched. He thought about me, about us, all of this time. I fight the urge to tell him it was not his fault. He did nothing wrong. It was me. I changed our lives with my recklessness. The desire to finally tell him what I had been holding onto for most of my life is so strong, I start to shake. I feel the tears well, and he becomes blurry across the table.

"Noreen never had one hundred percent of me, and she knew it. And she loved me anyway."

We drive back to Daniel's in silence. When I pull into his driveway, he turns to me.

"Beth…"

"I have to go. Alan is waiting for me."

He watches me as I stare through the windshield, like a coward, before finally, he sighs, grabs his bags, and pushes himself from the car.

"Yes, of course."

I drive home in a daze. What have I done? I betrayed this man not once, but twice in his lifetime. My relationship with him—whatever I could call it—was a lie. I have lied to everyone: to Daniel, to Noreen, to Alan, to myself. I actually made myself believe that things were okay. My whole existence is a fabricated story, wrapped in a handicapped, crippled box.

I have to pull over and wipe my eyes, blind to what I should do. Soon, a knock on the window startles me. I turn to see an officer peering in, concerned. With a hiccup, I slide the window down.

"Ma'am, you've been sitting here for ten minutes. Is there something I can help you with?" He looks around the car, and back at me. "Are you okay?"

No. I am not okay. I want my friend back. I wanted to have my career, working in Washington D.C. I want to have married the man of my dreams, and not have a limp, and a crooked smile. I want to see my dad, hug him. I want Nancy, and Noreen. I want....

"Ma'am, would you mind stepping out of the car?"

Back on the road, humiliated after having to walk a straight line, and touch my nose for a man who was more afraid of me than I was of him, I decide to turn around and tell Daniel everything. I have held onto the truth for too long. I owe it to him, and to myself, to tell him what happened. He should know that I didn't leave him because I didn't love him. He deserves to know.

When I pull into his driveway, Daniel comes to the door, looking perplexed. He steps onto the porch, and watches me get out of the car. I stand at the start of the walkway, and freeze when I see the look in his eyes. Does he know why I am here?

My legs won't move.

Finally, he walks to me, and stops inches away. What is he thinking? I stare up into his green eyes, and let myself wallow there. He waits.

"I have something to tell you." I start.

He is still.

"What is it?"

Like a whirlwind in my mind, various pictures from my memory swirl in my head: our last embrace at the airport, our lives ahead of us, meeting again ten years later, forming a friendship, the talks we shared over the years–scattered at first, but growing more and more frequent...Our trip to St. Lucia, things he said, that I took as pity at the time: compliments and looks when Noreen wasn't aware.

Or had she been aware? Oh, God.

The door slams, and I look past Daniel to see Devin watching us. He is on the porch where his father stood moments ago, confused.

What am I doing here?

"I have to go." I can't be here. I have not thought this out. I am irrational, and unfair. What purpose will it serve if he knows?

Before Daniel can react, I am in my car, and back on the road. In my rearview mirror, I see him standing in the same place I left him, with his son still on the porch.

Alan is in the kitchen when I get home, putting plates on the table, and smiles when he sees me.

"How'd it go? Did you get everything done? Beth, what's wrong?"

I start to cry, and he walks to me, and pulls me into him.

"Shhh. It's okay. It'll get easier. I promise."

I look up at my husband. This is the man who fell in love with me when I believed that I would be alone for the rest of my life. A man who looked past the clouded eyes of my soul, forever shattered, and wanted to be with me anyway. In all of the weeks I have been giving my time to Noreen's family, he has not voiced concern, impatience, or distrust. This is the man whose heart I never fully accepted. I am ashamed.

I put my arms around Alan and hold him tightly. "I'm sorry." I whisper over his shoulder. "I'm sorry. I just miss him so much."

He returns my hug fiercely, with soothing words, whispers— It's okay, It's okay—believing, I'm sure, that I am referring to my father.

Chapter 40

November 2007

"How about this one?" Stacy asks.

I stand, and slowly walk around my daughter, who is regal on a platform before a tri-fold mirror. I finger the tulle on the back of her dress, and gently lay it down over the train.

"I like it." I turn to Nikki. "What do you think?"

Nicole, who at twenty-three, is as gorgeous as her mother, grins widely from her perch on the small sofa in the back of the bridal boutique. "I love them both."

"Ugh! I need more from you two! Please, tell me which one you like. I love them both, too. You're not helping! Do I need to bring Annabel with me next time?" Stacy stomps over to the rack, and starts sifting through more dresses. Nicole grins at me. We exchange entertained shrugs and watch the bride-to-be stress over what she will wear to her wedding.

"Stace. I'd go with the first one. It's simple, elegant." Nikki says.

"I agree." I add, knowing her best friend's opinion would weigh more heavily than mine, anyway. I always relied on Nancy for final approval over my own mother.

Stacy stops shoving hangars aside. "Really? The first one? Are you sure? I want it to be perfect. It has to be perfect."

My daughter stands before us, exasperated, and adorable.

"You should worry more about your marriage than the wedding. Just remember that. Jeremy is wonderful, and you're going to have a beautiful life together. Try to focus on that. The wedding lasts five hours. Try to gain some perspective." I say.

Stacy looks at Nicole. "Nik?"

"Don't worry." Nikki grins. "The dress is perfect, the party will be perfect."

Six months later, I take Stacy to lunch after our visit to the florist.

"Okay, so the flowers are done, the band set, one more fitting for the dress, the bridesmaid dresses are in, flower girl dress. Right! We just need to still find that headpiece. I'm sure I can make one for you. I saw something in a magazine that made it look easy."

Stacy listens as she bites into her sandwich. "Mom, eat. We'll go over the list later. I think we're all covered."

I put down my pen, and move the list to the side.

"You're right. You're in good shape. I think."

"Thanks to you."

"Well, that's what a mother is for."

Stacy's face clouds over, and she puts her sandwich down. "What is Nikki going to do next year?"

I look at my child, and deep pride fills me. She has worked hard, and graduated with honors from college–something I never did. She landed a strong position at an advertising company, and found a wonderful man with whom to spend the rest of her life. She and Nikki had remained close, even when they split up to go to school, and Stacy is still looking out for her. Noreen died almost eight years ago.

"Well, we'll help her with all of the things she'll need. Her future mother-in-law seems like a very nice woman. She has all of us."

Stacy picks at her nails. I put my hand over hers–something I know she hates, but I can't help it.

"Honey, I want you to focus on your own day. Nikki will be fine. She doesn't want you to worry about her."

She pulls her hand free and sips her iced tea.

"Nikki told me her dad is bringing a date to my wedding. Someone he's been seeing. I wonder what she's like. If she's like Noreen." She put down her glass. "Mom, are you okay?"

"I…" I clear my throat. "I'm fine."

I think about that afternoon when I almost told Daniel the truth of who I really am. After the holidays, I started spacing my visits until, as if weaning from an addictive drug, I managed to keep a safe distance from him. I resorted to reaching out by phone, and the occasional visit with Alan, until we both fell out of the habit of seeing each other regularly.

Stacy sighs and leans back in her booth. "Mom? How did you know that Dad was the one for you? You know, 'The One?'" She uses her fingers to make quote marks in the air.

"Why? Are you having doubts?"

"No. Of course not. It's just that, well, so many people nowadays are getting divorced. How do I know I won't be one of those people? I love Jeremy more than anything…but I'm afraid. What if he doesn't love me ten years from now? What makes you and dad work?"

I sit back and ponder the question while I envy my daughter. She floats on an effervescent high, making her wedding plans. She and Jeremy enjoy a mature relationship. Alan and I have spent many evenings with them—over dinner, movies, and conversations—and we know he truly loves her. I believe with my whole heart that they will be together forever. For one, she will be marrying the man of her dreams.

"Well, first you fall in love, and you float in that wonderful, delicate bubble of romance, and newness. Then, ultimately, the bubble returns to Earth, and when it subtly disappears, you're left with a partner who has thoughts, and faults, and opinions, and certain ways that may differ from your own. You have to understand each other. Talk to each other. This is the most important thing—more important than intimacy. And you must respect each other."

"I hope I am as happy as you and dad."

"I hope you're happier."

The ceremony is simple, but lovely. The bride and groom recite their own vows, and as I watch them profess their love before God and witnesses, I recall my own wedding to Alan, who sits beside me, holding my hand. Specific moments were lost along the way as years floated by, but I can distinctly remember what I felt as I was escorted by my father down the aisle. At the time, I shared none of the exuberance Stacy exudes. As a bride, I was unsure of myself, my feelings, my future, and before my married life even began, full of regret.

I look to my husband as I see him struggle to keep his chin from quivering. I squeeze his hand, and he looks at me and smiles.

At the reception, the band plays the wedding song, At Last, and my husband and I are entranced by the couple who waltz across the dance floor, oblivious to everyone but each other. We don't have much time to dwell on how fast life passes by, as we are thronged by guests, and it is not until dinner is served that I can finally sit down.

Stacy's friends soon monopolize the floor, bumping, and swaying to an unfamiliar beat that seems to move the room. Then it's time for Alan to escort Stacy alone to the floor, and dance with her. They are good together; they always have been. She looks at her father with adoration, and suddenly I pine for my own, knowing I will never stop missing him.

The dance ends to enthusiastic applause, and I gratefully wipe my eyes, wondering briefly how my face must look. Happy tears do as much damage to makeup as sad ones. I look to my mother, seated at the next table, and wonder why she isn't telling me how terrible I look, or to go to the bathroom to check myself. She must not be feeling well.

The bride and groom cut the cake, and the party is seated for dessert as we near the end of the reception. The cake dishes are cleared, and the dance floor becomes crowded once again. This will be the final hour of the evening; guests pouring themselves out to enjoy the music, a wonderful celebration of love, before they return home, and back to normalcy.

Alan's sister, Tiffany, and her husband entertain me with the saga of their younger daughter, while Alan is somewhere on the dance floor, trying not to embarrass himself, I hope, when the band slows down one more time. Couples form quickly, and I smile when I finally find Alan with his aunt Charlene. She is eighty years old, all of four feet tall, and still on the floor at the end of a party. I lose my sister-in-law too, and find myself sitting alone when I feel a tap on my shoulder.

I turn to see Daniel looking down at me. He extends his hand, and I allow him to lead me to the corner of the dance floor. We fit, as I knew we would, and sway in perfect rhythm to the music. In all the years we've known each other, this is our first dance. He takes it slow, so my limp is not so pronounced. I almost feel as if it's not even there.

"You should be ashamed of yourself." He says.

I lean back and give him a look.

"You're as beautiful as the bride tonight."

I snort out a laugh. "Liar."

Daniel pauses, and holds me still. "I don't lie, Beth. You know that." He is not smiling, and it is a full minute until we start moving again.

"Why do you do that?" I ask.

"Do what?"

"Say things like that to me when it's so blatantly not true. Why do you tell me I'm beautiful? I know what I am. And I don't appreciate your patronizing me."

Our eyes are locked, and I feel the heat of my anger reach my cheeks. My daughter is perfect, with large, almond eyes, glossy blond hair, and a strong, shapely body that is as natural to her as it is for my mother. There is no comparison between myself and these women. For years this has bothered me; how easily he says the words, and how difficult it is for me to get over them each time he does. They are a cruel reminder of what has been taken from me. As if I could ever forget.

Daniel slows us down until we are barely moving. His hand tightens against my back, as if he wants to ensure I don't walk away. I stare into his eyes, and try to anticipate his next comment.

He has never been predictable, and I am not prepared for what he says next.

"Do you honestly believe that I can't see past a face? Or a body?" He shakes his head and appears as angry as I feel. "Do you think that is what I am referring to? Beth, I can see you, who you are. And you're beauty goes deeper than your skin. I'm talking about in here." He pulls my hand with his, and points to my chest, my heart.

We resume our dance, and I cannot look at him.

"I thought you knew me better than that." He adds, and I close my eyes with regret. I have known Daniel for thirty years. For much of that time, we've been friends, part of a foursome, support for each other in a time of loss; and we've never stood this close for any length of time. Yet, the way I feel in his arms, as we move on the floor in time with the music, and each other, is as natural to me as taking my next breath.

He is the other half of me; but he is not mine. I try to think of something to say, to replace the thoughts in my mind, my desire to tell him the truth right now. I have known in my heart since Noreen died that I will never tell Daniel who I am.

"I like her." I say, referring to his date.

"Good."

We don't say more, and I work to rid myself of thoughts. I can't. I ask myself the same question that pierces my mind since standing in front of his house eight years ago. Does he know it's me?

The music ends, and he gives me a sad smile that breaks off a piece of my heart and sends it pulsing through my blood.

∽

Chapter 41

March 2009

"Alan!" I yell, holding my hand over the receiver. "It's Stacy! Where are you?"

I listen for him in the bedroom, and put the phone back to my ear. "Honey, he may be in the bathroom. When are you and Jeremy planning to come out?"

"I'm not sure. We're still working on the rooms. You have to come and see the new paint colors, Mom; the den came out beautiful!"

I hear a click and know that Alan is on the phone. "Alan, is that you?"

"I'm here. Hi babe. How is my second favorite girl?" He says.

"Hi Dad. I'm good. I was just telling Mom that you guys have to come out here and see the house. Daddy, you'd love it here."

He sighs. I know what he's thinking. Why did you move so far away? Stacy and I wait for his response.

"Maybe your mom and I will take a few weeks and visit. I'll try to clear my schedule in spring. I hear San Francisco is nice in May."

I smile into the phone. Alan is not happy when he's too far from his practice. The extent of his time off reaches to long weekends, or an afternoon here and there. I know he wants to make Stacy happy, and he'll try.

"That'd be great, Dad. Mom, I'll call you. Love you both."

I hang up the phone and finish the dishes while peering out into the dreary March evening. We are nearly out of winter, a season that fills me with longing for the people I miss, and I am eager for May; warmth, light, and my daughter. The house is too quiet. It's funny how one person can change the dynamic of an entire household. Stacy has been married and out of the house for a year, and Alan and I are still adjusting to being alone. Since I was pregnant at the onset of our marriage, our alone time seemed like a fleeting moment, and an idea to which we haven't yet grown accustomed. Sometimes we just stare at each other across the kitchen table without words.

What is there to say now that we don't have to drive our daughter somewhere, or help her study for a test, or listen to her rattle on in her perky, positive way? We don't verbalize it, but we're also sorely missing another couple in our lives. We get together occasionally with the Manetti's and Schwartzs, but it's not the same. I miss Noreen. I miss Daniel. I pain for the quartet we were for so long.

I shut the light off and go to the bedroom to talk to Alan. The thought of visiting Stacy fills me with hope. She moved across the country six months ago, but it feels like I haven't seen her for longer than that; time plays tricks on me. But Stacy seems happy, and Jeremy is doing well in his new position. So well, she can take her time finding a new job, and can focus on her new home.

Alan is not in the bedroom, so I check the den and the living room, which is rarely used anymore, and both are empty. Maybe we should consider moving, find a smaller place where I won't have to look so far to find my husband. I know my idea would be met with resistance. Alan loves this house, and I'm sure we will call this home for many more years. Where the hell could he have gone?

I return to our bedroom to change, and that's when I see his feet from behind the bed. "Alan!" I go to him, and he is unconscious. My heart drops to my feet, and I shake as I check to be sure he is breathing before reaching for the phone.

We're at the Medical Center in less than twenty minutes. I ride in the ambulance with my husband, and two medics, holding his hand the entire trip. I wait until he is finally in a room—four hours—before I call Stacy and tell her. Her words betray her shaky voice as she tries to assure me he will be okay, and she will get on the next available flight out. I sit by him, holding his hand as he sleeps. He's lucky to be alive, his doctor tells me, fortunate I was there; he had a massive heart attack, and is weak.

I didn't even know he was at risk.

I stay with him all night, never letting him go, whispering to him occasionally, willing him to wake up and see me.

I must have dozed, because the next thing I know, Alan's hand is moving, and it reaches to my face, resting on his bed. My eyes sting when I open them, taking in the light through the blinds, and I smile.

"Hi." He says.

"Hi, yourself." I say, as tears spring to my eyes.

The nurse asks me to wait outside while she performs routine checks on my husband, and cleans him. Subtle pain shoots from my lower back to my ankles as I work to stretch my legs; my limp is more pronounced after sitting in an awkward position for most of the night. As I slowly make my way up and down the hall, I try to avoid looking into the rooms. Hospitals depress me, and I am reminded of why Noreen chose to die at home, with her familiar smells, colors, and noise. It feels more natural to die where you lived. I wonder, though, if it was harder for her children to know their mother died in their living room; a conundrum, Noreen would have joked.

I am on my way back to Alan when I see Daniel enter the wing. He is rushing through the doors and doesn't notice me until he is close. Without a word, he takes me in his arms, and we hold each other.

Eventually, he lets me go. I want to stay in his warm arms longer, but I know I can't.

"Why didn't you call me?" He asks.

"I…I don't know. I wasn't thinking. How did you find out?"

"Stacy. She called this morning. I'm picking her up at one. But I wanted to come here first. To see you. How is he?"

I nod, tears in my eyes. Exhausted, my emotions overtake me, and I can't speak. I haven't seen Daniel in months. He looks at me, and pulls me toward him again. At once, I am safe.

~

Chapter 42

Stacy flings the door open and enters the hospital room in her wonderfully dramatic style.

"Oh, Daddy!" She throws herself on Alan, and starts to sob. "I'm sorry I wasn't here!"

I stand back to take them in, and glance quickly at Daniel, who remains near the door. My daughter looks tired, but I am so happy to see her. I feel everything will be okay. The people I love most in the world are contained in this room, right now.

I leave my husband and daughter to themselves–a duo so tight, there's barely enough room for anyone else–and Daniel follows me out of the room.

"Have you eaten?"

I shake my head. We walk slowly toward the elevators, and find the café near the lobby. It is alive, and colorful, and warm, and feels good to be out of the hospital room for a while. He buys me a cup of coffee–tea isn't going to cut it today–and we find seats at one of the long tables.

"How've you been?" I ask.

He takes a sip, and looks around the room, then back at me.

"I'm okay. Work is fairly busy, so…"

"The kids? I haven't talked to Nikki in a while."

"She's well. I told her about Alan, and she'll be here later. You should see how big Matty is getting. He started walking." Daniel reaches into his back pocket and opens his wallet. Showing through the plastic window, a photo of a beautiful little boy replaced the picture of his own children.

"He looks like her, don't you think?"

I hold the wallet and stare at Matty's face. Noreen's eyes look back at me. I look at Daniel and smile.

"I'll bet he'll be a terror, like Devin."

"God forbid!" Daniel laughs, and puts his wallet away. "Speaking of Devin. He's still finding his way, working and dating, having too much fun to settle down yet. He's in an apartment in Reading, so he stops in every week to check on me."

I don't want to ask, but I feel I have to. "How is your girlfriend?"

"Fiona? She's fine. We're fine."

It takes time for him to get around to it, but I knew he would ask me. I am waiting. We are barely finished with our coffee when it comes out.

"Why have you been avoiding me?"

I look down, and rub my hands against my pants.

"Hey." He says. I look up at him.

"What did I do?" The look he gives makes me want to touch his face, his hand, some part of him; but I don't. I can't. There's no point, I learned, to maintain his friendship without Noreen. It is too painful for me, and not fair to Alan. I made a resolution years ago to focus on my husband, and it's one I don't plan to break.

"You didn't do anything, Dutch. I've been busy."

He knows I'm lying.

"I miss our talks. I miss seeing you. I'd like you to get to know Fiona." I stand and want to bend over from the pain of his words, feeling like I've been punched in the gut. I don't want to know Fiona. I don't want to know anyone with him that isn't Noreen. He follows me back toward the elevator. There are three other people waiting, and when the doors open, I turn to him.

"I miss you, too. I miss the four of us. Everything we had."

The look on his face brings me to him. Over his shoulder, I thank him for bringing my daughter to the hospital.

Time seems to stand still while we wait for the doctor to come and tell us what is going on. Teresa spends the entire afternoon with us, and I am thankful for her poise and composure–the antithesis to my daughter, who intermittently cries and converses through the hours.

In the early evening, Nicole visits, and convinces Stacy to take a break and get something to eat. I urge her to go, and reluctantly, she hugs her father carefully around his tubes, whispers something to him, and leaves. Teresa follows shortly after with a quick peck and a promise to stop in again in the morning, before heading to her book club.

Alan and I are alone again, at last. He looks exhausted, and slightly gray; but everyone who enters the room takes on a sickly hue, so I don't look too much into it. The doctor finally checks in and reviews his chart. He informs us that Alan is scheduled the following morning for surgery, to bypass two arteries that are ninety percent clogged. If all goes well, I can take him home by the end of the week.

When the doctor leaves, we sit quietly together, holding hands. The light flickering from the television casts a glow on the darkening room, as dusk settles outside. I stare at the screen, unseeing, while I try not to focus on how close I came to losing my husband, relishing the feeling of his warm hand in mine.

"Beth?"

"Hmmm?" I turn to see him looking at me. He wants to say something, so I turn the TV off, and put the clicker down on his bed, giving him my full attention.

"I just want to say, in case anything happens tomorrow, that I love you."

"I love you, too."

"Please." He squeezes my hand. "Let me finish."

I straighten, and squeeze his hand back. "Okay."

"I know I may not have made you very happy. And I'm sorry. I tried to give you….Just please know, you made me the happiest man in the world. And I hope that when you look back, you feel some happiness, too."

I stare at my husband through my tears, and hold his hand tightly. I have hurt the man who loved me the most, and now as he lies in a hospital, with a broken heart, I wonder who really put him here…

"Alan, you've given me a wonderful life. A beautiful daughter. And I will never, not once, ever feel anything but joy when I think of what we have. Please know that."

He closes his eyes and nods slightly, as I watch closely, believing what I tell him to be true. I lay my head on his chest and cry, without fear, without remorse, while he strokes my hair.

The next morning, I leave Alan with a kiss as two nurses wheel him to the operating room. While I wait in the café with Stacy

188 | *Kimberly Wenzler*

and Teresa, I offer a silent deal with God to give my husband more time on this earth so that I may prove to him that he is my life, and the man of my dreams. Three hours later, the doctor finds us sitting in the small waiting room at the end of the hall where Alan is staying. I stand, clutching my daughter's arm, while my mother puts her arm around her granddaughter, and listen to a cautiously optimistic prognosis.

Alan is released the following Monday, four days later, with a list of dietary and medicinal instructions to follow. At home, we dine with Stacy on grilled chicken, steamed broccoli and sweet potatoes, enjoying light conversation, joking on how boring our meals will be now that we have to adhere to a diet regiment. She is a breath of spring air in the house again. I know Alan feels the same way by the way he looks at her when she's unaware. He loves her more than life itself. I've felt that way, too. To love so much, it hurts.

Two weeks later, when Alan is settled, we drive Stacy to the airport, and watch her walk to the concourse until we can no longer see her. Alan and I walk back to the car together, and drive home.

I can't help but wonder what goes through Alan's head as we watch television in the den, or eat dinner by the dim light overhead in the kitchen. Our conversation in the hospital was meant to alleviate uncertainty, but I find it only caused tension. How can I assure him I'm happy? How can I assure myself I am? I move through the days, burdened by his confession of what he believes was our whole life together. I can't undo it.

When Daniel calls–frequently, at first–I quickly pass the phone to Alan, until eventually the calls come at longer and longer intervals.

With some regret, Alan refers his patients to a longtime colleague until further notice and we pass the days taking leisurely walks through the town park, embracing the thaw in the air. Visits to the library, and the occasional evening with friends break up the monotony. Our routine is comfortable, and I don't push Alan to go see Stacy because he doesn't look like his usual self yet. I figured we'd go see her in the summer. I can detect his unspoken concern about our antisocial behavior, and work to show him how little I need of anyone else in our daily lives. This is the way I am most comfortable.

Alan and I were together for less than a year before we were blessed with Stacy. For much of our life together, there have been three of us, and our conversations revolved around our daughter, her needs and our friends. Alan worked six days a week, and when we travelled or went out, we did it with Noreen and Daniel. Now, alone again after twenty-four years, I understand how little Alan and I talked, and now that we have all of this time together, I find it difficult to conjure up things to say. Silence sits between us on the couch, at the kitchen table, and lies with us in our bed.

My agreement with God gives us only one more year together. In February, his heart stops again, and we find ourselves in another ambulance ride to the hospital. This time, I call Stacy right away, knowing I shouldn't wait. Before she arrives, I wait for the nurses to finally leave us, taking with them their machines, and their silent gazes that tell me what I already know. I hold Alan's hand while he lies with eyes closed, and whisper over and over again, *Thank you.* He waits for his daughter to arrive twenty-four hours later, before he lets go of this world.

In the intensive care unit, behind a light blue cotton curtain, with the murmuring and bleeping sounds of others several feet away, others struggling for their lives, for more time, Stacy and I say goodbye.

Daniel and Nicole are the last to leave my house after the funeral. By ten o'clock in the evening, we all feel like we've been up for days. The house is in order, thanks to my mother's nervous energy. I watched her during the afternoon as she flitted about between quiet conversations, picking up plates seconds after they were set down, wrapping food, and wiping down tables and counters. I didn't ask her to stop, knowing how important this task is to helping her cope. She argued to stay with me earlier, but now she looks tired, and gives in easily when I implore her to go home to rest.

At the door, Daniel turns to me, and tells me to call him if there is anything I need. I assure him I will, and we both know I'm lying. We've grown apart. I've pushed him further away in light of my knowledge that Alan believed he failed to make me happy, and now I cannot fathom resuming our friendship.

Stacy and I sit alone in the den while Jeremy is inside on the phone, checking his messages. I feel as exhausted as she looks. Her long legs rest on the coffee table, and I stare at knees that were once covered first with small tights, and then with bandages and dirt. The years have melted away without mercy, and I pine for the beginning again. I want to wake up my five-year-old for her first day of school, and wait for her to step off of the bus so we can chat over snacks, coordinate birthday parties, and hide Christmas presents. She watches me as I wallow.

"Mom? We want you to come live with us." She says.

"Where? California?"

She nods.

I rest my head, and stare at the ceiling. I have only known Pennsylvania my entire life. Everything I've ever done has been here. Not a valid reason to stay, but I don't want to give life to the real reason. So, I turn to my daughter.

"I can't go. Your grandmother needs me."

Stacy snorts. "Grams? Since when has she needed anything but herself? She's so independent, Mom. Besides, you never really got along. You said so yourself."

"Stacy, she's my mother. She's alone. And she's old. I can't."

My child sighs, and pushes herself up and off of the couch. She starts to gather what's left of the dishes, the few overlooked by her grandmother, and stands at the door.

"You're always welcome to come to us, Mom. I want you to know that."

I look at her, grateful.

Jeremy returns to work two days later, and Stacy stays with me for another week. Slowly we sort through the paperwork in the house, and meet with my lawyer, who helps me make a financial plan for my future. Alan had the foresight the past few months to straighten his portfolio, making it relatively easy for me to read and understand. He knew he was not going to be with me long. He was always a planner, right to the end. Among other things, what he has given me is the freedom from worrying about money, having saved enough to carry me through to old age.

At home, Stacy urges me to go through Alan's belongings while she is with me, fearing I will allow his things to sit, a museum of his life, if left to do it on my own. I concede by allowing her to help me with his closet, but ask her to leave the rest. I want to wait awhile, let his possessions sit with me a bit longer, to keep me company. I remember Daniel waited for months before calling me to help him sort and box Noreen's clothes. He decided to donate them to the Brothers and Sisters Club. By that time, he was able to perform the exercise with little hesitation. I think I had a harder time dealing with it than he did. Every shirt I folded reminded me of a different memory with her. We'd had so many. I thought him callous at the time, but I can see now it was a survival technique. He had a better attitude. They're just clothes, right?

At the airport, through tearful goodbyes, I assure Stacy (and myself) that I will be okay. Life moving forward is inevitable, and I cannot burden my daughter with worries of her poor mother. She has her own life now, and I want her to live without a cloud of guilt or neglect hovering overhead. It is not the way I brought her up. Alan would never accept it.

On the drive home, the sun fails to warm me, and I look forward to spring, weary of the dark winter. I want flowers and heat and hopefully, optimism I so sorely need. I try to tell myself I will be alright; I have hobbies, friends, my mother. Okay, I am reaching; but Teresa is all I have here. If she only knew my thoughts.

I pull up to my driveway and walk to the door.

I step into the foyer and stand still, listening to the empty house. The couch and chairs are poised, waiting. I can't avoid the deafening sound of loneliness as it comes crashing down on me, and I sit right down on the Mediterranean tile near the door until I am ready to walk in and resume life without my husband.

Chapter 43

Stacy checks in on me daily, and I begin to wait for her calls, starting my day only after I hear her voice. Before long, boredom brings me back to the gym. I go three days a week and work the circuit, as Daniel taught me years ago. I go in waves, and my body becomes a balloon: thinner when I'm working out, and thicker when I grow lazy.

My heart isn't in the process; but when I think of what is waiting for me at home, I re-focus, and get through it. Sarah and Pete Manzilli have me over for dinner, but the conversation seems thin without a fourth voice, and eventually the calls are infrequent. Threesomes rarely work. I understand, and hold no bitterness.

My weekly lunch dates with Teresa eventually morph into standing appointments on the second, and fourth Wednesday of each month, to accommodate her social calendar, which is still full at eighty-one. Teresa is already seated when I arrive at the restaurant, and I wait for, and am awarded with, a subtle glance at her watch. *Yes, Mother, I'm tardy again.* I still cannot show up for an appointment on time. Pleasantries are followed by our orders taken (always cranberry, apple salads), and then we are left to sit across from each other while we wait.

Today, my mother is impeccable in a cream suit, and I am awed by her consistent beauty and grace, feeling as I often do, mediocre in her presence. She rests her forearms on the table and leans toward me.

"Elizabeth, how are you holding up?"

I straighten my posture as I meet her eyes. It's a trick I learned long ago. If I meet her gaze directly, she believes what I say.

"I'm doing well." I respond.

"Bullshit."

Okay. It doesn't work all the time. I am taken back by her brash response and lean away from the table.

"Mom, it's been only a few months. What do you expect? How long did it take for you to feel like you wanted to move on after Daddy died?"

Teresa's face softens, and she sighs.

"I'll let you know when it happens." She says.

"What?"

"He's been gone for twenty-one years. I figure if I fill my days, then I won't think of him. Don't get me wrong, I do enjoy myself much of the time; but he's still my first thought in the morning, and my last at night. I'm still here, and until the good Lord decides it's time for me to join them, I will live my life. I don't want you to sit around and do nothing, Elizabeth. You're young. Don't wallow. It's pitiful."

The waitress steps to the table, giving me a needed reprieve from this conversation. I don't like where it's going, and I don't want to hear what I already know. Quietly we dress our salads and I start to eat, focusing on my dish, hoping she decides we've touched enough on the subject.

She doesn't. She places her fork down. Teresa has an agenda today, and nothing will deter her from it.

"What are your plans?"

I look at her mid-chew. Plans?

"I haven't given it much thought. Yet."

What I want to tell my mother is that I'm afraid. Afraid of everything; of living alone, of the long, empty hours I have to face each morning, of the blatant clarity of my empty life. I have relied on others to fill it, and now that they're gone, I am left with just me.

"I feel like I wasted my life." I say, as surprised by my own admission as she is. Teresa's face clouds over, and I sense the storm approaching.

"A waste of life? Really? What were you supposed to do? Save the world? Do you think it's much worse off because you weren't there, in the thick of it?"

"That's a cruel thing to say, Mom." I whisper.

She sighs again, and sips her water.

"It wasn't meant to degrade your inspirations. What I want to say is, you're looking at what you didn't accomplish, when you ignore all that you did. You raised a wonderful daughter who, because of you, will raise her own wonderful children. You supported a dedicated doctor who saved countless lives. He could do that because you took care of him, and allowed him to focus on others. If every parent and spouse were as devoted as you were, this world would be a much better place than it is now. It already is, because of you."

Her words sink in, and spread through my body, warming me. I had no idea she felt this way, and I realize how important it is for me to hear it. What she said next I will hold with me forever.

"You're your father's daughter."

My conversation with Teresa stays in the forefront of my mind for the next several days. The power she holds over me is underestimated, to say the least. Her supportive position gives me pause for thought, and I feel strength that I hadn't held before. On my way to the grocery store–which is always a dismal visit, as I now shop for one–I pass a small storefront with a "Volunteers Wanted" sign that catches my eye. I must have passed this establishment a hundred times and never bothered to take notice of what is through the thin, glass doors. The sign over the door says "Give Trees A Chance." I decide to walk in, and inquire what type of work is needed.

A young woman–Trish, she says–greets me kindly and explains that what they're looking for now are people to man the phones, answer questions about the upcoming Annual Healthy Food Local Farms Conference, and sign people up for the conference: take payment information over the phone, reserve seating, and the like.

"You look confused." She says.

"What does this have to do with trees?" I ask.

"Trees?" Trish is perplexed, until she understands I am referring to the sign out front. "Ahh. The sign. It's a play on words. You a Beatles fan? Anyway, we moved here a year ago and started a campaign to try to preserve the existing trees, and plant new ones around the world. Sort of a *Let's save the rainforest* type of thing; tried to get donations and such. We have since morphed into doing various local drives and fundraisers for the state environment. It's more our speed. I've been here since its inception. There are others up and down the East Coast-kind of a smaller, inexperienced Chapter of the Sierra Club."

Trish goes on to explain there is a one day training program I can sit through to understand fully about the conference, and I can make my own hours.

"If you have the time, we would love your help for other projects when this is over. We could use the extra hands, and it's never boring." Trish says.

Though frightened, I feel pulled to the cause, which is something that always struck a nerve. When I think of how little I was able to accomplish in the schools while Stacy attended, I know this is something I want to do. I need to do. I have nothing else.

Trish smiles widely when I ask her when I can start. On the way home, I wonder what I am doing, and hope it's the right thing.

It takes less than one week for me to feel comfortable fielding calls, answering questions and signing people up for the conference. I am pleasantly surprised at how much I enjoy the work, and when the conference is over, I transition easily into the next project, which is to make outbound calls, inviting community members to a presentation and discussion on getting local waters tested more often.

I work three days a week, and enjoy lunches with Trish, who at twenty-five, reminds me a bit of my old self, when I had dreams of healing the world, and felt so passionate about environmental issues. Trish is an ex-patriot of Texas, where she went to Rice University to study Civil and Environmental Engineering. She explained that she followed her boyfriend to Pennsylvania two years ago, and in September, planned to enroll at Juniata College to finish her studies. I almost let it out that she would be attending my alma mater, but held back, preferring to keep to myself the chain of events that led me here, to this place, doing minimal work, instead of making a career out of helping the environment.

I enjoy my time with Trish. Though half my age, she is engaging, funny and the only friend I have, at the moment.

Chapter 44

I am volunteering steadily for five months when Teresa calls to tell me she took a fall outside of her friend's apartment after canasta. She's laid up with a broken ankle and cracked clavicle.

"Mom, I'll stay with you." I say.

"Don't be ridiculous. You have your life. You can't drop everything and stay with me." She sounds tired and disgusted.

I want to tell her that, outside of my volunteer work, I don't have a life anymore. My life ended last year due to a heart attack and a move to California. What I have now is time. I cannot tell my mother this, but her accident came at the most opportune moment. I keep my thoughts inside, knowing she would be more upset by my pitiful existence than anything else.

"You're my mother. I want to take care of you."

"And as your mother, I'm telling you, I don't need you."

I clutch the phone with white knuckles and count to ten, glancing up at Trisha, who thankfully, is too preoccupied at one of the other tables to notice my ire.

"I'll be by with dinner." I hang up before Teresa can retaliate.

I stop in daily to see her, bringing lunch or dinner, depending on my work schedule. Two weeks in, I am washing lunch dishes in her kitchen when, from her perch on the den couch, my mother asks me to fetch her lipstick. I do as I'm told, but question her as she applies the ruby red to her thin lips.

"Mom, no one is visiting today. Who are you doing this for?"

She has enjoyed regular visits since being laid up: friends from her canasta group, her book club, and Irish-American club. I realize, not for the first time, how different we really are.

Teresa places the stick on the side table. "I do it for me." She looks me over. "It wouldn't hurt for you to do the same."

I leave the room, swallowing her words like bitter lemon, forcing myself, again, to keep them down.

Later, as I button her nightshirt–a task still difficult for her to manage alone, due to her constricting bandages–she sighs.

"Elizabeth, you really need to do something with your hair. You haven't changed that style in years. It's a mess."

I raise my hand to my head, impotently pushing fly-aways back into my ponytail. Really? My hair is an issue?

"And what are you going to do socially? You can't keep hiding in that tiny office with only a few women. Get out and meet people. Do something."

I've had enough. I clasp the last button, and turn to walk toward the bedroom door when Teresa stops me.

"Did you have a happy life?"

I stare at her, confused.

"Elizabeth. Answer me. Please."

"Yes. Why are you asking me?"

"Sometimes I'm not so sure."

I look at my mother carefully. Is this her way of apologizing for any wrong I may have felt she'd done to me? It turns out, it is not. She pulls her legs onto the bed and lays back on her pillow, her hair fanning around her, and I watch her eyelids flutter, thinking, she suddenly looks... old.

"You made your own choices in life, Elizabeth. The only person you have to blame is yourself. What you do with the rest of your time is entirely up to you. Always remember that."

I turn on my heels and head to the front door as my eyes well. I pull the door open, and pause at the threshold. Taking a deep breath, I step back and close the door, keeping me inside. Filled with courage, fueled by adrenaline, I stomp back into her room.

She appears surprised to see me standing in her doorway.

"Yes, Mom, I have made choices in my life. But do not, ever, tell me that the only person I have to blame is myself! I have been angry with you for most of my life. I blame you, Mother, for my agony, for a lifetime of mediocrity. You had the love of your life for years. I had mine for *five months*. My love for Daniel lies dormant in my heart, still. The basis of my whole life is a throbbing thorn in my core that has pained me every day since we've been apart. You don't know what it's like to feel this way–to be crippled far beyond a crushed face, or wobbly stride. And far worse than even the pain, is knowing you were right–that I should leave him, that *my own mother* showed me my shortcomings, flaws I could not control and do nothing about. I blame you. Maybe I shouldn't, but you made me feel…unworthy."

My body shakes, and I struggle with breath through my hot tears, as words that I have held inside for so long pour forth in a torrent of rage and regret and sorrow. Teresa lies frozen on her bed, staring ahead.

"I needed more from you. I needed you to take me in your arms, and tell me that I was worth loving, if not beautiful. But you never gave me that. I wanted to be nothing like you." I whisper. "And I realize that I am. I am just like you. My daughter has no idea who I am. I have hidden my past as if I, too, am ashamed of what I have become; like if I were to tell her what happened, she would look at me the same way as you do. I would lose her like you lost me. Well, I'm still here. I'm still your daughter. I'm not in a costume, a mask I've been wearing for thirty-five years to spite you. This is me. You've never accepted me. And I don't know why…"

My hand over my mouth, to stifle the sobs, I can barely see the woman who gave me life, and caused me so much distress. As I stand heaving, I don't know she's pulled herself up and walked to me until I feel her arms encompass me. When I calm down, she whispers to me over my shoulder.

"Elizabeth, you did what you needed to do. Your father and I supported you. I don't know what else you expect of me. I thought we were doing the right thing. We'd never met the boy— how did we know what he would do? We were scared for you."

She pulls back and looks at me. There are tears in her eyes and her voice shakes. "I never believed you would harbor this love for him all of these years. You were so young. How would we have known…?"

I step back and swipe my arm across my nose like a kid. My mother clears her throat and wipes her eyes. "You've been carrying this anger around like a shield. I could see it as clearly as if you wore a sign, telling the world your life was my fault. I didn't write that letter. You did. You married, had a family–and still, you're angry."

She leans to the dresser and hands me a tissue.

"I've been carrying this cross for you and it's too heavy. I'm putting it down. Stop being a victim. Take some accountability."

"Oh Mom. I'm sorry." I fall into her arms again.

She kisses my head as it rests on her shoulder. "You are a beautiful person, Elizabeth. I never wanted to make you feel less than worthy. It wasn't my intent."

It feels strange and wonderful to be in her arms. It is also strange and wonderful to see that she's right. Why didn't I see what I'd become?

"You know," Teresa says, breaking our silence, "I think you need to revisit your memories and see what a wonderful life you had with Alan. You'll never know if Daniel would have stayed."

I squeeze my mother more tightly, as my thoughts remain my own. *No, I'll never know.*

Late in January, Trish informs me there is a new conference, planned for the middle of February, and asks if I can work longer hours. I am so relieved to hear it that I answer yes before the full question passes her lips. I dread passing the winter alone, and use the work to tether me to sanity. It is the work that keeps me from packing my bags and following my daughter to the West Coast.

On my days off, I wrap myself in my full length wool coat, scarf, gloves and hat and walk to the library to sit in the warmth, paging through books, losing myself easily in stories. I go for humor, especially during the darkest months, content to pass the afternoons until I finally decide to head home to make myself dinner. These hours are the hardest to endure; the silence but for the sizzle of the pan, or ding of the microwave, Ted Koppel droning from the den, and me with my thoughts until mercifully, I crawl into bed to do it again the next day.

ॐ

Chapter 45

Nikki calls me in June and invites me to dinner. Her invitation is accompanied by a sincere apology for the delay. Her new baby is six months old, and she confides in me over the phone how hard it is for her to manage two young children. Matty is four and requires much of her attention, especially with the new addition to his world.

I pick up several outfits for her new son, Cole, and a set of farm trucks for Matty, and arrive at Nikki's the following week with the gifts and my crumb cake.

She comes to the door holding Cole, and immediately I take him from her. I am so totally focused on the baby–holding him close, breathing in his intoxicating newness–that I don't notice Daniel standing in the dining room for several minutes. He is watching me, smiling. When I finally surrender the baby back to his mother, I walk to Daniel and give him a hug. I close my eyes over his shoulder. I have forgotten how happy it makes me to see him. It has been so long. When I finally pull away, I wonder if he feels the same way.

Dinner with Nicole's family is loud, warm, and delicious, and brings to mind the family gatherings I so sorely miss. There is no focus on me, my loss, or what I am doing. Instead, I am thrown into idle chatter of current events, humorous anecdotes of Matty's antics, and Nikki and Rick's back-and-forth saga of trying to get two boys to bed so they can have an evening. Daniel and I laugh all night.

Nikki hints–more than once–that she would like Daniel to start dating again. I learn that he and Fiona stopped seeing each other shortly after Alan's passing two years ago. I remain especially quiet during this gentle, well-meaning attack on his stubborn reluctance to socialize. Daniel is uncomfortable, and glances at me occasionally during this interlude. When Nikki moves onto another tale of Matty, Daniel's visible relief makes me smile.

When the men retreat to the den with the babies, I help Nikki clear the table, happy to have some time alone with her, as together we put food away and wash dishes. While I stand beside her with a towel, she asks how I am doing without Uncle Alan. I tell her the truth. She is like a daughter to me, and expects, and deserves nothing less. I admit to the loneliness, especially with Stacy across the country. She nods thoughtfully, handing me another pot.

"When Mom died, Dad still had us, so he kept busy. I wonder if it's easier that way. You don't have time to really think. He relied on you, you know. The clearest memory I have after Mom's death was how his face lit up whenever you walked into the house. You were so capable, and made things better. It was kind of like still having her there, in a way. You and Mom were always together, so it felt half of the puzzle was still in place when you were with us. Then eventually, when you started to stop by less and less, we were able to stand on our own. Dad had more confidence. Of course, we weren't babies, so it was easier. The loneliness set in for him after you stopped coming. I think you filled a void for him that we couldn't. I'll never forget what you did for us. I'm sorry I can't do the same for you."

I put my arm around Nik's, and lean my head in to hers. "Thank you for having me. This is the nicest time I've had since… well, in a long time."

Daniel walks me to my car at the end of the night. He opens my door, and is still leaning on it when I start the engine.

"It was good to see you, Beth."

"You too, Dutch."

As he leans on my door, I feel a chill down my spine, though the air is balmy. He wants to say something. I wait patiently, nervous.

"Beth, do you think I can take you to lunch? I'd like to catch up, without drooling, screaming babies in the room."

I smile. "Of course. I'd love lunch. Call me tomorrow." He closes my door and with a wave, I pull out.

I drive home, trying to ignore feelings of butterflies in my gut. He only wants lunch, but I can't help feeling excited at the prospect of seeing him alone. I walk into my bedroom, undress and slip into my sheets, thinking of Nicole with her babies, and how Noreen would have been crazy about them. I hope, I pray, she can see them now; see how well her children are doing, know how well Daniel did after she left them.

I think of Alan, as I always do in the waning hours of the day, when it is most quiet; I am thankful for him, for the years, for Stacy; for my comfort and stability. Tonight I add thoughts of Daniel. I missed him more than I care to admit out loud. It's strange, how the two of us are left. We have come full circle. Only he has no idea he is back to where he started.

With me, and a date for lunch.

When I fall asleep, I think I must be smiling.

I am waiting on the driveway when Daniel pulls up at one o'clock. He takes us to Luigi's, and after we're seated at our usual table, makes a declaration over wine.

"Let this be the last time we eat here." He holds his wine glass to me, and we lock eyes, knowing this place has too many memories to bring us back.

I nod, clinking his glass with mine, and we drink, talking nonstop for two hours, catching up on each others' lives. He fills me in; details about his work, his upcoming projects, and his plans for the next five years. I update him on Stacy, the last days of Alan's life, and my volunteer work.

It is nearly four o'clock by the time we find our way to his car. While the motor idles in the restaurant parking lot, Daniel looks at me.

"I don't want to take you home."

"It's where I live." I joke, but I know he is serious. I'm just not sure what he wants.

He turns the key, and the motor quiets, leaving us in the car, breathing. Can he hear my heart beating? He must be immune to it by now, for it has always responded the same way over the years, on those occasions when he and I have found ourselves alone.

He moves his body awkwardly in the seat to face me. I do the same.

"I can't stop thinking about you." He shakes his head. "I miss you. I miss our friendship. You pulled away, and I respect that; but I want to know if we can see each other. Again."

After all of these years, I can no longer wish that I had never planned to go to the party and drive the car that fateful night. If I hadn't, I know in my heart that we would have met at the café at Juniata, and our relationship would have flowered into a beautiful, unalterable bouquet of love, family, and memories; but then I also would not have experienced the joy of my daughter, the treasure of my friendship with Noreen, and my comfortable, loving, easy life with Alan.

Daniel and I were brought together by some unexplainable fate. Maybe this is how it should have been all along. I look at him, at his green eyes, and have to believe this is true. It's the only way I can accept the chain of events in my life.

Still, I'm forced to accept one simple fact: I don't care what he wants. I don't want to go home. I want to stay with this man forever.

"Well, what do you want to do now?" I ask.

Daniel smiles, and starts the car. He makes a left onto Route 39, in the opposite direction of my house. An hour later, we pull up to a small lake. Daniel takes my hand and leads me to a long dock that extends over the water. Silently, he helps me along the uneven planks, interrupting my step every few feet, while the gentle lapping of the water bobs beneath us, to a weathered bench at the end of the dock. I wonder, but decline to ask, how he found this perfect place.

We stare over the water, at the evergreens across the lake.

"I stumbled onto this last year, while trying to find a new site for a building. I thought of you, of how you would love it." His gaze remains ahead as he speaks. "I come here to think, and reflect. I'd been hoping to bring you here, to enjoy the view with me."

The sun is setting, and the colors it exudes are gifts from God, irreplaceable to me. I have never seen anything so beautiful. We sit with our hands clasped, as the last of the sun falls behind the horizon of trees, leaving a wonderful hue of oranges, softened by my tears.

Daniel calls me every week. I look forward to hearing his voice, and soon we are spending platonic weekends together. He comes up with different excursions, and I anticipate our next adventure with the exuberance of a child waiting for a surprise; a seamless segue from despondent widow to happy camper.

He takes me to an amusement park, and we are like children again: squealing on the roller coaster, eating cotton candy, and giggling over prizes won by blowing up balloons with water guns. We meander through forests I didn't know existed, and have picnic lunches.

My favorite days are spent at the lake, though, quiet hours of lying on the grass and watching clouds float along the Pennsylvania sky. We talk about anything and everything that comes to mind. We reminisce about memories with Noreen, and Alan, and they bring me bittersweet pleasure. I think Daniel feels the same way, for after these conversations, he is quiet and reflective. I leave him to his thoughts.

As summer makes way for autumn, the days subtly become cooler. Before long, we are wearing sweaters and sipping tea, watching a different sky. Thanksgiving looms near, and Stacy invites me to California for the holiday. Daniel drives me to the airport, and I realize as we walk into the terminal that we will be apart for two weeks—the longest stretch since June. He waits with me on the check-in line, and, too soon, it is time for me to continue on alone.

"So, safe trip. Please give Stacy my love."

I nod silently. I am a teenager all over again, inexperienced and unsure. The last time we were at an airport together, we had to be pulled apart by the looming announcement of his plane departure and last call for boarding.

He thinks this is our first time with goodbyes on a plane.

Daniel solves my inner turmoil by pulling me into one of his hugs. He holds me for a long time, and I melt into him, wondering if he has any idea what he does to me. He whispers in my ear, *I'll miss you*, and lets me go.

I walk away without looking back.

Chapter 46

Stacy's house is in the heart of San Francisco. The two-bedroom space is decorated in a traditional style with warm colors, prints and big, comfortable couches. They set up the spare bedroom for me, and, after allowing me just minutes to settle in, whisk me out to see the city.

I am taken with the winding, charming streets—and the trolley, which I ride with my head sticking out as I gawk unashamedly at the architecture. I am awed by the Painted Ladies, the view of Alcatraz across the bay, and Fisherman's Wharf, silently wishing Alan could have seen all of this, too. I collapse into bed in the evening, my body retaliating after the marathon day I put it through, and fall into a deep sleep.

The next morning, Stacy and Jeremy take me to Napa Valley, where we enjoy a tour of Robert Mondavi and Beringer wineries. Having never seen a vineyard, or tasted wine from a barrel, I am exhilarated by the experience. At Beringer, Stacy and I decide to walk among the tree-covered paths while Jeremy takes a call from his office.

The weather is cool, the sky is brilliant cobalt, and with my daughter holding my arm, surrounded by beauty I never imagined, my eyes water with joy. Before heading back to San Francisco, we decide to stop at Tra Vigne, a charming Tuscan-style restaurant in the valley. Here I fill Stacy in on Nicole and her children: how Matty looks just like Noreen, and after several months, is finally accepting Cole as part of the family.

She and Jeremy exchange glances at one another while I talk, and I think I am making them feel bad with my constant chatter of home.

"I'm sorry." I say, during dessert. "I don't mean to keep talking about Nik. I thought you'd like to know how she's doing."

Stacy smiles at me, and sips her tea. "Nikki sends me pictures and we speak on the phone almost every week. I'm glad you saw her. She promised me to have you over."

"Well, you don't have to worry about me, honey. I'm fine. I have a little of your grandmother in me." I smile.

"Oh, God forbid!" Stacy laughs. She looks quickly at Jeremy, and back to me.

"Mom. You seem really happy. Nik says you're spending a lot of time with Dutch. Could that have something to do with it?"

I look at my daughter and try to decipher her tone. It seems pleasant, but I can't be sure if there is a twinge of underlying skepticism.

"Well, you know, we're friends. We've been friends for a long time. We pass the time together, so we don't get lonely." Why am I explaining myself? I know why. It must look suspicious to the girls. How odd it must seem to have two unrelated parents spending so much time together.

"We're just friends. That's all. I'm too old to go looking for new ones."

"Mom, you're fifty-three. That's the new forty-something. Don't kid yourself. You're young enough to date. And so what? Why shouldn't older people have romance?"

I continue to eat my key lime pie. Why is she saying this? Romance?

"Honey, my days of romance are over." I put down my fork, reluctantly–the pie is so delicious. "Does it bother you that I talk to Daniel?"

"Daniel?"

"Excuse me. Dutch." Still, after all of these years, I cannot call him Dutch without forethought. I haven't slipped in a long time. My daughter watches me closely. Jeremy remains quiet, taking this in.

"Mom, you have history. You're best friends, and he's a nice man. He's been alone for God knows how many years, and Dad's been gone for two. We want you to spend time with each other. We don't have to worry if you do."

Ah, yes. It's about guilt. What will we do about Mom if she's all alone? I love my daughter; but she is my daughter, and not my mother. I can't have her worrying about me.

"Listen to me. I'm fine. Dutch and I are friends. And yes, we spend time together because it's easier than trying to join clubs, and play cards, and knit. Please stop worrying about me and focus on your life here. I'm fine. I'm happy."

"Good." Stacy puts down her mug and takes Jeremy's hand. "Then maybe you can bring Dutch out here in June when you come out to meet your grandchild."

I almost choke on my tea.

Thanksgiving is quiet and beautiful. Jeremy's parents fly out from New York, and spend the long weekend with us. They stay at the Plaza, a few blocks away, because there is no other room in the house. We toast to the news of the baby, and there are congratulations around the table.

The spare bedroom, where I have been sleeping for the past four nights, will be transformed into a nursery after Christmas. I lie in bed on Sunday night, and imagine a baby in this room, my grandson or granddaughter, and I am overwhelmed with emotion. My baby is going to have a baby. The thought brings me such sadness; Alan will not be here to share this experience with me. Stacy is the true love of his life. I know it, and she knows it. How must she feel?

We talk about it the next night, while Jeremy stays late at work. Stacy and I lay on the couch, feet to feet on her plaid sofa, full from turkey pot pie and more dessert. I have walked so many miles in this city, I have no guilt about the sweets I've consumed. She lies on her back with her hand on her flat belly.

"How are you feeling?" I ask her. She knows what I mean.

"I miss Dad. I wish he were here."

"I know. I miss him, too. He would have been crazy for a baby." Stacy smiles and nods.

"I'll come out to help you before your due date, if you want. I'll be here whenever you need me."

"Why don't you live here with us? I don't mean right here. We can find you a place close by, so you can be a part of the baby's life."

My daughter is going to need me. I am going to want to see everything–every first, each experience–and help her through it. I wonder if I am strong enough to leave my home. San Francisco is an entirely different monster than the slower life of Hummelstown.

I know nothing, and no one outside of two people here. Would this be enough?

I sigh. The truth rises to my throat, and I push it back down. I can't leave Daniel.

"Why don't we see what happens? Let's focus on the next few months, okay?"

Chapter 47

My ambivalence upon returning to Pennsylvania, after my two-week hiatus out West, prevents me from calling Daniel to pick me up at the airport. I left my daughter and her husband, expecting a baby, with a promise to return in spring, and again for the birth in June. They presented a strong argument for why I should make a new home with them. I promised to think about it, and I will. It's a lot to digest, and I need to be alone, in my space.

The taxi pulls away, and I stand in front of my house with my bag, Tonight, it seems way too large for me. Abandoning my suitcase in the foyer, I walk into every room, and turn on every light. I walk through the rooms, back and forth, taking everything in: the pictures on the walls of Stacey at nearly every stage of her youth, the lamps; Tiffany's that replaced the ones I bought at the thrift store when Alan was still building his practice: the dressers, tables, knick-knacks from trips, and special occasions.

Can I leave this? It is part of me. The walls tell my story.

I eat cereal in the den, in front of the television, trying not to see myself in this scenario. I climb into bed, but my internal clock is still on Pacific Time, and sleep eludes me. I start rummaging through my closet, and come across old photo albums that have been tucked away forever. I bring them to bed, and, slowly, look through every page.

The album on top of the pile is filled with Stacy's baby pictures: young Alan holding her, and a woman I still barely recognize as myself, with the skewed smile and crooked nose. I allow myself the immense luxury of wondering what Stacy's baby will look like. Will he take on her lineage, or Jeremy's?

Another album is older, holding the memories of my parents' lives together. I had forgotten my mother gave me this and a few others albums years ago, when she went through her basement and started purging. I just carelessly tossed them onto the pile, having too many other things going on to spend any sort of time. Now, it seems time is all I have.

Their pictures tell the most wonderful love story, and my heart swells as I see my parents at the cusp of their lives, smiling, holding each other, filled with promise, to memories from their honeymoon on Nantucket, and numerous excerpts taken from all of their trips and experiences together. I wonder if I could sit with my mother and listen to her stories behind the photos. What were they laughing at so heartily here? Where did they eat on the island? Question after question fills my mind, perhaps never to be answered. Maybe it doesn't matter. They discovered something so few have the privilege to know.

Yawning, I decide to take a quick peek through the last book. Under the cover, I am surprised to see photos I thought were lost. They must have been part of the pile my mother gave to me. They are pictures of me. The old me. The young me. I look at them as if I am seeing them for the first time. With more than a few, this is the case. I have not seen many of these before, and cannot recall the instances where they were taken or the memories behind them. I stare at one where my father is holding me, perched on his shoulders, and my five-year-old face stares into the camera, as if daring it to interrupt my time with him. On the opposite page, Nancy and I have our arms around each other, laughing in our caps and gowns. I touch Nan's face, framed by her gorgeous curls, and as hard as I try, cannot recall what she said as the shot was taken, to break me up.

The book ends in the middle, with blank pages unfilled. The last picture taken is of me leaving for college my senior year. I remember this picture, how I stood in the driveway and posed for my mother, smiling, full of myself and possibilities. That was the year I met, fell in love with, and lost Daniel: the most wonderful, traumatic year of my life.

My long, blond hair blows slightly across my flawless cheeks as my eyes glimmer with pleasure. I take her in for a long time, willing myself to remember what it was like to be that beautiful. The girl in that photo had no inkling of what her future held. Does anyone?

I gather the pile, and drop it back in the corner of my closet. As I lie in bed waiting for sleep, I think of how my own daughter never really saw me before. All she knows is what her mother looks like. She knows nothing of the girl I was before she came along.

Daniel calls the next day and asks me to dinner. I dress carefully, not sure of how I will feel when I see him. Standing before the mirror, I clasp my long, beaded necklace, not missing the irony of how I used to dress with him in mind. It's only been two weeks, but a lot has happened since he dropped me at the airport. I will be a grandmother. I am considering moving my life across the country. I'm sure if I tell him about my plans, he will be happy for me and want the best for me. Don't friends want what's best for each other?

Dressed early, I feel restless while I wait for him to arrive. In my bedroom, I look at Alan's dresser, the items within all but forgotten in the two years he's been gone. I run my hands over the detailed woodwork along the edge, allowing him more time in my mind. I pull open a drawer and see his tee shirts, meticulously folded, and smile as I push it back in. There's a comfort to having his clothes where he left them, and I wonder if I will ever gather the courage to empty these drawers, pushing back my daughter's fears from my mind of never letting them go.

Pulling the second drawer, I find all of his ties wrapped neatly in a row. I bought Alan most of these ties, and try to remember the occasions, and order in which I had given them. I touch each one, and move the top layer over to see the next when my finger rubs against a thick piece of paper. I pull it, and see a photograph that had been hidden underneath.

I move to the bed, and sit to look at the picture. It is of the four of us: Alan, me, Daniel and Noreen, the picture that was taken by the waitress at dinner the night we first went to Thurston's. In it, we are all smiling, happy, toasting one another. I don't even remember taking it. Upon closer inspection, I notice I am looking at Daniel across the table, as I hold my glass to the others. He returns my gaze, and if I didn't know better, would believe there was something there. The way we're looking at each other indicates that there is a shared feeling, a deeper connection between us. It is obvious to me. Why then, didn't I ever see it at the time?

Oh, Alan! What is it you thought when you saw this? Why is this photo hidden in your drawer? Why didn't you show this to me?

I would have explained our satisfaction in deceiving Noreen. We were planning a surprise party for her. You must have understood. How often did you look at this stupid picture?

I have this discussion with my dead husband, wishing that he would have confronted me at the time. I could have put his mind at ease. Or would I have? Is that what brought his statement to the surface at the hospital, when he had his first heart attack? Were my feelings for Daniel obvious? Were his for me?

Like a wave, the reality of my relationship with my husband washes over me. Our mutual respect was evident; but we communicated our deep, inner thoughts so seldom that I wonder if we really didn't know each other.

When I open the door later, Daniel is standing on my porch with a bouquet of flowers. His collar is pulled up to protect from the chilly air, and his green eyes crinkle when he sees me. I am overwhelmed by the sight of him, and my ambivalent feelings from moments ago dissolve like morning fog in sun.

He hands me the flowers. I walk to the kitchen with the fragrance pressed to my nose and smile as I un-wrap the bouquet, and pull out a vase from the cupboard above the sink. I can feel Daniel behind me as I gingerly arrange the flowers.

I don't want to turn around, knowing what's on the other side. Daniel will be patiently waiting to leave and get dinner, for he is nothing if not polite. There is no other thought. I am a comfortable pair of shoes of which he can't get rid. They fit, and he knows what to expect. This is why, I'm sure, he never found anyone permanent after Noreen. He is not a shoe-shopper. He said so himself. Noreen was pushed on him by friends, and he was coerced into marriage. I am a safety net, someone to help him pass the time. It's what I've always been.

When I do finally turn to face him, having willfully lowered my expectations, I am taken with what he does. Daniel stands close to me, with a look I have not seen on him in thirty years. It is a look of longing that I'm sure must mirror my own. Without a word, he leans in, and puts his muscled arms on the counter around me, holding me in place. My eyes drop to the floor. What is he doing?

"Hey," he whispers, as he tilts my chin up with his hand forcing me to see him. I search his eyes, not knowing what I'm looking for.

I don't breathe. His lips gently graze mine. It is a whisper of a touch and I nearly groan with desire and trepidation. Daniel smiles, and his arms surround me as he kisses me again, slowly at first, before allowing himself to let go. His tongue is warm, and immediately, I am brought back to my youth: to the days when we used to kiss as passionately after declarations of love.

We stay this way, in my kitchen, with the hum of the water heating the pipes through the house, the pattering of my heart music to my ears. When I finally lean away to take a breath, he steps back, but keeps hold of my arms.

"I'm sorry. I took a chance. I've been wanting to do that for I don't know how long."

"You have?" I am shocked by this confession. How long has he wanted to kiss me? Noreen's been gone for eleven years. No. Couldn't be.

He is still holding onto me. "Of course. I thought you knew how I felt. Didn't you? All of these years of being together, I've wanted to kiss you, to tell you..." He shakes his head. "I've waited so long."

I am speechless. Having believed I was alone all of these years in my desire, the truth is hard to accept. In fact, it is unbelievable.

"I know you feel the same way. I know it. I can feel it." He watches me. "Please say something."

There is so much to say. I have been waiting my entire life for this moment, and now that it is here, I am unprepared. This very conversation occurred in my dreams countless times, and in my own world, I knew exactly how to react—what to do to make the most of the moment. Reality plays out so differently, doesn't it?

Suddenly my desire to tell him everything feels inept and wrong. I want to tell this man that I am in love with him, that he is the love of my life, that every moment we have ever been together has been torture for me. Then I think of Alan, of the picture I just found, and how hard it must have been for him to know my feelings for Daniel. I know I don't deserve to have what I want, when I should have wanted simply what I had. Isn't that the secret to happiness?

Instead, while the taste of him still lingers on my lips and tongue, my first word is the last word I'd expected to come out of my mouth. "Noreen."

214 | *Kimberly Wenzler*

Daniel's face morphs from contentment and longing, to sad resignation as he steps back, letting me go.

"I loved Noreen. Believe me. I thought..." He stares at me as if seeing right through me, and nods as if he understands. What does he understand? As he starts to turn around, he says, "I'm sorry. I never meant to...I'm sorry."

He walks through the kitchen toward the door. I watch, dumbfounded.

As he crosses the living room, I realize that if I don't go to this man now, he will walk out of my house and I may never get another chance to make this right. I will not have the strength to go find him and tell him how I feel. From the depths of my soul, where I have hidden all of my feelings for so many years I lost count, I try; but I cannot push myself to him.

As he closes the door behind him, my whispers of *"Daniel, don't go"* are frozen on my lips.

Chapter 48

"Are you sure you're okay?" Trish asks, for the second time this afternoon.

Veronica is obliviously ranting about her eldest son, as she adeptly stuffs envelopes across the office, while Trish watches me closely. I throw a smile on my face and nod. I even toss an eye roll in Veronica's direction, which is enough for Trisha not to push further, and leave me to myself.

I am preoccupied, and don't want to burden Trish with my troubles. There doesn't seem to be enough room in this office for two sets of problems, by the sound of our co-volunteer's unending rant.

As I sort through table seatings for next week's seminar on Pennsylvania's ecology strategies, thoughts about my conversation with Stacy earlier this morning creep into my mind. At seven months along, she sounded tired today more so than usual and twice abdominal cramping interrupted our conversation. I am worried about her, and feel helpless being stuck more than a thousand miles away. After making her promise me she'd call her obstetrician, I finally allowed her to hang up.

When I finish with the charts, I file them and straighten the table in preparation to leave. As I grab my sweater from the wobbly hook in back, I can see Trish waving her hand in an effort to get my attention. She holds a phone to her ear and mimes for me to please wait until she's finished. I nod. Of course I'll wait. Where am I going?

Standing near the door, I relish the warm rays pouring through the glass as I watch the budding trees outside, their arms reaching to the sun as happy as I am to feel her after a long winter. Trish finally hangs up and asks me if I can come in every day next week for some special mass mailing that's been delayed.

She already knows my answer, but I go through the ritual of saying of course I can, both of us aware of my reliance on this work to keep me busy and sane. Outside, I walk to my car and ponder my situation. Give Trees A Chance truly did save me after Alan died. After my last encounter with Daniel four months ago, I threw myself back into the work, trying desperately to anesthetize the pain of losing him again. The numbing I learned is temporary, for the pain is always present.

In the car, I robotically head in the direction home, and wonder at my bleak future. Should I join some clubs, as my mother had done? Teresa certainly would not have found herself in this miserable situation, and would have some choice words for me now, if I gave her the opportunity. I think of an earlier conversation, before my outburst; before our fractured, tenuous talks, where we are slowly trying to come to a peaceful plain.

Elizabeth, you disappoint me! What are you doing with your life?

Mom, I'm fine. I am doing just what I want.

Oh, please! Volunteer work at a dinky little office? Haven't you been there long enough? What do you see in the big picture? Didn't you tell me you have dreams? Think about it Elizabeth. You have control of your future. You always have.

I watch the road before me and am awed that even in her absence, my mother can put me in my place. I think of my father, as I often do, bringing up from my memory the talks we shared, his support of my dreams and goals, and a pang of sadness stabs me. As I see the sign for my exit loom ahead, I know at once that I don't want to go home. I don't want to sit in my house and watch television, eating a microwaved dinner, waiting for darkness and sleep. For sleep brings Daniel to me, and I can no longer bear the thought of him. I need new thoughts, a new purpose.

Propelled by determination and a tiny inkling of fear, I speed past my turn and continue on the highway to a new destination.

When I pull the heavy door and walk into the building ninety minutes later, the familiar smells welcome me, and I am overcome with nostalgia as I peruse the list of room numbers hanging on the wall. Okay, 114. I glance around, embarrassed, and work my way through the main floor until I stand outside the office, taking deep breaths before entering. It is quiet, and I am thankful no one else is here, for I know if I had to wait in line, my courage would evaporate and I would run outside to my car and leave, never looking back.

A woman on the other side of the counter smiles at me and I smile in return, silently pleading with myself not to break down.

"Can I help you?"

"Yes." I whisper. Clearing my throat, my voice gains strength. "I'd like to register for your fall semester."

218 | Kimberly Wenzler

꩜

Chapter 49

After my registration yesterday, I stopped on the way home, bought a bottle of champagne and enjoyed a small celebration: party for one, in my honor. I was proud of myself. The woman at the Juniata registrar's office was able to pull up my records (from a century ago, I had joked), and together we figured out what I needed to complete the requirements and get my degree. When I walked out of the office, I was ready to go home and toast to my new future.

This morning, a little woozy, I incorporate a ringing into my dreams, until I finally realize the phone is bringing me (slowly) to consciousness. When I finally move to the side of the bed and reach over, it falls silent. On the pillow, through a slit in my lids, I glimpse the light gray sky behind the curtains. It is early morning; dawn, maybe? Who could be calling? I have nearly returned to slumber when the phone explodes into the quiet room again.

It takes a bit of effort for me to read the incoming number, and I struggle to push back the pitifully hopeful thought that it might be Daniel. I still hope he will call again, though I'm not sure why. What would change? It is an unrecognized number and I am about to ignore it when I realize the call is coming from another state. *Stacy.*

As I put the receiver to my ear, I wonder what time it is in California, and my heart is in my throat.

Jeremy's voice sounds strange. "Mom? It's Stacy. There's something wrong. We're at the hospital."

"How's the baby?" It is not due for another five weeks.

"I don't know. We just got here. Stacy woke up with severe pains and some bleeding…" He chokes up, and stops talking.

His voice clears my head, and I sit up. "Okay. Jeremy. Listen to me. Go to her. Remain calm. I will be out there as soon as I can. Do you hear me?"

"Okay. Okay. I'll tell her you're coming. She's been asking for you."

I disconnect the line and immediately call information for American Airlines. I took their flight out last month and say a silent novena that there is a flight later today. I am in luck—for a fee, of course. The agent moves at the speed of melting molasses as I start to tear through my drawers and closet, tossing clothes onto the bed while I wait for her to enter my flight information and reserve a seat.

I grab a suitcase and duffel, stored conveniently in Stacy's old room, and stuff them with the items strewn about. I make a quick call to Teresa to let her know what's happening and she instructs me to check in when I get to California. Two hours later, I am waiting for a taxi to take me to the airport. I walk out of my house without thought to what my plan is. All I know is my baby is in trouble.

The flight is nearly full. When a bulky man squeezes into the seat next to mine, I close my eyes to avoid any conversation. I have five hours of sitting here, and it will take me that long to calm myself. I breathe deeply, in and out, in and out, until I can think straight. When I called Jeremy to tell him I would be there by noon, he sounded better. The baby is okay. Stacy is resting. This information will keep me sane for the duration of my flight, which seems interminable to me as the attendants smile benignly, walking up and down the aisle bringing chips, soda, napkins.

As I stare out the window, praying, chewing on my nails until they bleed before working on my inner cheek, waiting for the plane to descend, I think of Daniel and how much I want to talk to him, to see him, to have him here with me—calming me, soothing my ricocheting thoughts of doom.

I have been pushing him from my mind for months; but today, outside of my daughter, he is on the forefront of my mind, and I let him stay here. When I registered for my classes yesterday, I reached for the phone to tell him what I'd done before stopping myself. What would I say? I'm going back to Juniata to finish what I started? Shouldn't that include my life with him?

As soon as I see Jeremy, any thoughts I held of anyone else drops away. In the car, he explains in fits what happened to bring us to this point. Stacy had been feeling sluggish for the past week or so. When she first called the doctor complaining of pain, he explained she was experiencing Braxton Hicks contractions, a normal occurrence up to a month before delivery. Essentially, her body was getting ready for labor.

Stacy kept Jeremy from calling the doctor again two days later, when she was doubled over, not wanting to be one of those annoying patients Alan used to complain about over dinner. She finally relented when she saw blood in the toilet. Jeremy brought her to the ER and then called me.

I walk in to see her lying peacefully in a room, her large belly a small mountain with a black monitor strapped along the peak. When she sees me, she starts to cry. She has an IV in her arm and the strap on her stomach, and as much as I want to hold her, I don't want to disturb the monitoring process. So, I take her hand and pat her face, trying to exert some calm, assuring her she'd be okay, praying I am right. The baby will be fine, I tell her.

"Oh Mom! I'm too early! He's not due for another five weeks." She is sobbing now, and I am worried this will upset the baby.

"What is the doctor saying?"

She wipes her eyes with her arm, and works to compose herself.

"He wants me to stay in bed for the rest of my pregnancy. To be sure."

I take a seat beside her. "Well, then that's what you will do. I'm here. I'll take care of you. Let Jeremy go to work. You'll want him home when the baby comes."

Stacy nods, visibly relieved.

"Are you sure, Mom? You don't mind being here so long?"

I remember the afternoon Alan brought me to the hospital, leaving a blood-stained couch in our wake, and how afraid I had been–that I did not ask for my mother.

"I've never been so sure of anything in my life."

I sleep on the couch in the living room, since my old room now belongs to my grandchild. I don't mind; the cushions are wide, and the bedrooms are upstairs, so I have privacy and so does my daughter. Jeremy is gone before Stacy and I wake up in the mornings. It doesn't take me long to familiarize myself with their kitchen, and I make Stacy's favorite breakfast in between healthy servings of oatmeal with fruit.

Today is an eggs Benedict day, and I enjoy watching my daughter devour my meal. I've been here for a week, and our days have taken on a routine. After breakfast, we watch the morning talk show while we lounge on her king bed.

Lunch consists of soup or sandwiches followed by some basic leg exercises to keep the blood moving. We spend the afternoons catching up and reminiscing. I cherish these hours with my daughter, free from daily stress; talks I know will occur with less frequency once she is thrown into the daily requirements of parenthood. She has so much ahead of her, and I look forward to it.

Today, Stacy admits she is concerned about me.

"You look sad." She says as I stand over her to bend and straighten her left leg.

"I do?" I push a smile across my face.

"I don't mean here, Mom. There's a sadness about you. It reminds me of how you were when I was growing up."

"Really? You thought I was sad?"

"Well, not all of the time. But sometimes, when you didn't know, I would watch you and you seemed to be sort of, I don't know, melancholy. As I got older, I wondered if you and dad would split up. But you never fought, so…"

"You did? Stacy, why didn't you say anything before this?"

She shrugs, but doesn't waiver from my gaze. "Other times you seemed really happy. I just thought that was the way you were. You know, some people just aren't excitable. But when you came out a few months ago, you were a totally different person, and I almost didn't recognize you. You were glowing, Mom; and that was *before* I told you about the baby."

My daughter pats the side of the bed, inviting me back to sit. "I want you to tell me what's going on. What made you so happy then that you don't have now?"

I take in my daughter, in her glorious state, and wonder what we did to make this wonderful person. She is going to be a loving, caring mother, and I anxiously await meeting my grandchild.

I place her leg down gently and walk to Jeremy's side of the bed, climb on and start talking. I start at the very beginning: with meeting Daniel at the library at college, the semester we spent together, our agreement to meet in September after we would be separated all summer, my accident, Nancy (who Stacy knew nothing about), my rehab, therapy, surgeries, eventually meeting Alan, our courtship, pregnancy, early marriage, meeting Noreen, and finding Daniel again.

As I regale the story about the me she never knew, Stacy remains quiet. Although Stacy was privy to the details of my life at this point, she only knew it from her perspective. I assure her I was faithful to and in love with her father. It had never occurred to me to leave him. We had a life, and Daniel was part of my past.

I touched on Noreen's illness, and how Daniel and I remained friends, leaning on one another. How we lost touch by the time Alan was sick. How we were both at Nikki's for dinner and picked up at that point. I admitted to my daughter that we'd kissed, that Daniel said he'd had feelings for me; but that I'd sent him away, that he still doesn't know it's me, and I haven't seen him since.

I have no regret about what I have just told my daughter.

I can't for the life of me guess what her reaction will be.

"Mom. You have to tell him." She says first. "You can't end like this. He's the love of your life. And you're the love of his. How else could you explain that he came to you *twice?*"

I look at this woman through my tears. My daughter has become a friend with whom I can share my thoughts and secrets. I never imagined how comforting this would feel. All of these years, I have held my inner most thoughts and hopes to myself. My best friend could not know of them for obvious reasons, and I certainly could not share them with Alan. My mother proved to be less than objective, leaving me to struggle on my own, grappling with my inadequacies at being a good wife and friend.

When Daniel and I re-connected for those few months, a dam burst open, relieving me of years of inner turmoil. I smiled all day, noticed my surroundings in fresh ways; colors, sounds, music– everything came alive.

When he walked out of my house that evening, the dam was back in place, thwarting my inner happiness.

"I don't think I ever will. I've lived with a lie for so many years, it's impossible to undo it. But I did do something that I think will make me very happy. Something I should have done long ago."

My daughter raises her eyebrows.

"I went back to Juniata and pre-registered for fall classes. Your old mother is going to finally get her degree."

Four weeks after I arrive, Jeremy wakes me at two am. Stacy's contractions are minutes apart, and we shuffle through the house getting ready to take her to the hospital at once. I sit in the back seat with her while Jeremy capably speeds through the dark, quiet streets. We don't speak on the way. I hold Stacy's hand, and breathe along with her.

I stay in the waiting room while Jeremy and Stacy are whisked into the labor/delivery wing. Jeremy comes out to see me every few hours with an update. At the first update, he tells me that Stacy is comfortable now, with an epidural. Two hours later, we are still waiting. He informs me a third time that the epidural has slowed down the delivery process, and the baby is no longer looking to push his way out. By the eighth hour, I am agitated, and demand a visit with my daughter.

She is in the bed with a monitor strapped to her belly, in much the same way I found her four weeks ago. Her weak smile does little to calm my nerves. Eight hours is a long time to be in this position. I silently hope the doctor knows what he is doing and isn't putting undue stress on Stacy or the baby.

When we find ourselves in the tenth hour, I am beside myself. Jeremy tells me to go home and rest, but I can't. I am back in the waiting room, working off the caffeine I'd ingested earlier. I need to hear one man's voice, but I can't bring myself to call him, sure he would not want to speak to me.

So I call the next best person.

"How is she?" Nikki asks, when she hears my voice.

"She's been in labor for ten hours, Nik. I just wanted to give you an update. Jeremy's a bit preoccupied."

I hear her breath in my ear.

"Okay. A little longer, and they'll do a C-section. They won't let her go on too much more."

"That's what I thought. Okay, I'll keep you posted. Please give my best to your family." And to your father.

"Okay, Aunt Beth. Don't worry. She'll be fine."

I smile, thinking of Noreen, and how alike they sound. "I know."

I call Teresa a little while later and give her the same information. She sounds as calm as Nikki did. I am somehow comforted by her unruffled demeanor.

At two pm, Stacy undergoes a Cesarean operation and my granddaughter, Abigail, is born. I let Jeremy take me back to their house once I know Stacy is comfortable, so to speak, and finally out of recovery, in a regular room. Jeremy jumps into the shower, and I fall quickly into a dreamless deep.

Stacy is in the hospital for four days. I do my best to keep out of the way, allowing Jeremy to spend time with his family, while I cook meals to freeze, and clean the house -anything to keep my mind busy. Each afternoon, I spend a few hours getting to know my granddaughter, drinking in her beauty and smell. I watch as Stacy nurses her, and marvel at how quickly the two adjust to each other. Stacy was bottle-fed from Day One, and I admire her capable maternal instincts.

I am lost in wonder with Abby in my arms when I hear my daughter whisper something from the bed. I look up perplexed.

"She looks like you, Ma." Stacy says again.

"No, she looks like you. She's beautiful."

Chapter 50

Abby is eight days old when Jeremy drags himself back to work. He'll take off more time when I go home. It's a good plan, and everyone seems happy. I dread the idea of going back to Pennsylvania, but I certainly cannot overstay my welcome here. I am in limbo, in the air with no place to land.

Stacy is exhausted, and still uncomfortable after her operation. She is up all night nursing and sleeps whenever Abby sleeps during the day. I cook dinner every night, and I am pleased when Jeremy returns from work, famished, gobbling my food with compliments interspersed between grunts.

Abby is two weeks old when Stacy begins to resemble herself again. The bags beneath her eyes are smaller and she is more active, helping me with laundry and cooking.

"How long can you stay, Mom?" She asks as we sit on the couch behind a mound of tiny onesies and burp cloths.

My nose is filled with the wonderful scent of Dreft, newness, innocence and simplicity.

"Not much longer. I think it's time you and Jeremy have the house to yourselves. When are his parents due out?"

"They'll stick to their original plan. Beginning of August."

I add a tiny T-shirt to the growing pile. "Good. You'll have a month by yourselves."

Stacy places the neat piles in the basket. They support each other like little towers.

"You can stay, you know. You're not in our way."

I smile at my daughter.

"Yes. I am. But thank you for saying I'm not. I understand. I was a new mother once. I remember what it was like. You and Jeremy need to work out your rhythm with Abby, and it's not going to happen with me here. I wanted to make sure you were feeling well first. And now that you are, well, I think it's time I go home."

Optimism and anxiety about my future course through my veins, and I feel better than I have in ages.

Four days later, my suitcase stands in wait at the door and I am hugging my daughter while Jeremy waits to take me to the airport. Stacy holds me tightly, sniffling over my shoulder, and I am touched. I have been here for six weeks, and the time has brought me back to the years in which we were a family, under one roof. I will miss her terribly when I get home. I already do.

A fleeting thought passes through my mind. Perhaps it is not an impossible idea to live out here. I can find a local college. How else will I watch my granddaughter grow?

I held Abby all morning, well after she dozed in my arms, looking like a perfect doll. She is already changing. The thought of leaving her clutches my heart, squeezing it until it hurts.

Stacy lets me go, and we look at each other.

"Thanks, Mom, for coming to our rescue."

"Don't thank me. I'm your mother. I will do it again if you call. Maybe I'll consider moving toward this neck of the woods."

I watch my daughter's reaction. Is she happy? Mortified? I can't tell. Her face softens a bit after some thought.

"I don't think you should make any hasty decisions."

I hide my hurt, knowing I was right in believing I've been here too long. I'm in the way, meddling. Is my smile wide enough to cover my pain?

"I wasn't going to say anything, because we won't know for sure until September, but Jeremy requested a transfer back to the East Coast." Stacy lifts her eyebrows and waits for me to say something.

I grab her close and hug her tightly. "I'll let you know as soon as we find out." She whispers. I close my eyes and say a prayer that this move will come to fruition. I need my family near me.

Jeremy is quiet in the car, and I watch the beautiful streets of San Francisco whiz by in a blur. We arrive at the airport in forty minutes and he steps out of the car, takes my bag and stands with me at the curb check in.

"Thank you, Mom, for coming out like you did. You really have no idea how much you helped us." His voice shakes, and I wonder what kind of relationship he has with his parents. He called them a full day after I arrived. I enjoy that he calls me Mom. I've wanted to hear that from more than one person my whole life.

"Stacy told me about your request to transfer."

Jeremy puts his hands in his pockets. "Yes. I may end up in New York. Did she mention that? There's a spot that opened up in the midtown office. We figured it's better to be within driving distance..."

"Well, I just want you both to be happy. But I will be waiting to hear."

We say goodbye and I head to the concourse with an ache in my heart.

I have five hours to think. Too much time. I spend two in the glorious recap of the first days with my granddaughter. The word still sounds strange on my lips. I can't keep from smiling as I retrace her perfect eyes, tiny nose and pink, pouty lips. Abigail. Alan would be proud of Stacy. My daughter is a woman I enjoy. How many people can say that? I no longer have a best friend. I've lost the only two I had, and I don't know if I have the energy to form new, impenetrable bonds like those I shared with Nancy and Noreen. My daughter will fill some of their voids, I know; but she is going through a part of her life I've experienced, and she will keep her closest secrets for Jeremy, I hope, and Nicole.

I follow the passengers like a herd of sheep heading toward the baggage claim. We quietly make our way down the large hallway, following signs, standing erect on the escalator down and to the still empty moving carousel. We stand and wait, keeping enough distance from each other, and stare at the hanging canvas, hoping our bag pushes through first. I try not to dwell on the symbolism of this moment, to where my life has brought me: standing on my own, just far enough from others to feel alone.

I wheel my bag to the exit and see my fellow travelers as they are received by loved ones and taken home. The outside heat feels welcome on my chilly skin. I almost don't mind the thirty minute wait on the taxi line before I climb in and head home.

Six weeks melts away as I gaze at the landscape of my state. I do love it here, and I hope that Stacy and Jeremy find their way back toward me. I pay the driver and with my carry-on over my shoulder, drag my suitcase along the walkway to the door and let myself into the house.

Chapter 51

The sun is shining brilliantly when I step outside of the building after my last lecture of the day—my favorite one: Environmental Ethics. Squinting to adjust my eyes, I grapple with my book bag in search of my sunglasses. Once settled, I sling my bag back onto my shoulder and make my way carefully down the steps, holding on to the railing. Two girls I recognize from class jaunt past me, wishing me a nice weekend over their shoulders, and I watch them stroll on ahead, heads together in conversation, on the cusp of their lives.

I am fifty-four years old, the eldest student by far in all of my classes, and I watch my peers with envy and weariness. *Be careful,* I want to warn, *don't take this part of your life forgranted.* Classes started a month ago, and though it took some time to get used to being back in school, I gradually fell into my new routine with ease.

As I meander along the footpath near the Arches, I feel refreshed in the October chill and, today, my slow gait doesn't bother me. Having nowhere to go for the next seventy-two hours, I decide to take the scenic route to my car and enjoy the glorious foliage on a campus I've missed. I'd forgotten just how much I loved it here, as I told Stacy earlier, when she called. Still no firm date on her move; but she did promise to bring Abigail to see me and Teresa next month. I can't wait. Hopefully they decide to visit after my midterms. I chuckle at the thought.

I stroll past the Quad and realize that I am not far from Lesher House, where I spent my freshman year…was it thirty-eight years ago? Oh Lord, where does the time go? That's where I met Mindy, who I eventually followed off campus junior year. I wonder briefly how Mindy is doing, surprised she hadn't found her way into my thoughts in years. I never reached out to her after my accident, and she didn't work too hard to find me. We were housemates, really, more than friends. As I pass buildings that were once so familiar, comfort lays over me like a veil.

Up ahead is my old dorm, and I am crushed by disappointment as I approach it; the beautiful brick entrance is marred by scaffolding, and the people dotting the roof and lawn are not students lounging and studying but workers armed with thick tool belts in place of book bags. Many of the buildings have endured facelifts in my absence, and it appears my old stomping ground could not evade modernization any more than an aging woman. We're relics in a young world. Everything must change, eventually.

With the once beautiful façade in disguise, I decide not to walk any closer and turn around when my peripheral vision catches a glimpse of someone who seems familiar. Shocked into immobility, I stare at a man across the lawn, talking to another gentleman. Holding onto to his hard hat, he looks up toward the roof, pointing and gesturing with his hands. His back is to me, but I have no shred of doubt in my mind that it's Daniel.

I know I should move, should walk on and head home; but I can't. Minutes pass as I watch him, feeling my heartbeat increase exponentially until I am sure the whole world can hear it. My reaction to him will never change, and I don't fight it anymore. I can't stop my heart any more than a dog can prevent his tail from wagging when he is happy.

The gentleman eventually walks away and now Daniel stands alone, surveying his workers. I make no sound, but something makes him turn in my direction. I am not sure what it is, and I expect him to turn back and keep working. He doesn't. He stands and, shielding eyes from the sun with one hand, recognizes me and gives me a smile.

I am thankful for the space between us, the expanse of lawn he has to cross before he reaches me, so I can compose myself and push my tears back to where they were hidden. Before I can react any further, he is standing in front of me, holding his hat.

"I was hoping to see you here." He starts to reach to me, but something makes him stop and instead, he gives me a smile. As always, I feel a throbbing in my heart, surprised there is anything left to hurt.

"How…" Then, judging his reaction, I understand. Nikki told him.

"It's one of the reasons I took this job." He looks around and back to me. "The other is simply because I love it here."

I nod, unsure of what to say.

"I'm proud of you."

I smile. "I'm proud of myself."

We fall silent. Daniel looks at me, wanting to speak; but he doesn't.

"So, how are you?"

He nods. "Fine. I'm fine." He turns to Lesher House. "This is the last building in our contract, so… How have you been?"

"I'm okay. Stacy had her baby, as you probably heard. She's due for a visit soon." His eyes hold mine, though I want to run screaming because I can't say everything I want to say.

"Yes, congratulations. Nicole told me. I am so happy for you. I wanted to call, but I thought you'd…"

I nod, and he lets the words fall. He thought I wouldn't want to hear from him. I certainly have given no other signals to keep him trying.

The leaves rustle above us and a cool breeze pushes his hair— still thick, now heavily salted—from his weathered face, making him more handsome than he's ever been. When we last stood on this campus together, our lives had barely begun. Now, more than three decades have passed, I am a grandmother and I can see the horizon not far away.

His green eyes shimmer and though I want to lose myself in them, I know I cannot stay here any longer.

"I'm sorry, I have to go." I say, surprising him with my abruptness. His face falls, and I turn before I can regret the decisions I've made, the mistakes I've lived with, any longer.

As I take a step from Daniel, I hear his voice; but it takes me a moment to fully comprehend what he says.

"Lizzie?"

I gasp and turn back to him. The tears in his eyes mirror mine. *Oh, God.*

"Were you ever going to tell me?"

"You knew?"

He shakes his head. His smile is sad. "It took me awhile. Your face changed, your hair." He swallows and a tear finds a lonely trail down his cheek. "But your eyes...I know every fleck of gold in them. I'd dreamed of them, of you, for years."

He takes a shaky breath and looks down. "I told myself I was crazy–that I was imagining it and each time I'd see you, I felt it. Inside. At the park, the diner, in the elevator in St. Lucia..." His eyes come back to mine. "My soul knows only yours, Lizzie. After all of these years, after our five months together, it speaks to no one else."

A sob catches in my throat and my hand covers my mouth.

"You didn't say anything." I whisper.

"I wanted to, God, so many times, but I couldn't."

"Why?" I can still see his face clearly, as the elevator doors separated us. At the time, my own distress enveloped me and I couldn't recognize his.

"Lizzie, you left me. My heart was broken. How could I tell you I knew, when all this time, you said nothing? I thought you didn't love me anymore. I tried to piece together the timing of your accident with your marriage. Wondering if you met Alan first, while I was away, or if it was the accident that made you leave me."

My gaze falls to my feet in shame. *No.*

"I thought, *She couldn't have left me because of her accident. She wouldn't do that. She knows who I am.*" He waits, and finally I bring my eyes back to him.

"Daniel, I never meant to hurt you...I thought I was doing the right thing...I'm sorry."

"Did you think that little of me, that you would doubt my love for you?"

Shaking my head, tears course down my cheeks. "I didn't want you to be stuck with someone like me."

Daniel lets out an anguished cry. "Someone like you? You mean someone who brought me to life? Someone who made me happy? Really? Are you not that person anymore? You can change every physical trait but you can't change who you are!" His voice is rising in anger; words that have been held for a lifetime are pouring out of him and washing over me like a frigid rain.

"I thought you broke my heart then. That pain pales in comparison to what you're doing to me now. Thirty-five years, Lizzie! How could you let us go? We were perfect!"

"I know. But I wasn't. Not anymore."

"That's bullshit! Don't you get it? You're all I've ever wanted. You're all I want now. And then, after Alan, you sent me away again."

He stares at his hat as he turns it in his hands. Finally, he looks back up to me. "Do you know how hard it's been for me? To have to stand near you and not touch you, hold you, tell you I've never stopped loving you? Do you? The pain..."

Tears fall freely down my face, and it takes some effort to catch my breath. Daniel watches me and waits.

"I'm sorry." I whisper, looking down at my feet, disbelieving. The silence between us grows.

He takes a deep breath and runs his hand through his hair as he lets it out. He does this again and when I look at him, his eyes are closed.

"No," he says. "I'm sorry. I should have fought for you then. I didn't. And I've lived with the regret all of these years. But no more."

I shake my head. These are words I've dreamt of hearing. But I am afraid, afraid of letting him down. I'm not Noreen, my body... he can't touch me.

When Daniel speaks, his voice is quiet, belying the tears that flow. "Stop it." As if he hears my thoughts. "I know you, Lizzie. You're beautiful, and you're mine. Just tell me one thing. And if you say no, I promise, I'll leave you alone forever. Do you still love me?"

Do I love you? For a fleeting moment, I think of Alan, and Noreen, and I know in my heart that I loved them both. But nothing can compare to what I feel for this man. Nothing ever did.

I never stopped, Daniel. Not for one minute of one day since we met. I am powerless to verbalize my thoughts; instead, I just nod over and over.

He drops his hat, lifts his hands and cups the sides of my face. Gently, with his thumbs, he wipes my tears, as he did at the airport decades ago, when we said goodbye. Then he glides his thumb down the side of my nose, the pitted cheek, and I squeeze my eyes shut. It feels wonderful and frightening.

He pushes my hair back and kisses my forehead. "No more. We have each other. Please. I want to take you home and show you all the ways I still love you. Let's take the years we have left and make them ours."

Daniel takes a step back and holds out his hand. I feel like I am in one of my dreams, and I fear any minute I will wake up, he will be gone and I will be alone again.

"Lizzie." My eyes close while I drink in the sound.

My hand reaches for his, and at once his warmth envelopes me. I open my eyes to see him smiling, and I know I've made it.

I am home.

Acknowledgements

My heartfelt gratitude goes to friends and family who read early versions of this book and provided valuable feedback and continued support. They are, in no particular order: Monica Carlsen, Suzanne Guacci, Jon & Katie Mittelman, Mary Jo Haggerty, Joanna Whitcomb, Sue Moran, Elaine Trumbull, Tracy Bianco, Linda Michaels, Cathy Michaels, Loraine Kehoe, Nora Katz, Ronnie Levine, Sandra Scully, Gayle Cassar, Beth Smith, Joann Kalfas, Janice McQuaid, Val Dietrich, Lynn Meyer, Joy Martinson, Shevawn Bannon, Terry Alexander, Ann (Mom) Wenzler, Tatiana Dashkin, Christina Russo, Sandra Catalanotto, and Jimmy Granauro.

Booked for Drinks (Sue, Mara, Patti, Liz, Kerri, Debbie and Eva), thank you for opening your hearts to read the raw manuscript of a stranger, for answering all of my questions, and for making me an unofficial book club member.

A special thank you goes to Katie Mittelman and Linda Shapiro for their enthusiastic marketing assistance.

Advice given by authors and friends, Gina Ardito, Harry Hauca, and Pat Wiley, was inestimable.

I am particularly grateful to my editors, Saryta Rodriguez and Mary Jane Tenerelli, of *Brave New Publishing*, for their invaluable insight and suggestions.

Thank you Suzanne Fyhrie Parrott, of *First Steps Publishing*, publisher and graphic artist extraordinaire, for your kindness, patience and beautiful book layout and cover design.

I am blessed to be part of a family who loves unconditionally and believes in me without question, especially Mom, Rose Baylis, who read *Both Sides Of Love* half a dozen times, cover to cover, and endured countless conversations about Dutch, Beth, and Noreen without complaint. Thanks, Mom.

Steve, Zach and Alex, you are my life and proof that true love really exists.

And to you, the reader. Thank you.

I hope we meet again.

Kimberly

About the Author

Kimberly Wenzler was born and raised on Long Island, New York, where she currently resides with her husband and their two sons. Wenzler writes primarily about families, love and friendship. *Both Sides of Love* is her first novel.

Drop by and say hi. She'd love to hear from you.

www.kimberlywenzler.com.

Made in the USA
Middletown, DE
11 November 2015